Also by David Sheppard:

Oedipus on a Pale Horse
Journey through Greece in Search of a Personal Mythology

Novelsmithing
The Structural Foundation of Plot, Character, and Narration

THE MYSTERIES
A NOVEL OF ANCIENT ELEUSIS

Volume One:
DAUGHTER OF DARKNESS

Volume Two:
THE DADOUCHOS

Volume Three:
THE TWICE-BORN
(at a later date)

by

David Sheppard

DAUGHTER OF DARKNESS

Being the first volume of

THE MYSTERIES
A NOVEL OF ANCIENT ELEUSIS

by

David Sheppard

FOR

All the brave women throughout history
whose stories have never been told.

Acknowledgements

The concept of this book is the outgrowth of a conversation I had with a friend of mine several years ago at a Starbucks in Boulder, Colorado. After listening to me talk obsessively about Herodotus, she suggested I write a novel set in ancient Greece. The essence of the story came to me immediately. She also mid-wifed it through the first draft. My sister-in-law, Nancy Sheppard, read it in episodes as it was written and offered encouragement. The expertise of my editor, Marilyn Mueller, has once again been indispensable. A special thanks to Richard Sheppard for the map and the cover design and illustration.

Author's Note

I am the author of *Novelsmithing, The Structural Foundation of Plot, Character, and Narration*. I used the methods of *Novelsmithing* to write *The Mysteries*. Since some instructors are using *Novelsmithing* in their creative writing classes, I thought it might be of benefit to expose a little of my plotting and research methodology. Therefore, I have provided some hints at story structure and the primary sources for *The Mysteries* at the end of the novel. I plotted Volumes One and Two of *The Mysteries* as one complete story and Volume Three separately. Practically all sources are a part of my home library. Anyone interested in the size and content of my library can find it listed at:

www.librarything.com/catalog/dshep/yourlibrary

For field research, I visited Greece twice, once for ten weeks in October 1993 and then for sixteen days in October 2009. I took a considerable number of photos and video clips, some of which I've provided for viewing at www.themysteriesofeleusis.com.

My readers can follow me on twitter at user name "novelsmithing" and on my blog www.novelsmithingblog.com. When I travel, I post at www.palehorseblog.com.

Ancient Greece in the 5th Century BC was a collection of separate city-states, loosely bound by a common language and religion. The ancient Greeks called the encompassing geographical area Ἑλλας, Hellas, and its people the Hellenes. No one called it Greece. I have used both: Greece/Greeks for narration and Hellas/Hellenes for dialogue.

MOUNT OLYMPUS ▲

DODONA
•

THESSALY

EUBOEA

MT.
PARNASSOS
▲
DELPHI •
ITHACA •

BOEOTIA

THEBES •
PLATAEA • KHALKIS •
• AULIS
PATRAS • GULF OF CORINTH ▲ MT. KITHAERON

ELEUSIS •
ISTHMUS ATHENS •
CORINTH • • BRAURON
SALAMIS PHALERON •

PELOPONNESE

OLYMPIA • MYCENAE • EPIDAURUS •
ARGOS • NAUPHLIA • SOUNION •

SPARTA •
TAYGETUS
MOUNTAINS

IONIAN SEA

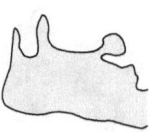

ANCIENT
GREECE
(HELLAS)

PROPONTIS

• ABYDOS
HELLESPONT
• TROY
LEMNOS

AEGEAN
SEA   ASIA

LESBOS
MYTILENE

SKYROS

SARDIS •

• SMYRNA
CHIOS

• EPHESUS

CYCLADES   TINOS   SAMOS   ▲ MT. MYKALE
MYKONOS
DELOS

DODECANESE

KOS

THERA   RHODES

AEGEAN
SEA   KARPATHOS

CRETE • KNOSSOS
• PHAESTOS

Contents

Daughter of Darkness

CHAPTER 1: PERSIA CROSSES THE HELLESPONT

A great bonfire burned on shore where fast water flowed through the strait separating Europe and Asia, the Hellespont. A man of war, dressed in a short black tunic, stepped forward with a hot iron, the tip glowing brilliant red, and slipped it into the hurrying current. Steam hissed into the cold morning air, and its froth trailed downstream, dissolved. Warrior after warrior appeared carrying glowing irons, and they too branded the water, marking it for the Persian King, King of Kings, Xerxes. Men carrying jangling fetters emerged from the crowd and ceremoniously heaved them far into the unbridled flow. Another thirty stepped forward, each with a coiled length of lash used to force reluctant men into battle, and, leaning over the current, dealt it three-hundred stinging lashes, all the while shouting, "You salt and bitter stream, Xerxes punishes you for your insults and will cross you without permission, without sacrificing. Your acid and muddy waters deserve neglect."

Ten more were brought forward, unwilling men, their heads laid upon the chopping block. These were the engineers who'd built the bridge across the strait recently decimated by violent storm and churning surf. Another man emerged from the throng, dressed in black, hooded. His pale legs stuck from beneath his tunic as healed tubular wounds. He swung his ax with the confidence of one who'd performed the task a long bitter time, as from a god's bidding. The swift stroke of the ax fell, and each severed head, all ten in turn, rolled among tender wildflowers. The mouths moved as if to articulate some ancient wisdom. Bodies slumped, releasing pulsing spurts of life-giving blood. A leg, a hand quivered as though stricken by a fit of nervousness.

A Greek, Harpalus, not a prisoner but a traitorous engineer, stepped forward to execute the order at which the Persian team of ten had failed so miserably: to bridge the Hellespont. Horns bellowed, men shouted as they labored against the elements. Anchored ships bucked and pitched in the restless current while wooden winches groaned, stretching taut giant coils of papyrus and flax cables, straining to fulfill an oracle. The arched lines hissed in the wind like snakes. Two more bridges, formed of biremes, triremes, rope and plank, stretched the width of the channel.

The strait bridged, the king burned incense, broadcast myrtle bows over the road, and put his troops in motion. When an old man begged the King for his eldest son to remain behind to protect his family and tend crops, the king cut the son down the middle and, leaving a bloody half on each side of the road, drove the army between them. A total eclipse of the sun reduced the landscape to darkness, causing birds to roost, and giving the king pause, but the Magi put the King's mind to rest. "'Tis but a sign to the Hellenes of the future eclipsing of their cities," they said. For seven days and nights, the troops crossed, one million seven hundred thousand under the lash of the impatient king. All Greece shuddered.

As she stepped off the bridge into Europe, a mare gave birth to a hare.

CHAPTER 2: NIGHT HORSEMAN AT ELEUSIS

On the far side of the Aegean in a quiet bay lay the small town of Eleusis, an ancient city, sacred, known for worship of the two goddesses: Demeter and her daughter, who was referred to as Kore, the Maiden. So feared was the divine daughter that her name, Persephone, was never spoken in public for she was Mistress of the Underworld.

Within the stone walls of the semi-sacred quarter where the priests of the Mysteries made their homes, slept the priestess of Demeter, her dreams tainted with worry over her own daughter. The clap of a horse's hooves on cobblestone and the bark of dogs roused her. She recognized the booming voice of her brother-in-law, Aeschylus, who'd been away to the north with the Greek army. His presence at Eleusis could only mean that something decisive had happened.

Myrrhine's handmaid stood in the stone doorway, vestiges of sleep casting a blank expression upon her face. Myrrhine dismissed the woman back to bed and, slipping into her robe by herself, hurried from the room and down the hall, now populated by sleepy-eyed children and scolding mothers. A hungry puppy whined at her feet. She entered the large chamber built around the hearth of Hestia, the flickering sacred fire.

Aeschylus already stood before the flames rubbing his hands, his booming voice addressed to the Hierophant, Myrrhine's aged father. She wondered if her father ever slept anymore. The room had filled with the acrid smell of a man who'd been long on the move.

She hurried to Aeschylus, feeling a renewed safety in his pres-

ence, but restrained herself from embracing him, as was the custom. She kept her eyes averted. "I hope it's good news that brings
you home so unexpectedly," she said to the man who reminded
her so much of her late husband.

Aeschylus' eyes glowed coal-like beneath a bushy bank of eyebrows. He shook his head. "Myrrhine, my brother's wife and he
in Hades now ten years, I wish I could say something to console
you, but you'd see through me. I'll speak nothing but plain truth.
The Athenians have decided against opposing Xerxes at the Vale
of Tempe and have dropped back to Thermopylae. They'll force
Xerxes' hand at the Hot Gates."

The priestess looked questioningly at the Hierophant, but
could read nothing in that wrinkled face. He'd seemed distant
the last few years, as if only matters of the other world, the Underworld, concerned him. He creaked about the house like an
old ghost. She turned back to Aeschylus. "That's still a good way
north. Is Eleusis in danger?"

Aeschylus' face filled with a disillusionment she'd never witnessed in this man who'd fought at Marathon, where her husband
had died. He stared into the fire. But he didn't respond to her, instead turning again to her father. "Listen, Zakorus," he said, using
the Hierophant's name instead of his title, "I was born and raised
at Eleusis. My line of descent here goes back as far as yours. I'll
not see all these women, children, and old men slaughtered like so
many sacrificial goats. I've seen Xerxes' forces with my own eyes,
stood on a mountaintop and first thought them the very grasses
of the earth, Demeter's gift. The locust horde of Persian warriors
filled the valleys and overran hills. Xerxes has forced into service
all those conquered on his way here. His army has swelled to five
million. We have but five-hundred thousand."

"But the same was true at Marathon, and we killed them like
flies." Myrrhine turned away as she spoke, remembering it was
also Aeschylus who'd returned from battle bringing Kynegeiros'
body.

Philokleia, Aeschylus' wife, rushed into the room, fell into her husband's arms, and sobbed softly. Myrrhine knew well the woman's gloomy disposition. Philokleia whispered that their two boys, Euphorion and Euaion, had taken ill.

"Myrrhine is right, Aeschylus," the Hierophant said, ignoring Philokleia's presence. "The odds were heavily against us at Marathon, but the great god Pan took our side and spread terror through the Persian ranks. Even Theseus, though dead eight-hundred years, was seen leading the charge. The gods won't allow Persia to destroy Hellas."

"Not true," said Aeschylus. "The gods have decided against us. Xerxes has many Hellene allies, not only Ionia, but also Karia and the rest of Phrygia. Our neighbors, Thessaly and Thebes, have gone over to him. You must evacuate. Themistocles has given the word for Athens. Persians will descend on us here like the waters of Deucalion's Flood."

Aeschylus then held Philokleia at arms' length and quietly questioned her about the children. He told her they'd best prepare to evacuate. "Everything and everyone," he said. "We have little time for such a large task." Then Philokleia left the room, nodding to Myrrhine as she passed.

The Hierophant relaxed. "We'll never abandon Eleusis," he said. "We didn't evacuate before Marathon. We have sentinels at Oak Heads pass to the north, and our own army mans our walls. If the Persians don't use the route through the mountains, they'll come at Eleusis from the east and have Athens to contend with first."

"Their forces will be brushed aside with a single stroke."

"You don't understand the significance of Demeter's sacred temple. To abandon Eleusis is to abandon mankind. The gods will never forsake Eleusis, nor will we."

"My ignorance isn't the point!" Aeschylus shouted. "This new Persian threat, I tell you, it's not like Marathon." He turned his back on the Hierophant and looked at Myrrhine, warmed his hands over the fire again.

His shouting scared Myrrhine, but she could say nothing to

arbitrate between men.

The Hierophant continued. "I'm not concerned about Xerxes. He knows nothing of war strategy. As long as he's in command, Hellas will survive. It's that cousin of his, Mardonius, who scares me. He was defeated and wounded in Thrace a year before Marathon. Ever he covets a power base, and he's vowed to govern Hellas some day because of his humiliation. His strategy drives Xerxes invasion."

Myrrhine let silence lie between them before she spoke. "At the very least we might retrieve Melaina from Brauron. I've been uneasy with her away from home lately, and several women in labor have asked for her. She has such a gift for comforting during delivery."

The Hierophant glared at her, and his voice hardened. "You protested me sending her. She'd never leave your side if it were up to you. She must stay at Artemis' temple until the ritual of the Bear. Her education, so important to Eleusis, is at stake. I won't disobey the will of the gods because of the Persians. They've been here before."

Aeschylus raised his hands to the sides of his head. "You've left Melaina at Brauron? You old fool! Your miscalculation could cost her life. At the very least, send a soldier to Brauron to protect her, stand guard over her day and night. I've heard rumors of Persian raiders on horseback penetrating far into Attica. And with Brauron on the coast, one ship could sack the entire sanctuary."

The old Hierophant seemed to lose confidence. "We're that vulnerable?" he said to himself, then looked up at Aeschylus. "Myrrhine can see to it tomorrow. But when you rejoin the troops, remember our greatest strength." He looked away, quiet in thought. When he spoke again some of the tension had left his voice. Myrrhine thought perhaps he even smiled. "We're a free people, Aeschylus. Every man who takes up arms against Persia does so to defend his own home. Persians go to war under the lash."

Aeschylus calmed. "I know you speak from the heart, and I

don't deny the importance of the Mysteries. For a thousand years they've influenced our institutions, over-influenced to my mind. Their emphasis on the worth of the individual was undoubtedly the seed that put political power into the hands of the people, but you haven't seen Xerxes' army. We're but a handful of city-states against the entire Persian Empire."

Myrrhine was accustomed to their arguments. Aeschylus had steadfastly refused to be initiated into the Mysteries though he was born and raised in the sacred city. His presence was a constant provocation to the Hierophant. And now this matter of evacuating stood between them. She left the room but didn't return to her chamber. Concern for her daughter's safety flared like a mania. She walked the stone corridor to the back of the house, stopped by the kitchen to draw a cup of wine, then passed through the courtyard to another stone enclosure, a small one with no door. An oil lamp flickered on a square stone beside a mound, the tomb of her late husband. She breathed the cold, thick air.

"Dear Earth, born of Chaos, mother of all mortals and immortals, hear me and call forth my dear husband, entrusted to your care. Call him from the magnificent Elysian Fields deep within your womb so he might listen to my words." She poured half of the cup of red wine into the recess of the burial mound, prayed again, louder and with greater confidence. "Beloved Kynegeiros, husband ten years dead, I beg forgiveness for this intrusion into your new life among the gods and know how my beauty pales beside that of the goddesses who now share you, but come, Kynegeiros, listen to me. A great storm stirs to the north."

She poured the remaining half-cup of wine, listened as if for footsteps of the dead, then continued. "The enemy who slew you has returned, vowing to waste all Hellas. And our daughter, Melaina... O Kynegeiros! How can I tell you what a beauty she's become? Only a goddess' flashing eyes and smile could be more radiant. Now she's on the east coast of Attica at Brauron, the temple of Artemis, to dance the Bear. I have such great fear Persians will take her. If you could speak to Artemis, virgin goddess, protectress of children, about Melaina, such great comfort would come from it."

She stopped for a moment searching for some further enticement for her husband's help. "Through the great solitude since your departure, I've remained faithful though I've not been without suitors. I take heart remembering the chasteness of Penelope during her long years of waiting for Odysseus. I have no hope for your return, still I remain yours, and so I shall be though I live an eternity. O how I long for thy gentle touch! Fare thee well, Kynegeiros, fare thee well, fare thee well. May earth rest lightly upon thee."

After leaving his tomb, she considered returning to bed, but thought of one more way to voice her desperation. She entered the walkway between stone buildings, the sparkle of stellar constellations spread above. At the wall around the sanctuary, she greeted the guard standing below a burning torch and entered through the back gate. The altars of Demeter and Kore stood before the Telesterion, marble statues glistening with the half moon. She supplicated herself on the cold steps before Demeter, then came to her feet, touched a hand to her lips and with outstretched arms prayed aloud.

"Divine mother, august but gentle goddess, Demeter. You alone can understand the grief of my daughter's absence, you who suffered so when Kore was ripped from your bosom. Send Melaina to me, O Divine One. Cure this desperation, and deliver us from Persia. Around your throne, whirl and howl with ecstasy, filling the enemy with terror if he knocks upon your gates. Preserve your glorious sanctuary, so we may ever celebrate your sacred rites."

She hurried home, accompanied by roughhousing dogs. Reentering her chamber, she slipped from her robe, pulled back the bearskin blanket, and as she lay down, gathered her breasts in her arms and fell asleep.

CHAPTER 3: THE BURNING OF BRAURON

On the opposite coast of Attica, in swampland at the mouth of the oft-flooded Erasinos, stood the temple of Artemis. During daylight, the hillsides echoed with shouts of young maidens, and during evening, sweet lyre music lofted with the rustle of oak leaves to sweep cold temple walls. Darkness was dense before dawn, and the girls lay silent as corpses.

Melaina saw them coming to kill her first, then all the rest, woke realizing it was just a dream. She lingered in misty visions of so many girls, all her friends, slaughtered at the temple of Artemis. As Hermes' world slowly faded, she knew the upcoming ceremony had precipitated it. She would be dead by nightfall; they'd all die that day, symbolically sacrificed for the sake of Greece, as had been Iphigeneia centuries earlier. But they'd be reborn as young women, to assume roles as wives and mothers, and to run the households of Greece.

Her dream had seemed so real, the screaming, the blood. She still trembled. They'd even killed the priestesses. Many deaths would actually occur that day, but the girls would do the killing, slitting the throats of she-goats representing their maiden-selves. Melaina worried over it, not ready to leave behind her childhood friends to run the home of some man she'd never met.

She listened to the soft breath of the three friends sharing her chamber and snuggled against Theodora, worried. Their days at Brauron were coming to an end, and her mother should have arrived yesterday. She'd missed her mother so much these past months.

But it was more than that. Lately, she'd noticed a familiar

face stalking the grounds of Brauron, a soldier from Eleusis. He lingered about, always in the background, even in areas of the sanctuary ordinarily off limits to men. His appearance was also troubling, sword strapped at his side, shield in hand. He carried a spear. Melaina knew the priestesses were trying to keep news of an impending war from the girls, but the overheard whispers simply magnified their fears. Several families had pulled their girls out of Brauron. Rumors of an evacuation were on every girl's lips, and the hateful word "Persia" would send the littlest screaming.

Melaina untangled her legs from Theodora's, reached for her chiton, pulled it over her head, and slipped from the room. She went directly to Hestia's hearth, poured the morning's libation there, noticing that Kynthia, priestess of Artemis, had already added sacred oak to rekindle the coals. Melaina whispered a prayer to Asklepios, the god who resurrected them from Hermes' dream world into the new day, and found Kynthia at the slaughter stone. Melaina helped the young priestess sacrifice a cock to Asklepios as bright sunlight broke the horizon. Afterward, Melaina told the priestess of her dream.

"Entry into the world of adults can be frightening," Kynthia said, "and with war looming it's particularly difficult. That's why we have divine Artemis help make the transition. Are you to marry when you return home?"

"I've not been given away yet," answered Melaina. "I dread leaving my mother. If my husband won't allow me to read and write poetry I'll wither. Here at Brauron I've fallen in love with Sappho's poetry. I want to be a teacher, too."

Kynthia smiled, seemed to wrestle with a thought. "I know another course should a young woman not choose marriage." She hesitated again. "You could follow the divine virgin. I myself have chosen the path of Artemis. But you'd not marry, never have children."

"Oh, mother Kynthia!" responded Melaina. "To follow Artemis would be a miracle. I'd settle for being like Sappho, but I'm afraid grandfather already has my future planned."

"Perhaps you can persuade him."

"Demeter and Kore are such strong influences at Eleusis. And my grandfather is the Hierophant."

The two of them spoke no more of it, letting the thought lie between them as a shared dream. The rest of the girls and priestesses joined them, forming a procession to the temple. During the day, the girls reenacted the life of Iphigenia, Agamemnon's daughter, who'd founded the temple there at Brauron. Seven hundred years before, when the Greek fleet left to fight the Trojan War, it mustered in the bay at Aulis, just north of Brauron. But Artemis calmed the winds, so the Greeks couldn't sail and demanded that Agamemnon sacrifice his most beautiful daughter to her. Agamemnon brought Iphigeneia to Aulis under the pretext of marrying her to Achilles, greatest of Greek warriors, but once there, the seer Kalchas dragged Iphigeneia to the slaughter stone. Just as the blade touched Iphigenia's throat, Artemis whisked her away and substituted a deer to die in her place. Iphigenia became Artemis' priestess at Brauron. She never married but assisted women in childbirth.

The girls danced around Iphigenia's tomb and brought a hind into the temple, a symbol of the sacred deer killed by Iphigenia's father. They ran footraces in tribute to the plight of the animal, but in the end, sacrificed it and held a great feast.

Melaina worried all day, and not only for her mother or the fate of her homeland. Her short conversation with Kynthia had infected her with a quick-growing discontent. She lost interest in thoughts of marriage that occupied the other girls and that had been the thrust of their training at Brauron. She wanted one thing more than anything else: the freedom to choose her own life. She wondered anew about her girlfriends, Agido and Anaktoria, back at Eleusis. Melaina was the oldest, and her mind was fast formulating a plan to remain among them.

Melaina watched for her mother, glancing up the sanctuary road for a trail of dust, and listened for the clop of horses' hooves, rattle of carriage wheels. She searched the faces of the other girls' mothers, but the priestess of Demeter from Eleusis wasn't among them.

That night was to be the finale of the Brauronia, the Night of the Bear. At sunset, the initiates and priestesses gathered just outside the temple before a barred, cliff-side cave where an adult she-bear nervously paced. One priestess played the aulos, a double-reed wind instrument, and another, the lyre. The initiates donned bear masks, formed choruses to sing elegies to Iphigenia, and then joined hands to dance before the caged beast. Soon the wildness of their young hearts would also be caged within the homes of their husbands, a thought that flashed anger in Melaina. The patter of the girls' tender feet set the rhythm, and they twirled and shook their hair in defiance at the caged she-bear as her roars sent shivers through them.

As darkness encroached, the girls gathered in the temple to meet death. Melaina worried about her she-goat. She'd selected her months ago, having chosen this particular animal because of her feisty, independent nature, the way the little she-goat stood off from the crowd and made a run at Melaina when she tried to corner her. But Melaina had tamed her, and now the goat trailed along behind her on a leash. The temple was crowded with animals: rabbits racing along the floor, doves fluttering in and out of torchlight. Melaina watched the she-bear pace inside her cage.

As female family members gathered to view the proceedings, Melaina scanned them. What could have happened to her mother? Melaina's feet still ached from running barefoot, her sunburned legs and shoulders tingling under her saffron chiton.

Melaina heard Kynthia call her from among the scores of initiates. She'd be the first to sacrifice. She was the oldest and, as an Eumolpid, from an aristocratic family. As Melaina stepped forward, Kynthia donned a bear mask and slipped a bear-claw glove over her right hand. Kynthia dropped the upper part of Melaina's chiton to expose her right breast and, without warning, sliced the claw rapidly across it just above the nipple. Melaina flinched, screamed, as beads of bright blood formed.

Scattered laughter came from the crowd.

Brandishing a shiny bronze blade, Kynthia led Melaina to the slaughter stone. Melaina sprinkled her she-goat with holy water and watched her shiver, an assumed sign of assent. Kynthia put the blade to the animal's throat while the chorus broke out in a hymn, faltered, then fell silent. A clamor had erupted from behind the temple. Melaina heard shouting, the clash of steel. Kynthia removed the mask and stepped away from Melaina, stood silent.

A stranger raced into the temple, carrying a knife. As Kynthia froze in fear, the she-bear rose on her hind legs and let loose a bloodcurdling roar. The soldier from Eleusis, who'd been shadowing the sanctuary, rushed into the fray but was immediately cut down by two more strangers. The man with the knife came for Melaina, and she felt her knees weaken, saw the world fade.

Kynthia stepped in front of Melaina and struggled with the man, showing more strength than Melaina could have imagined. It appeared as though Kynthia might even wrest the knife from him, when she went limp, cut down by a single stroke, the knife buried deep in the small of her neck.

Screams, a flurry of doves, and scurrying rabbits sent the temple into chaos. Melaina felt the assailant's steel fingers wrap her arm as several Greek soldiers charged into the battle. Leading them was a fierce-looking man in heavy armor, who shouted, and when her captor hesitated, grabbed him from behind and slit his throat in one swift motion. Still more blood gushed onto the altar.

The man lay gurgling out his life in wordless mouthings as light faded from his eyes. Kynthia breathed laboriously beneath him. Melaina was struck dumb, but gathered herself and rushed to the priestess, who with each raspy breath brought forth crimson froth. Kynthia's wound emptied in a slow stream, mixing with that of her murderer who lay between her legs. The two were a strange couple, mated by their simultaneous deaths on the altar of Artemis.

Melaina looked up at the man who'd saved her life as he ripped off his bronze helmet. His curly black hair was tied in a ponytail and held in place by a bright-red headband. He was the Dadouchos, a priest from Eleusis. What is he doing here? she wondered. No sooner had this thought crossed her mind than he grabbed her hair and pulled her head backward.

Melaina realized he'd just exposed her throat. To murder me also, here on the altar, she thought. The world has gone insane, and I'm also to be a victim. He again raised his knife to strike, and as she brought her hand to her throat in a final act of defense, the color drained from the world again.

But the blade's stroke only tingled her scalp, and the blond lock loosed into his hand. He held aloft the knife in one hand, her golden curls in the other as he dropped to one knee. The she-bear let forth another mighty roar, followed by the Dadouchos' voice ringing throughout the temple.

"Artemis! frenzy-loving huntress, goddess of all things wild. Among the din and cry of beasts these two have given their lives, willingly or no, so this tender virgin may die as maid and be re-born as woman. Accept them as her sacrifice. Divine virgin, dear goddess of swift birth, receive this initiate, offspring of this grue-some delivery, to thy bosom."

He raised Melaina to her feet, her knees quivering. "Quick-ly!" he said. "We must leave, now."

"Why did you do this to me?" she said, feeling the bald spot in her scalp cut so close he'd drawn blood. "Look what you've done." She felt he had purposely terrorized her.

The Dadouchos shouted to the startled crowd of initiates and onlookers who'd scurried for cover behind the marble columns. "Everyone! Listen to me! You must vacate the temple. Danger stalks us all. My men just scattered a larger band of Persians in back of the temple. They'll return when they find their courage. Yesterday, to the north at Thermopylae, the Persians routed the Hellene forces under Leonidas. Attica is under siege and must be evacuated. Leave everything and make for Athens."

He said again to Melaina, "Follow me! Quickly!"

She ran after him to a grove of trees outside the sanctuary

where a lone man stood restraining a team of four black horses harnessed to a two-wheeled chariot. Nearby, another horse stood reined to a tree. Melaina realized she had none of her possessions and bolted back toward the temple. The Dadouchos shouted after her, but she pulled her chiton to her knees and raced madly on.

At the dormitory, she entered the dark room she'd shared with the other girls and quickly rummaged among her things. She felt her own tears fall onto her hands. The image of Kynthia giving up her blood on the altar stood between Melaina and everything she saw. How would Kynthia get to the Underworld without proper burial?

She discarded the terra-cotta figurines, a bear and a likeness of Artemis, but clutched tightly to her heart a small bundle of papyrus bound with leather straps. "Oh Sappho!" she cried. She stuffed them into a leather sack along with a two-reed aulos just as the Dadouchos entered the room, huffing and fuming.

"You've put all our lives at risk," he said. "Have your senses abandoned you?"

Melaina hoisted the bag to her shoulder and walked past him, but a dark Persian stood before her, blocking the doorway. His sword thrust was aimed at her heart, but the Dadouchos' naked hand brushed it aside, and once more he slew her would-be assassin, his quick blade opening the man's abdomen so that his entrails poured forth.

The Dadouchos pushed her out the door, and they hurried back through fading light into the deep shadows of the grove. There he spoke quickly to the young man holding the team of horses, and the Dadouchos and his charge climbed aboard the chariot. The carriage, supported on two six-spoked wheels, was made of carefully shaped wood, overlaid with leather and gated at the aft end. The glistening gold railing came to her waist. The floor was soft but steady, formed of interlaced leather thongs. It was empty except for a deerskin blanket carelessly cast inside.

A flickering light fell on the grove, and Melaina looked back to see flames licking the sanctuary roof. She heard shouts, women screaming. People poured from the temple.

"The Persians have returned!" shouted the Dadouchos. "But for the maiden, more blood would flow from my sword." He grabbed a coiled whip from the front of the chariot and cracked it over the horses' heads. "Forward!"

The chariot lurched, almost throwing Melaina from it. She shouted into his ear as they entered the dirt road west, "They'll all die if we don't help."

"My cargo is more important than all of Brauron, and more danger lies between here and Athens. I've orders from the Hierophant to return you to Eleusis."

"But my mother! We must find her."

The Dadouchos cracked the whip over the horses' heads, and the chariot squeaked and groaned as they flew into the deepening night, her protests silenced by the thunderous hooves of the four ink-black horses. A great sadness enveloped Melaina. Kynthia dead, and what had happened to Theodora? Where was her mother?

CHAPTER 4: FLIGHT IN DARKNESS

On they sped pulled by demons into darkness, full moon casting pale light for the horses. As the moon disappeared behind a thick bank of clouds, the chariot slowed, and the young man, who'd held the horses in the grove, came alongside and talked briefly to the Dadouchos. He called the Dadouchos by name, Kallias. Melaina repeated it to herself. "Kallias." She felt her raw scalp, and her anger grew.

The rider lit a torch and went on ahead, holding it high, hair glowing in the light. Sparks streamed behind. The silhouettes of the four horses rose and fell against the flame. At times, the rider would guide them around a boulder or hold the torch while they negotiated an erosion channel. The wheels frequently fell into ruts cut by years of wagon use, and the chariot slithered through.

Melaina tried to soften her anger at Kallias. He'd saved her life, twice. Instead of her she-goat, two people had died. She was now supposed to be grown, a woman, but she felt smaller and less significant than ever.

★

Melaina jolted from her daze. The rider stopped and came back to the chariot, motioned for Kallias to get out and follow him. Kallias tied the reins to a tree, and the two disappeared into the brush up the hillside. Melaina developed a chill, and the night noises frightened her. Soon, Kallias and the young man came running back. They led the horses off the road into a grove of trees, stopping to listen.

"Horsemen," Kallias whispered. "Probably friendly, but…"

After dousing the torch, they calmed the horses, silencing

their snorts with hands held over the horse's noses. Kallias put two of them in Melaina's charge, and she felt soothed by their warmth, the velvet-soft nostrils. Her heart pounded, but she focused on the sounds of crickets, the rustling wind in treetops, and hugged the long bony heads to her.

Hearing faint voices from the road, Melaina made out her native tongue.

Kallias said, "I know one of them." He stepped from their hideaway. "Hey! Kimon, by the gods, is that you, man?"

The horsemen's torch extinguished and all went quiet.

"It's Kallias, Kimon. Have you forgotten your old boar-hunting companion?"

The response was slow in coming and little more than a whisper. "Kallias? That you? Or some daemon calling us to our doom?"

Kallias stepped forward to greet them, lowering his voice to match theirs. The young man traveling with Kallias relit the torch, and she saw not two but four men traveling together. After a few words, Kallias motioned for the young man to join them. Melaina, now alone, was grateful for the stout presence of the horses. Shortly Kallias and the young man returned.

"I'll not deceive you, Melaina," said Kallias. "Two of these men are from Paiania, a village not far ahead. They were trying to get home but ran into a band of Persians and Thebans blocking the road. These men turned back, not realizing the countryside behind us also swarms with the enemy. We've but one hope: come upon them swiftly, catch them asleep, and pass through their camp before they know what's happened."

Melaina avoided his eyes. He was the most muscular man she'd ever seen, arms bulging from his sleeveless tunic. She hoped he hadn't noticed she was trembling.

"These men are joining us," he said, leading the horses from the grove. "You'll lie low in the chariot wrapped in the deer skin." He mounted the chariot and turned to her again. "Under no circumstances are you to raise your head above the railing. Do you hear me, Melaina?"

She finally managed a weak, "Yes."

They groped by the light of the full moon as it peeked from behind clouds. Melaina tried to calm herself by thinking hard thoughts toward traitorous Thebes. The ancient city was north of Eleusis, opposite Mt. Kithaeron, and a natural enemy since the time of Oedipus. But she'd never imagined that the Thebans would side with Persia. Each moment seemed interminable. She hardly breathed, expecting the Persians to descend upon them at any moment. Still, on they went without being molested, horses' hooves clattering a steady beat.

Their five companions in the lead slowed. "Persian camp ahead," one whispered back.

A loud voice erupted from up the road, sliced sharply through the cold night air. "Halt! Identify yourself!"

Kallias cracked the whip. "Ha!" he shouted, and the chariot lurched forward.

Melaina sunk to the floor and covered herself with the deer-skin, peeking from a frayed edge. She was thrown about until she was sure all her bones would be broken. As they came into the torchlight, a great commotion erupted in the Persian camp. Barking dogs and the bray of a donkey mixed with shouts of the barbarians.

The chariot took a shattering blow to its undercarriage as fire exploded around them. Looking back, Melaina saw they'd over-run the campfire. But the horses reared up, pawing skyward and bringing the chariot to a standstill. A foul stench hung in the air.

Melaina could resist no longer. She raised her head and looked beyond the horses at a sight she couldn't believe was real. Something, perhaps an animal, rose up before them, a huge deformed beast not born of anything earth-walking, and staggered into the road. It was as if the great god Pan himself had appeared to inspire panic in the horses. Melaina's scream escaped before she could suppress it. Kallias plied the lash to the stallions, cursed them un-mercifully.

The chariot lurched forward as the horses regained their courage under the stinging whip. A rain of arrows and spears descended on the carriage. As they swept past the hovering shape, Melaina ducked back below the rail just as a spear penetrated the sideboard, ripped into the deerskin and lodged in the carriage's opposite side. Melaina's head hit the rail with such force that she momentarily went senseless, the pain in her side so great she thought the spear had dealt her a fatal blow.

As the chariot cleared the Persian camp, Melaina, lodged beneath Kallias' feet, was kicked, beaten about and stepped on. The once-proud horses regained their wits on the far side of the foul beast and, manes flowing, hunkered down to the business of putting it behind them. Persian torches gradually dropped from sight.

When they were in the clear, Kallias reined in the horses and called the others to him. "We may have lost the maiden," he said, his voice without its usual strength.

Melaina thought he might be right, but her groans and complaints at having being trampled on were welcomed with cheers and smiling faces. After they extracted the spear from the chariot and released the deerskin pinning her against the sideboard, she could finally breathe. Except for her throbbing head and some bruised ribs, she was sound. Her saffron chiton, on the other hand, had been penetrated front to back, which caused the men to murmur. "Eyie!" said one.

"Wasn't the Persians that frightened me," said Melaina, "but the fell beast."

"You sons of a mountain goat," Kallias said, turning on the men from Paiania. "Why didn't you tell me about the camel?"

"We didn't know. As Iris, the Oathgiver, is our witness," said Kimon.

"No horse can endure the sight or smell of a camel. We could've died."

"What's a camel?" asked Melaina.

The young man traveling with Kallias walked off laughing, causing Melaina to blush at her own ignorance.

Kallias shook his head at the young man. "A poet with a strange sense of humor."

So the quiet young man is a poet, Melaina thought. This pleased her no end.

Satisfied they were all in one piece, the group proceeded, without light, the terrain gradually becoming more mountainous, the forest crowding in on the road. They entered a village, and the road disappeared into a maze of dark, abandoned streets. A barking dog came to greet them. The men talked among themselves, then Kallias came to Melaina. "This is Paiania," he said. "We were to stop here, but it's deserted. We'll go on to Phlya."

The weary riders passed through the village, again braking out onto the open road. Just when Melaina wondered if they'd ever stop, at the foot of a mountain thrusting up into the stars, the chariot took a less-traveled trail north. "We're beneath Mt. Hymettos, sacred to Zeus," Kallias told her. "Soon we'll be at the farm of Mnesarchides."

The trail steepened up the foot of the mountain, and they picked their way through deep woods, which finally opened onto a clearing where the light of a home shone as a beacon. The stone building sat on a moonlit hilltop. Kimon and his three companions went before them, at times trading shouts with sentries. The black stallions whinnied at the workhorses pulling wagons stacked high with goods, which were on their way to Athens and the coast.

As the chariot drew closer to the home, Melaina saw that the place swarmed with people. Bonfires twinkled in the surrounding forest, and she saw a herd of horses, fully loaded wagons and oxen, fellow refugees sleeping in bedrolls. A baby cried.

The chariot pulled up before the stone building. At first she thought the men milling about were slaves, but some sported a hoplite's heavy armor. The hair on the back of her neck bristled. They were warriors. An army was encamped here.

As the riders dismounted, several men came to meet them, some to help with the horses, others to escort them inside. Women stared, whispered among themselves. Melaina overheard one say, "I tell you, it's her. The other is inside. Prophecies speak of the return of the two goddesses."

Melaina cowered under the women's scrutiny.

Kallias, with Melaina trailing behind, entered a large foyer through huge double gates that swung wide. Kimon followed, but the others remained with the horses. Melaina was disappointed that the poet who'd blazed their trail for them hadn't come with them. She'd wanted to get a good look at his face.

Slaves carried sacks of grain from storerooms lining the foyer and stacked them into wagons. Others carried clay jars. At the far side of the foyer, the large double doors into the heart of the home opened and closed on squeaking hinges, but Melaina was not to enter this area. Kallias took Melaina by the arm and led her to a side room through a small door to the left. As he pulled it open, bright light and voices spilled out. They were engulfed by the smell of food.

Just inside the women's room, the mistress of the house turned to inspect them, her stern face set hard as stone. The townswomen ate alongside their children. The room fell silent as all eyes fell upon them. The refugees' belongings were piled high along the walls: clothes, bedding, carpets, chests. The women turned back to eating, and the din returned.

Melaina felt uncomfortable as the stocky, heavy-set mistress scrutinized her. Though of no mean stature herself as the wife of a wealthy landowner, the woman was obviously transfixed by Melaina's presence.

Kallias and Kimon disappeared through the far doorway, but Melaina stayed put. She knew her place in the world of men. Still, she felt abandoned among all these strangers. Fortunately, the mistress came to her instantly, folded Melaina's small hands within her own chubby ones, and pulled them to her warm midriff as if they were precious. She led Melaina into a corner, where a sullen little boy with heavy eyelids sat on a carpet, pillows stacked about him.

"Are you injured, my dear?" the woman asked Melaina. "I administer to those who'll allow a woman."

Melaina blushed scarlet. She hadn't noticed that Kynthia had shed blood on her, but there it was, the spray of scarlet drops, now black, speckling her saffron chiton. The mark of the bear's claw across her breast had also soaked through. With one side of her head nearly bald as well, it was no wonder she attracted so much attention.

"No," answered Melaina, "just tired and sore."

"I'll give you something to lift your spirits, soothe aching bones." This large woman kept staring at Melaina. "May I ask your name?"

"Melaina, from Eleusis."

The woman relaxed, smiled, handed Melaina a steaming posset in a tiny clay cup. "I'm Kleito," she said. "Your mother and I were childhood friends, before we each married. And now the war has brought us back together. We've been anticipating your arrival. This pest is my little Euripides."

The little boy climbed into Melaina's lap, burying his head in her bosom.

"Drink slowly," Kleito said, "and conceal it from the others. The recipe is said to have come down to us from the centaur Chiron, who invented it to heal the wounds of warriors."

Melaina smelled the posset, spiced milk curdled with hot wine. Its taste sent a warm glow through her. Euripides moved about restlessly. Holding him was an unexpected comfort, even if his sharp-edged limbs poked into her tender ribs. His little body was as warm as glowing coals. He held a waxed tablet and stylus in his tiny hands and had scratched the first letters of the alphabet: α, β, and γ. The posset, beginning to do its work, Melaina relaxed and drifted toward sleep along with Euripides. Then Kleito spoke again.

"Your mother is here. Did you know?"

Melaina's eyes fluttered open, and she jumped to her feet, wondering if she'd heard correctly. Just then, Kallias returned.

"Follow me," he urged, leading Melaina down a hallway to a chamber of solemn men, who mumbled over a meal. Melaina saw mounds of cheese and barley cakes, boiled pigs' feet, lambs' legs, ripe olives and leeks, morsels of underdone entrails. Oh, she loved sweet entrails!

A shout rose up from amidst the din, and a woman rushed toward Melaina. It was Myrrhine, her mother. Myrrhine came out of the room and reached for Melaina, her hands all over the girl's face and limbs as if to check for the source of all the blood. "You look like a lamb led to slaughter," her mother said.

CHAPTER 5: THE WAR COUNCIL

Myrrhine had left home for Brauron the day before news broke of the Spartan defeat at Thermopylae. With the evacuation of Attica, the road east had been blocked at the foot of Mt. Hymettos. Realizing she couldn't get through, Myrrhine had sought refuge at the home of an old friend, Kleito, wife of Mnesarchides, and sent an overnight runner to the Hierophant at Eleusis telling him of her predicament. She asked that the Hierophant immediately retrieve Melaina. If he didn't, surely Melaina would be killed. Myrrhine had known nothing of her daughter's fate until she saw Melaina outside the banquet chamber with Kallias.

Myrrhine squeezed her daughter until the girl squirmed to free herself.

"My ribs are sore, mother."

"Why all the blood?"

Myrrhine listened to her daughter describe the events that occurred during the initiation, held her when she cried over Kynthia's death and her uncertainty at the fate of little Theodora.

"I also have so much to tell you, Melaina, things I couldn't before. The months you were away in Brauron seem years."

But Myrrhine didn't have time to elaborate. Kallias reappeared. He dragged them both inside the dining hall where a hastily organized council of generals was in progress. Hestia's hearth burned in the corner to the far right, flames licking high into the air through a hole in the ceiling.

One of the men was on his feet speaking. Myrrhine whispered in her daughter's ear, "He's Xanthippus, an Athenian general." Myrrhine wondered how Kimon would handle being in the presence of Xanthippus, as the general had sent Kimon's father to prison where the old man had died. Xanthippus was a short but broad man, deep-chested. His voice was quiet, and so the room fell silent under the soft swiftness of his words.

"... though defeated at the Hot Gates, we've learned a valuable lesson: how to fight Persians on land. Our fleet at Artemisium also proved it could hold its own at sea even when badly outnumbered. We've looked into the enemy's jaws and found his teeth dull, heard his roar, and found it less than frightening. Xerxes won a battle, but planted the seeds of his own destruction."

Myrrhine noticed that the men appeared restless, their eyes trained on Melaina's bloody chiton. Another man rose to interrupt Xanthippus. Myrrhine whispered in her daughter's ear, "That's Mnesarchides, Kleito's husband."

"Enough, Xanthippus," Mnesarchides said. "Kallias, richest of Athenians, has returned from Brauron, and by the looks of the maiden, though she be blood-splattered, his mission was a success. Torchbearer, what word do you bring from the coast?"

"Grim news," said Kallias, stepping forward. "But also an account of events forecasting great promise." The tie binding his hair had broken, and his black mane fell in ringlets to his shoulders, glistening against his ashen skin. "I've indeed retrieved unharmed the maid of Eleusis, out of the very hands of Persians. Only moments after I reached the temple of Artemis at Brauron, a band of Persians, who'd come by sea, tried to assassinate her. I witnessed the priestess of the temple trade her own life for this little priestess. Kynthia lies dead, the temple overrun. The five warriors I took with me are also dead. Last we saw, the temple was in flames. We barely escaped with our own lives."

Voices erupted, men turned to look at one another. "Great Zeus! Brauron burned, Kynthia dead. What's to become of us?"

"This knife," Kallias drew his own dagger, held it high for all to see, "took the life of two Persian assassins. I tell you, this is an omen of no small import. My own eyes witnessed the courage of this young woman, felt small standing beside her though I killed those who would have killed her. In the face of certain death, she stood her ground as did her father, Kynegeiros, at Marathon. Alas, that he died there! And all this yet but preparation for witnessing how the gods cherish her. Perhaps Kynegeiros himself watches over her, for during our brief encounter with the Persians just outside the gates of Paiania, a Persian spear pierced her through, but now she bears no wound from it. The holes in her chiton are there for all to see."

Myrrhine considered Kallias' words about her daughter, realizing his talent for hyperbole, yet the crowd listened trance-like. "Kallias," said one, "we haven't had such a favorable sign since the great god Pan was seen in the Peloponnese voicing his support for us at Marathon."

Kallias finished with a flourish. "School yourself in this young woman's courage! If the warriors of Hellas have half her mettle, we can defeat the Persians, no matter their numbers."

The chamber fell silent, all eyes transfixed on Melaina. Myrrhine saw her daughter blush deeply.

Xanthippus rose again. "Word that the Persians are burning our temples is of concern but not unexpected. Perhaps Hellas' salvation will come from divine outrage. No one could have foretold that long-dead Theseus would return to lead us at Marathon. Let us hope a new savior will deliver us this time."

Myrrhine felt a tug at her sleeve. "When can I eat?" Melaina whispered. "Will they never stop talking?"

Mnesarchides again rose to halt Xanthippus' monologue. "Kimon, tell us of your return from the southland. We, who remained behind to execute the evacuation, have been in sore need of your counsel. What can you tell us of our friends at Cape Sounion?"

Kimon was a great presence, heavier than Kallias but with the same dark countenance. He spoke with authority, emphasizing his words with a sweep of the arm, yet still projecting humility. His face was flushed from wine, and Myrrhine noticed that he never looked in the direction of Xanthippus. "My tale is much the same as Kallias'. Two Persian warships put ashore at Cape Sounion and quickly overran the temple of Poseidon. Before we were forced to flee north, we saw the nearby silver mines at Laurium fall to Xerxes. Zeus has turned his back on us for now." Having given his message, Kimon stepped back among the crowd for someone else to speak, but stepped forward again. "One more thing," he said. "I've spoken to those who've been behind Persian lines. They talk of Xerxes hiding his dead from his own men. Xerxes doubts himself, if I read it rightly."

Mnesarchides rose. "Perhaps Xerxes fears our will to fight as Leonidas and his men demonstrated at Thermopylae." He turned away from Kimon. "Kallias, I know your mission is urgent. During the priestess of Demeter's short stay with us," he looked toward Myrrhine, "I've learned of the Hierophant's concern for all Hellas should the Mysteries, only three weeks away, suffer neglect. Your word of this hearty but tender young woman certainly gives us courage. How could we expect less of the daughter of Kynegeiros? We'd hoped to catch a night's rest and depart tomorrow, but now see we must take what's packed and make our getaway before the pass closes. We'll detain you no longer, except for a libation and prayer from the priestess of Demeter before leaving."

Myrrhine noticed the muscles of Kallias' jaw tighten. After all, he was a priest and could have performed the ritual himself. She decided that her prayer would be to Kallias' divine ancestor, Hermes, from whom all Kallias' family of Kerkyes descended. Myrrhine pushed her daughter away, though the girl groaned at the separation, and walked toward Xanthippus. She received a cup of wine from him, averted her eyes to avoid contact, then splashed the altar stone with the red liquid and raised her arms.

"Hermes, guide of souls in the Underworld, protector of travelers; all who meet here tonight journey the road to death. Though for some it will come soon, others later, we are all yours. O Argeiphontes, father of lies and thieves, give false prophecies to the Persians and loot their courage. Grant us a safe journey home and strength for the dark days before us. Grant this and ever we'll roast glistening fat and thick thigh pieces in your honor."

As soon as her prayer ended, a long-haired slave boy approached and set a bowl of mint-scented water before Xanthippus, who dipped his hands, then dried them in the slave's hair. Another slave brought baskets bulging with barley bread, Demeter's gift—steaming loaves lofting mingled smells of yeast and honey. Platters of hot food soon crowded the table, and men tore apart great loaves, using the pieces to scoop stew.

The three of them left the room, and Mnesarchides followed. He and Kleito begged Myrrhine and Melaina to join them at their other home on Salamis after evacuating Eleusis. But Kallias, in his hurry, ushered them outside into the dark as Melaina protested her hunger.

"Quit whining," said Kallias. "You can eat at journey's end."

Melaina snatched a small loaf as the group left the room.

The young man, who'd come with Kallias and Melaina, was waiting alongside the chariot. The high-stepping horses, looking refreshed after being watered and fed, anxiously pawed the ground and rattled their bridles.

Kimon burst out the door to join their party. "If I stay behind with Xanthippus so close by, I'll kill him," he said. "Ever the call to avenge my father's death plagues me."

Myrrhine sympathized with Kimon. Her own husband had served and died at Marathon under Kimon's father, Miltiades. Yet a few years later, Xanthippus had had the victorious general imprisoned, where he died of gangrene from an unhealed wound. She wondered what would become of them if the generals themselves hated each other. She looked west where the glow from Athens lit the horizon. The great city hadn't slept either. The chariot was crowded with the three of them, oaken axle creaking under the weight. Kimon and the young man went in the lead ahead of the chariot.

Myrrhine held her daughter to her, and they slumped to the floorboard behind the Dadouchos. Slow-flowing time drifted by with the darkness.

★

Gradually came the dawn, and with it wagons, horses, sheep, goats and the people driving them along the narrow roadway to Athens. Behind them in the distance, wisps of smoke trailed skyward. When the sun broke the horizon, they entered the outskirts of Athens, where they learned of the overnight evacuation of its citizens, who embarked to Troezen on the Peloponnese coast, and the islands Salamis and Aegina. Myrrhine knew that many slaves and men of great age would have to stay behind. All could not be saved. The howls of homeless dogs echoed the countryside.

They stopped momentarily at a small township Myrrhine recognized as Kolonus. Kimon departed from them, taking a road to the west, and the young man dismounted, racing inside a smithy from which issued a great clang of hammers. She saw a statue of a horseman and heard a nightingale trill a clear note over the green glade. Soon they were back on the road.

Kallias skirted Athens' city walls, then turned west along the Sacred Way, shouting and cracking his whip at those who failed to step aside. Foamy sweat laced the backs of the horses though they never slacked their pace. They swept past wagons piled high with household goods, prized rubble stacked in rickety handcarts pulled by pitiful men and women, their poverty-gripped lives having been wrested from them. The rush of people to the sea became a flowing river of desperation.

Myrrhine realized that Athens was gone. She had a vision of great Ares, god of war, awakening from a ten-year slumber, rising above the landscape, irritable, bloodthirsty. She wondered about the strange occurrences during Melaina's initiation. If what Kallias said was right, Melaina's salvation had come in true Artemis fashion. The goddess had given her own priestess for Melaina. Perhaps a recent prophecy was also true. The oracle had come from the three priestesses at Dodona, who read the words of Zeus in the rustle of an old oak's leaves:

When all is lost and the smoke of great cities

darkens the bright passage of Helios' chariot
across the heavens so even those of great courage
whimper and cower in corners, the two
who are one will again take on mortal form
and walk among us. They will stand firm in the face
of great danger, against the barbarian's yoke.

They realized the "two who are one" must be Demeter and Kore, the two goddesses of the Mysteries. Still, during these restless times, prophecies swept through cities and villages like summer dust devils. One could pick and choose to suit the circumstance.

Myrrhine squeezed Melaina to her. She was so young, not yet fifteen. But in the time Melaina had been away, she'd changed, developed new confidence. Myrrhine now saw a hard look in her daughter's eyes, a loss of innocence. Oh, how she looked forward to hearing Melaina's voice echoing again in the halls of Eleusis.

Kallias' bare leg brushed against Myrrhine's arm, and she looked up at him. This was the closest she'd been to a man since her husband had died. This man's remoteness and countenance matched some dark place inside herself, where she'd put all her feelings toward men. With her daughter in her arms and a man so close, memories of her husband surfaced, and her body welcomed the opportunity to be its old self, hands tingling with the memory of sliding along a broad shoulder, down a hairy arm. She swallowed, realizing this man was her own age. Kynegeiros had been much older.

She'd heard sordid things about Kallias, that he'd taken his fortune from a Persian during the battle of Marathon. As the story went, the man mistook Kallias for a king because he dressed as the Dadouchos. The man had shown him the treasure to buy his life. They say Kallias killed him anyway to hide the source of his wealth. Myrrhine didn't believe it. Jealousy drove many to speak ill of the rich. Even though his family descended from Hermes, divine thief and murderer, she couldn't believe it of Kallias. She only knew he'd fought beside her beloved Kynegeiros and spoke nothing but praise of her husband's bravery. She felt a great kindness toward him because of it. And now he'd taken Kynegeiros' place and saved her daughter's life. She not only thought well of him; with his body so close, a woman's longing passed through her. But guilt came quickly, an old bitter companion. "Forgive me, Kynegeiros," she whispered.

As she held Melaina in her arms, she felt her daughter quake. Was this the return of an illness so frightening that years ago she'd not told even the Hierophant? She shielded her daughter's face with her own cape. Kallias mustn't see.

Melaina convulsed in Myrrhine's arms, limbs rigid, foam appearing in the corners of her mouth. Myrrhine shoved her fingers between Melaina's teeth to protect her tongue, ignoring the pain of her gnawing. Oh, divine Demeter! Not the falling sickness! Ten years before, when Melaina was first told of her father's death, Myrrhine found her little girl in the midst of a seizure on the ground before the Gates of Hades.

Myrrhine felt her daughter shudder in her arms, wake. Myrrhine smiled down at her, realizing Melaina knew nothing of the terrible tremor that had seized her while sleeping. The thunder of the horses' hooves filled Myrrhine's ears, and she watched the morning sun paint a warm glow on Melaina's cheeks as they approached the outskirts of Eleusis.

The chariot filled the sanctuary with dust as it came to a stop just inside the Greater Propylaea. Slaves rushed to assist, two men for the horses and a long line of women for the priestess and her daughter. As they exited the chariot, the Hierophant appeared in the gateway. Myrrhine had never seen her father look so old, and his face now carried a worried shadow. Melaina ran to him, throwing her arms about his waist. Myrrhine heard her daughter ask, "Who's the young man who accompanied us here?"

"Who?" asked the Hierophant.

"Him, the tall, bronze young man."

"That's Sophocles," her grandfather said.

CHAPTER 6: RETURN TO ELEUSIS

The Archon Basileus in Athens canceled the Mysteries without consultation. The Hierophant was bewildered. "They hold the Olympics but cancel the human race? Oh, for the days when Eleusis was its own independent state! Why do we have to subject the Mysteries to Athens' arbitrariness and political squabbling?"

Melaina heard Kallias sorely complain of not being in Olympia himself, having been recalled at the last moment to retrieve her from Brauron. His four black stallions had been the favorite in the chariot race. The Olympics were in progress even as the Persians murdered, pillaged, and burned throughout Attica.

Still, the Hierophant resisted evacuating Eleusis, and the city awaited its fate as the fires to the west grew closer, refugees streaming past to the Peloponnese. Not all planned to pass through, and the poorer of them, seeing the temple of Demeter as the ultimate refuge, brought their sheep, goats and cows onto temple grounds. The Hierophant couldn't bear turning them away, and still refused to evacuate.

The uncertainty created was whispered throughout the city. "The old man has lost his wits," said some. "Patience, he knows the will of the gods," said others. The poorer residents and slaves, those who could escape their masters, loaded their possessions into wagons, and took refuge in Corinthia beyond the Isthmus. The rich had more at stake. They congregated in the streets and shouted at one another, laughing at their neighbor's indecisiveness and crying over their own.

★

Melaina heard the Hierophant's booming voice echoing down the hall. She crept closer. He and Aeschylus were at each other's throats over the evacuation, again. Aeschylus had been at Artemisium with the Greek fleet and claimed better judgment of the situation. "All Attica is deserted. Why not Eleusis?"

"Evacuate the town if you wish, but not the sacred quarter or temple of Demeter," was the Hierophant's steadfast response. "Delphi stood its ground even when the Persians entered the nearby sanctuary of Athena Pronaia. Apollo defended his own, hurling boulders until the Persians panicked and fled. Even Kallias, though he pulled all his possessions from Athens, hasn't stripped his home here. We're still gathering the harvest. We'll continue stockpiling fruit and grain until Xerxes is on our doorstep. We'll never survive if we lose the entire crop."

"You're working for Xerxes. He'll take it all."

"You talk of Xerxes pillaging and burning all in his path, but refugees passing through Eleusis tell me a different story. Xerxes is showing considerable restraint in Boeotia and Attica. I've heard scattered reports of burned temples, Brauron is definitely one, but most still stand. Even looting is sporadic. And Xerxes hasn't burned Athens."

Melaina heard Aeschylus storm out, and ran to the hilltop to watch him catch a boat to Salamis to rejoin the fleet. She felt uneasy herself, having experienced Persian wrath firsthand.

★

All Eleusis lived in the shadow of the great temple of Demeter, and Melaina's home was within the nearby semi-sacred quarter where the priests lived. Having spent her entire life—until the months at Brauron—at Eleusis, she hadn't realized the luxury of her own home. Just outside the large double doors stood the herm, a boundary pillar topped by Hermes' head and bearing an erect phallus, a male watchdog to ward off intruders. The Hall of Men was just inside the double doors: a courtyard lined with separate chambers spread in a vista of bronze-paneled walls with azure moldings. A colonnade stood in the center, enclosing a small altar of Zeus Herkeïos, protector of the home. The women, and Melaina in particular as the young mistress of the house, were permitted in this hall only rarely, and then when no strangers were present.

The doors at the far end of this courtyard opened into the great dining hall where golden pedestals held aloft bright torches of pitch pine. Great chairs lined the walls strewn with fine embroidery made by slave women under her mother's close instruction. This was where, in evenings of days long passed, her father had stalked about extolling the virtues of this philosophy or that to his enthroned dinner guests. Melaina's dim memories of her father were of him in this great hall during the evening, and of a singer of Homer's great poems come to charm them and their friends.

Hidden away in one corner of the courtyard was a small chamber for storing papyrus scrolls. This was her grandfather's library of ancient writings. Melaina had always loved lounging on the floor, a scroll spread before her. Early on, her mother had taught her to read, and Melaina thrived on it, studying Homer's ancient texts of the Trojan War, Odysseus' wanderings, and stories of Agamemnon's daughters, Iphigenia and Electra. In particular, Melaina studied the ancient book of prophecy called the Sibylline Oracles. Melaina had a great interest in the future and thought seercraft a magnificent profession. She read the tragedies of her Uncle Aeschylus along with many others. Her grandfather delighted to see that Melaina was such a scholar and questioned her from time to time, marveling at her capacity for learning. "What an odd little girl," he'd say. In the minds of Greek men, intelligence in females was a rarity.

Her mother's bedchamber, which she'd shared with Melaina's father until his death, occupied the space to one side of the dining hall. That of the Hierophant was directly opposed.

Through another set of bronze-plated doors stood the Hall of Women and another pillared courtyard. Here, daily, twenty maids sat around the mill grinding grain, or weaving upon their looms

and twirling distaffs. These women were as skillful at weaving, as
were the men of Eleusis in ship navigation. Their wool-hardened
hands were a constant blur of activity. As with the Hall of Men,
the women's rooms lined the periphery of this great hall. There,
Melaina took possession of her new sleeping quarters.

Until she left for Brauron, Melaina had slept in her mother's
large chamber, rolled up on a small cot in the corner. Her efforts
toward her dowry, she kept at the foot of her bed. This consisted
of woven quilts, blankets, rugs, and her formal attire. Since her
return, though, she'd slept in her own chamber just inside the
bronze doors, the only room in the Hall of Women with a window to the outside, providing a sunlit airiness during the day and
giving her a sense of insecurity at night.

Her receipt of the room from her mother was accomplished
with a private ceremony. Through the years Melaina had known
it as a strong room, closed and locked by a sliding timber. Once
opened, her mother revealed the reason for the security: it contained Melaina's inherited dowry. Though Melaina had never
known it to be open, the room had been immaculately kept, no
speck of dust allowed to fall on the treasures within. Her mother
revealed what her father had hoped one day to say himself, that
his mother had left her own dowry in his care, trusting to fate that
one day he would have a daughter. And indeed a treasure it was:
finely embroidered tapestries and delicately woven carpets were
stacked about, some woven with fine threads of gold.

"I'm a Eumolpid," her mother told Melaina, "as was your father, descendants of Eumolpus himself, leader of the people when
Demeter, during her travail, appeared at Eleusis vainly searching
for Kore. Your father's mother was my aunt, your father, my cousin. We shared the same great grandmother. Much of your dowry
has also come down from her, you being the latest in a long line
of women priestesses of the Mysteries."

Melaina said nothing, not particularly liking the implication
that she would also be a priestess, but not wishing to spoil the
moment with controversy. And, the dowry was quite a spectacle.

Her mother opened the old chest. The outside was common, carvings and markings of some ancient script, now worn faint. As the lid squeaked open, exotic aromas and glimmers of light scintillated from contents that seemed to light the interior.

"This chest contains great wealth, Melaina. We've never been poor, and some of what you see is believed to have belonged to Eumolpus' wife, whose name is lost to us. Since this chest is in the domain of women, which is also true of the Mysteries, even your father knew little of its contents. Although none of it is really secret, it's best not to make the contents common knowledge. Could well incite jealousy."

Her mother lifted the fine linen clothes from one end of the chest, stacking them neatly on the floor until she uncovered the bottom. From within that wood foundation she lifted a small, hinged hatch to reveal a hidden compartment.

Melaina couldn't restrain herself. She plunged her hands into the darkness and felt a cold mass of loose coins, withdrew a handful. It was a wealth she could have never imagined. A mixture of coins, some so old and tarnished she'd never seen the like, others shiny enough to have been minted yesterday at Eleusis.

Melaina knew little of such coins. Her mother explained. "These," she said holding up a bean-shaped pellet, "are called 'dumps' and are hundreds of years old. The maker struck them to show that they are solid and not plated. These," she said holding up a shiny but worn coin with a lion's head, "are made of electrum and come from Lydia during King Gyges reign. They are at least two-hundred years old." Her mother got lost in the naming of them, and lingered on the Athenian "Owl," a coin with the likeness of Athena on one side and an owl on the other. It was a tarnished silver tetradrachm, and minted rather recently. Then, she held up a smaller coin, made of gold, with a profile of a king on one side and a ship at sea on the other. "This is the daric, from Persia," she said with a touch of venom. "King Darius minted it. It was he who is responsible for the death of your father. Our generals brought all these to me, taken from the Persian ship on which he died. I gave them all to you. Such a pittance for the loss of a father." She paused and stared at the coin, lost in deep thought. Then she recovered herself.

"Your female ancestors have added to it through the ages," her mother said. "Don't use it unless the necessity arises. This will be your daughters' legacy also. I could tell you many stories passed down with this dowry, but with the evacuation, I haven't time. Perhaps we can make some when we get to Salamis." With that, her mother made Melaina return the coins, then closed the secret compartment, and replaced the clothes. Myrrhine looked as though she had something more to say, as her eyebrows drew together. "This will give you a measure of independence for life. Should your husband put away your marriage and leave you, he must restore it to its original value."

Whatever it was that bothered her mother, she didn't put into words.

That night as Melaina lay awake, the sounds of refugees fleeing the Persian hordes drifted in from the nearby road. Her thoughts shifted to the chest and its marvelous contents. Her mother's words returned. "You are the latest in a long line of women priestesses to the Mysteries." She worried about telling her mother of her desire to follow Artemis. Is this the way I am to repay my mother's and ancestors' generosity? she wondered.

★

Melaina experienced many changes upon her return home. She saw none of her friends and cousins, who were kept indoors as their families readied their escape to Salamis. It wasn't just the Persian invasion, but also her mother's demand that she take command of the slave women, weavers and tenders of the sacred hearth, while Myrrhine orchestrated their own escape on the sly. Although the Hierophant forbade it, the entire sacred quarter prepared for evacuation, and Myrrhine was behind it all.

The caretaking of her father's grave now fell to Melaina. She'd purposely avoided her father's tomb since returning, but that evening she went carrying a wicker funerary basket filled with nourishment for the dead. There, she found herself overcome with guilt at being apart from him for so long. "Dear father," she said, "forgive my months of neglect while at Brauron. The only consolation I can give is that you never left my thoughts. My one great crime is that I can no longer visualize your appearance. How could I have forgotten your kind face? Still, it's done, and I hope you'll punish me for it." She sobbed softly.

Just as she was about to leave, a thought occurred to her, as if someone had spoken. In days of old, King Agamemnon's son, Orestes, and his daughter, Electra, had avenged their father's murder. She continued praying. "Having seen the Persian menace firsthand, I realize the depth of wrong done you. I'll do whatever I can to avenge your death, although I have no brother to help me as did Electra. I love you, father."

Then she slipped out unnoticed to the blacksmith's shop.

She'd desperately wished to see her friends and had set a plan in motion. Even as a child Melaina had been fearless and difficult for her mother to control. Within the stone fence in back of their home, a deep woods grew: black alder, poplar, and a small grove of cypress. It was Melaina's favorite place, where she came to watch birds from all over the Aegean rest their wings: horned owls that hooted evenings, falcons, cormorants, bustling flocks of finches.

Her favorite place for reading her grandfather's scrolls, those he'd let her borrow from his library, was within the shadow of a large pomegranate tree. The pomegranate was a symbol of Persephone, and therefore of the Mysteries of Demeter that fueled the ancient sanctuary. Melaina felt close to the divine Daughter of the Dead, particularly since her own father was among those who had passed to the Elysian Fields. She felt closer to him there beneath the pomegranate tree.

Around the smooth-stone wall ran crooking grapevines, the ply of green leaves hiding purple clusters. Here and there along the base of the fence, beds of violets and tender grasses grew. Melaina was forever climbing the fence, peering over its edge and into the smithy beyond. When she was older, she scaled the fence to get a closer look, and there the hysterical slave women, who were supposed to be watching her, would find her keeping company with the blacksmith. Her mother would then set Melaina down, provide a lengthy dissertation on the expectation that women would leave their homes seldom, if ever, and that the most cherished girls were those whose faces had never been seen in public.

But Melaina had a scandalous appetite for adventure. She developed a reputation. Her mother secretly thought it amusing and rather appreciated the blacksmith's parental attitude toward Melaina. The little girl sorely missed the male influence of her father, and the blacksmith helped fill the gap. But her mother hated the smith's two workmen, "fashioners of evil," she called them, and sternly warned Melaina to stay away from them.

Earlier in the day, Melaina, heedless of impropriety, had sent a slave girl to ask Agido and Anaktoria, her two best friends, to meet her in the smoked-filled precinct of the blacksmith. As she left her father's grave and crept out into the bedlam of the dark street, she fell in behind a herdsman and several bleating sheep, their tiny hooves echoing sharp cries against stone. She had to step aside as a man pulling a two-wheeled cart plunged by out of control. The flashing blacksmith's fire was her guiding light.

She loved watching the smith work, and he made jewelry for her, anything she asked. He was a disciple of two gods, crippled Hephaestus, god of fire, and Prometheus, Forethought himself, who stole fire from Hephaestus and gave it to mankind, so we might not dwindle into nonexistence. Thus, the blacksmith owed his livelihood to Hephaestus and Prometheus, and he repaid them by telling and retelling their myths. Melaina would sit and watch him, winds of the two bellows delivering great gusts or faint puffs at his bidding, the smiting and counter-smiting of his great hammer and anvil working the woe on woe of beaten metal as it shaped to his will.

Melaina entered his open shop from the back, coughing at furnace smoke. She stood watching him, busy as he was at the bellows, from the open door to the room where he kept his precious metals and where her friends would soon join her. The blacksmith, Palaemon by name, suffered from a birth deformity, as had Hephaestus, and limped on both feet. This resulted in a rocking motion as he moved about, a hesitating forward roll of his entire frame. His upper body had strengthened to compensate for weak legs, so that he appeared a composite of two people, a giant from the waist up, somewhat of a dwarf from the waist down. He was from the island of Rhodes and likened the lower portion of himself to that of the Telchines, the mythical dwarfed metalworkers of the Underworld who practiced magic beneath Rhodes. "With these withered legs," he'd told her, "all my hopes are for the next life. That's why I chose Eleusis when I left Rhodes."

Melaina had hoped to talk to him while she waited for her friends, but a constant stream of warriors passed through demanding immediate repairs to weapons and armor. As the blacksmith pounded new spear points and reshaped damaged swords, Melaina heard them ask if he'd evacuate, but Palaemon shook his head. He'd left Rhodes years before to escape the Persians. He'd not run again.

Two of the smith's workmen, Akmon and Damnameneus, labored at the anvils. These two sullen giants were her mother's "fashioners of evil," whom Melaina had never heard speak and thought them perhaps mutes. A third, dwarf-like man with bow-shaped legs sat at a table working cold gold into jewelry and mumbling something about tears of the gods and the birth of metals.

Melaina spotted her friends peeking into the shop and motioned them to her. How good to feast on their smiling faces. Anaktoria was tall, thin and stately, as the ancients described Artemis. Agido was short, round. My little dumpling, Melaina called her. How she loved Agido!

Melaina made each of them tell what had happened during her long absence. Agido's father had given her older sister in marriage to a man from Ithaca. Her mother was shattered. "Oh,

Melaina!" Agido cried, pearl-drop tears spilling from her eyes, "I may never see her again."

"Take heart, little Agido," said Melaina, thinking Agido reminded her of Theodora at Brauron. "Ithaca is a fine island. Odysseus, the man of many wiles, once ruled there. At least she'll be safe a while longer from the tight fist of Persia."

Melaina had never seen Anaktoria so excited. Although her friend tried to keep it hidden, her eyes fairly sparkled, and her hands couldn't keep still. Anaktoria stood behind Agido with her hands on Agido's shoulders. "This summer I went with mother to the great healing center at Epidaurus. She dreamt of Asklepios."

"God of healing?"

"Exactly."

"Why did your mother go?"

"She'd not had a child in two years. She feared her womb had dried up. She got pregnant the very next month."

"Wonderful! I know you'll enjoy a little brother or sister."

Melaina grew serious and reached for the leather bag she'd snatched while escaping Brauron and over Kallias' objection. She raised a few notes on the aulos, told them of her new proficiency on the lyre and of her newfound love of Sappho's poetry. But finally she told of her plans.

"I've decided to follow Artemis," she said. "I'll not marry but remain virgin and teach here at Eleusis."

She didn't get the response she expected. Agido was confused. "Why?" she asked. "Marriage is every girl's one wish, her fulfillment as wife and mother."

Anaktoria's eyebrows pulled together.

Melaina told of her desire to start a school for girls at Eleusis. "Like Sappho's school for girls on Lesbos," she said. Then she realized they knew nothing of Sappho and would never understand. She grew irritable and dropped the subject entirely. Instead, she told them of the burning of the temple at Brauron, the death of Kynthia. She was about to relay the story of the camel when they heard a noise from outside, a growl. Melaina turned just as Agido's mother pounced on them.

"I might have known she'd be with *you*," she said, jerking little Agido to her feet and scowling at Melaina. She turned on Anaktoria. "Your mother is beside herself with worry." As she dragged Agido from the room, Anaktoria's face grew grave. "I'd better go too," she said, and charged after them.

Left breathless and guilt ridden, Melaina realized she should have known better than to drag others into her little outing. She'd been gone longer than planned herself and tried to sneak past the blacksmith to hurry home, but he caught her eye. Palaemon sponged his face, hands, massive neck and hairy chest, then taking up a stick to lean on, came limping to Melaina.

"Little mistress," he said, his kind face still with beads of sweat. "I'd heard you returned to us."

"It's good to be back in the warmth of your shop once again, to hear the music of metal on metal. I was afraid you'd forgotten me."

He smiled through a grizzly beard but said nothing. Instead he shuffled to a box he kept against the wall, raised the lid and retrieved something shiny. "So you're a woman now," he said, but his voice showed no irony. He seemed to be groping for words. He sat on the chair before her, where Agido had sat only a moment before, and held in the light of an oil lamp a magnificent gold broach.

"On Rhodes," Palaemon said, "I learned the art of fine metal work. This is the first I've attempted in years. The magicians who live beneath Rhodes developed the subtle working of granulated gold many centuries ago."

He stopped for a moment to catch his breath, and Melaina realized his excitement. He brought both her hands forward and placed the object in them. "It's an eagle, a special one made by the marriage of metals, male and female ores."

Melaina found its beauty spellbinding. The eagle had been created from tiny gold granules merged but not melted onto a gold surface. It seemed to retain the spark and flame of the metalworking process, throwing both light and shadow. "Its beauty defies saying," she said.

"Thousands of years ago when Prometheus stole fire and gave it to man, Zeus ordered Hephaestus to chain Prometheus to a Scythian mountainside at the edge of the world. For thirty thousand years an eagle came every day to eat out Prometheus' liver, which renewed itself every night. This golden eagle is a reminder of that one, but also contains a warning. When Prometheus gave us fire, something came with it. His act was one of arrogance, and it's tainted our existence ever since. It's as if the fuel with which all fires burn, even those of the soul, is arrogance. Our arrogance tells us we control our fate, and we're unable to accept that the gods give us our lot in life. In fact, we're but the beaten metal molded in the smithy of the gods. Remember that, little mistress, and the world is yours. The gods punish arrogance swiftly."

Melaina had hardly heard his words, so captivated was she by the ancient symbols etched on its underside. The sharp scratches seemed to release the broach's own internal light. "And the script?"

The smith's eyes rose to meet hers, but he hesitated. "It's not so much the words but the power locked within. The language is very old. Comes from ancient Crete before even king Minos or his mother Europa, stolen from Tyre by Zeus himself, walked the craggy shores of the giant island. So old we've lost the sound of the words. But when I was a child, the Telchines of Rhodes still knew the ancient writing and taught me to render the letters. They also taught me a bit of their magic, pale though it's now become even in their hands. It's not a good-luck charm, more a divine commandment."

Palaemon sat for a moment lost in thought, eyes mesmerized by the gold light coming from the object she held. He woke from the trance. "Off with you!" he said, looking alarmed, "before your mother finds you here and renders my head as lame as my legs."

"I'll study it well, keeping in mind your words. Perhaps its insight will be revealed when I need it most." She clutched the broach to her heart, bent and kissed him on the sooty cheek. Then she was off.

★

The indiscretion of Melaina's appearance in public, along with her friends, didn't escape her mother's ears. For the next two days, Myrrhine pushed and shoved Melaina about. First, it was the potters needing her immediate attention, then the spinning room where the slave girls struggled with evacuating, and finally the kitchen, where so much had been sent on to Salamis that fixing a meal for the Hierophant was no longer possible. Melaina found the panic of the slave girls contagious and resisted a pull toward screaming herself.

To escape the frenzied activity and her mother's scrutiny, she climbed the hill to her favorite overlook of the bay where she had, in the past, been allowed to go only with adult supervision. Now, she was an adult and escaped under her own recognizance. She hadn't had a moment to herself, and although usually she avoided solitude, now she noticed a definite longing for it.

From her vantage point, she could see a long ant trail of people and beasts of burden coming from the north. These were refugees from Plataea, Eleutherai and the legendary foothills of Mt. Kithaeron, where Oedipus had been exposed as a child and the frenzied maenads of Dionysus ripped apart wild animals and ate their flesh raw. The trail came to the very edge of Eleusis where it turned west to the Isthmus and Corinthia. Through the low rumble of all this traffic, Melaina heard the sharp ping of the blacksmith's hammer.

She found a seat on a stone shaped by ancient hands beside a laurel bush and pulled a small clay tablet from her bag. Strumming her lyre, she sang. "Artemis, arrow-pouring virgin and divine nurturer of moral youths, I sing to thee and ask not for a bow and swift arrows, not for a gift at all, but only for something I already have. Give me forever my maidenhood to keep, and stay the hand of Aphrodite when she comes bringing weak knees and limb-gnawing passion. O don't forsake Melaina now that she's grown, Artemis. Instead, bring Melaina..."

A noise stopped her, something on the other side of the laurel, and she looked around it to see Sophocles' tall form gazing
out to sea. If he's heard me, I'll die, she thought, but he seemed
to be judging the magnitude of the sunset or the thickness of
distant smoke from Persian fires. He looked less formidable than
that night before Kallias' chariot leading their escape. Perhaps he
doesn't even know I'm here, she thought. Her heart sank when
he finally spoke.

"Who is this poet you quote with such confidence? Though
it rings of Sappho, the rhythm seems fresh, original. Such a delicious weaving of melody and rhythm. Is it a poet of the past that
my education is sorely lacking, or someone too recent to be in
the curriculum?"

Melaina tried to take a breath but found no air. Why didn't
he return down the hill? she wondered. He must know it's not
proper for me to be alone with a young man. "Surely, you make
fun of me, sir. It's my very own poetry. A man of any manners
wouldn't eavesdrop on a lady who, thinking she's alone, opens her
heart to a goddess."

Young Sophocles, barely three years her senior, his cheeks
covered with something more than fuzz but less than beard,
peeked around the laurel bush, alarmed. "Forgive me. Until you
spoke, I thought I was alone myself. Still, I wouldn't trade hearing
your poetry for a season at the Dionysia."

"Perhaps if you hadn't laughed at me over the camel, I'd think
more kindly of your intentions. Your flattery does me no credit.
I'll be ashamed to open my mouth henceforth."

"No! Don't be. Truly, I'm grateful to have heard you, but
ashamed it embarrassed you. I too am a poet still in training and
hope one day to present tragedies at the City Dionysia. I've been
laughed at and told my gift is modest, so would never think un-
kind thoughts of another's poetry."

"I've heard it said, the slow-maturing soul gains the deeper
insight."

"Perhaps. Still Lamprus, my music teacher, says dancing is my only talent."

"I would have thought you'd be home evacuating instead of leisurely roaming a hilltop. Do you live in Eleusis?"

"No. Beautiful Kolonus. You might remember. We stopped there briefly on our way back from Brauron. It's just north of Athens. We evacuated to Salamis several days ago."

"Yes, indeed I do remember. And a marvelous site it seemed. Is that where you receive training to become a famous poet?"

"Now it's you who's playing with me. My father is but a simple blacksmith. We use my teacher's home in Athens and his second one here in Eleusis. That's why I'm here. I'll never be a famous poet, but he encourages me, perhaps beyond my measure."

"The smith here at Eleusis is not simple, and I suspect your father isn't either. They speak of blacksmiths as the 'priests of metals'. But who might be this famous poet teaching you?"

"The greatest in the world, Aeschylus."

"Uncle Aeschylus!" Mention of him brought her back to her senses. She panicked. "I must go before I'm seen. You've nothing to lose. I could be outcast."

"Here," said Sophocles, snapping a branch from the bush, "laurel is sacred to Apollo and has powers of purification." He reached it out to her. "For my lady," he said, "to cleanse her from an encounter with the forbidden."

She reached for it, averting her gaze, but not before noticing Sophocles' subtle blue eyes. She felt close to him because hers were blue also, but deep blue, not subtle. Gradually his stare drew her eyes upward until their eyes met. She saw him stagger, wondered at it. Their fingers intertwined, both refusing to let go the branch. His warmth seeped into her. Such exquisite warmth. She'd heard of the legendary hotness of young men, its superiority to that of women, and had always thought it a lie.

CHAPTER 7: THE ORACLE FROM DELPHI

The following day, her mother pulled Melaina from the chaos of evacuation and took her to the Hierophant. They found him in the library overseeing a scribe. Melaina's grandfather was castigating the man over the quality of his letters and left-out words, but changed his tone when he saw Melaina. He took the women to the temple of Demeter, the Telesterion, where she'd been initiated five years before. At ten, she'd been the youngest ever to witness the epiphany. They passed the altars of Demeter and Kore on the way and walked through the guarded entry. "Need a little privacy for important matters," he told the guards. Inside the Telesterion, they picked a path through the forest of columns, footsteps echoing. During the yearly initiation ceremony, three thousand initiates sat on the stair-stepping stone seats that lined the walls.

Melaina put on a hangdog look, resigned to punishment for the previous day's excursion and thinking that surely someone had seen her with Sophocles. Myrrhine walked in silence and looked worried herself. They made straight for the Anaktoron, where the Sacred Objects, the Hiera, Holiest of Holies, were kept and where everyone except the Hierophant was refused entry. His throne stood outside the bolted door, and he assumed his position in the great seat, a stately presence in his flowing wraps of colored cloth. Melaina's apprehension grew. Surely he was about to levy some formal punishment against her.

The Hierophant said he'd heard from Kallias of her final moments at Brauron, her initiation during the Night of the Bear. "But I want to hear it," he said, "from you. Details are important."

Melaina paused a moment to gather her thoughts, then told him all she remembered, eyes flooding with tears as she recalled the details of Kynthia's death.

"That's interesting," said the Hierophant, "particularly the fate of your she-goat, the fact the animal had not been sacrificed."

She continued and after she finished, he said, "I've heard nothing to compare with it, a goat refused and a human sacrificed provided, two actually, as Kallias read it. Remarkable."

"Not really, grandfather," said Melaina, "it was simply chance that the assassin intruded before I slit the she-goat's throat."

"'Twas the same as the casting of lots," he said. "The outcome of chance is ever the gods' handiwork. I've heard nothing like it since Iphigeneia."

"But I dreamed it the night before. And could have prevented it if I'd realized it was all to come to pass."

The old man raised his eyebrows, laughed out loud. "Simple guilt tells you that. Not even Zeus can change what the Fates ordain. But you've a gift for prophecy. I've known it for some time."

"What good is prophecy if it doesn't help?"

"Mortals don't always work toward fulfilling divine will. We all wear the gods' yoke, and those who know must spread the word. A priestess from Zeus' sacred grove was here not long ago on such a mission."

"Grandfather! One of the three doves of Dodona?" Melaina had never met a priestess from the most ancient of oracles and wished she'd not been away at Brauron.

The Hierophant nodded. "She brought word that Demeter and her divine daughter will come amongst us again."

"Still lamenting Kore's marriage?"

"More likely, concern for the Mysteries. Xerxes is a threat to Eleusis. You may play a role in the goddess' plans. When Artemis saved you at Brauron, she gave you a second fate. The goddess did that for a reason."

"A second fate? How extraordinary! What could the goddess want with me?"

"The gods have designs on all our lives, but you will be severely yoked. You've answered my question. Now, off with the two of you. I've the Dadouchos to contend with over this."

Melaina didn't particularly like the idea of her grandfather discussing her fate with Kallias, but stifled her objection. He may have saved my life, she thought, but that should be the end of it. The Hierophant returned to his chamber, but the mother and daughter lingered in the Telesterion. Melaina wanted to be alone, but Myrrhine wouldn't have it. "I have something to tell you," she said. "During the months of your absence, the Council of the Mysteries met and voted on admittance of new priests and priestesses. You were the only one approved."

Melaina started to protest, realizing she must reveal her plans for the future before the council decided for her.

"Please," her mother said. "I haven't finished. Ordinarily you wouldn't be told until the Hierophant decided it was time to assume the position, but word has leaked out. People will be whispering. He'll decide which vacancy you'll fill. Any will be a great honor, yet simply a steppingstone for your final life-long position. One day you'll take my place as priestess of Demeter, the most powerful position in the Mysteries other than that of the Hierophant."

Her mother paused, took Melaina into her arms and held her close. But Melaina stiffened. She felt none of her usual warmth and affection. Her mother continued talking, the words whispers in Melaina's ear.

"Perhaps now you can see the importance of not repeating the indiscretion at the blacksmith's. You're to stay out of the public eye."

Melaina started sweating, felt trapped. "But mother," she said, her voice a much younger whine. "I don't want to be a priestess. I want...." She pushed away, turned her back.

"What?" her mother asked.

Melaina wouldn't respond, felt an overwhelming sense of irritation.

"Talk, Melaina. What's wrong?"

When Melaina turned around, she'd changed. She was no longer the little girl she'd seemed a moment ago in her mother's arms. Melaina straightened and realized for the first time that she was as tall as her mother. "Never!" she cried, her eyes flashing. "I want to follow Artemis, not Demeter. I'll remain virgin and be a poetess like Sappho."

"That's foolishness. This is a different time, a different place. Sappho was below your station. You can't cast aside being the most important woman in Eleusis. Events and inscriptions will be dated by your name. You'll be in charge of the expense fund and receive an obol from each initiate. Your dowry will grow beyond bounds."

"But mother, why would the Muses give me song if I weren't supposed to sing? Besides, Sappho wasn't just a poetess." And Melaina assumed an adult stature she'd never shown, had deliberately hidden in fact. Appearing fragile had its advantages, but now she must show strength. "She ran a finishing school for aristocratic girls. Kynthia," and now her eyes filled with tears, "said my verses are sweet as Sappho's. And you have to admit that with my years of training, I'm the most educated young woman in Eleusis."

"Kynthia has filled your head with nonsense. You must realize that soon you're to be married. Sappho was married, even had a child. I warned your grandfather about sending you to Brauron where you could fall under Artemis' influence. The path of the virgin goddess is not for you. Demeter would be deeply offended. We've been close in the past. Don't let this come between us."

"No! Mother, you mustn't let them marry me off. I'll talk to grandfather." She fumbled in her leather bag. "I'm very good with the aulos," she said, "and Kynthia told me I had few peers on the lyre."

"The aulos is a sordid thing, disfigures the face. You want to be a common flute-girl?"

"Mother! I'm serious about poetry and teaching. The aulos is indispensable for a chorus."

Melaina saw her mother calm a little, although she still appeared determined. "Dreams of such independence can never
be. Women were allowed more freedom on Sappho's Lesbos one
hundred years ago. We're discouraged from even being seen in
public. Priestesses have a little more freedom than other women
but are still kept from the public. All must marry."

"You haven't remarried since father died."

"That's different. I've been waiting for a chance to talk to you
about that, but not while you're angry. Besides, you don't understand virginity. You would remain an empty vessel, your body a
sieve. Remember the Danaïdes, who in the Underworld were
condemned to carry water in bottomless jars? You'd be like the
people who haven't been initiated into the Mysteries."

"Kynthia wasn't an empty vessel. I can still be out of the public eye while running a finishing school. I could learn to teach
from Uncle Aeschylus. He loves me, mother, more than anything,
he once said. Sophocles says Uncle Aeschylus is the best poet in
the world." And then she blushed, realizing she'd blurted out her
latest indiscretion.

Her mother's voice filled with coarse anger. "When have you
been talking to Sophocles?"

Melaina turned her back again and walked away, her blush so
deep it reddened her bare shoulder.

"Melaina! Please come back. You're not well. I must talk to
you."

Melaina broke into a run, the clip-clop of her sandals echoing off the walls of the sacred chamber. She wondered what her
mother's last statement meant but simply couldn't bear to hear
anything conflicting with her own plans.

★

In the end, it was the priestess of Athena from Athens who
convinced the Hierophant to evacuate. She'd come to Eleusis after a harrowing escape to see Myrrhine. Melaina watched as the
woman collapsed into her mother's arms, sobbed long and hard,
then raised her red, tear-filled eyes. "We're done for, Myrrhine.

Athena, protectress of cities, bringer of civilization, has abandoned Athens. We put out the sugar-cake, like always, but the sacred serpent, whose form Athena has always assumed, didn't come to eat it. It turned hard and crumbly. The ants got it."

The Hierophant gave the word. "All but the sanctuary," he said. It wasn't just the priestess' tears. The Akropolis was under siege. A few of the more stouthearted Athenians had taken their lives in their hands to man the holy citadel.

The people of Eleusis gathered on the hill, where Melaina had surreptitiously met Sophocles, to view the distant spectacle. They stared toward Athens as black smoke trailed skyward. Xerxes had set fire to everything on the Akropolis. Even the women normally kept indoors escaped the confines of their homes to glimpse the horror. It caused a great stir among them. "By all that's divine!" said one. "Why would Athena permit the burning of the Parthenon?"

"And why would anyone, even a Persian, want to burn it?" said another.

"Persian sacrilege," said the Hierophant. "The gods mean nothing to the heathen." He turned back down the hill. "Evacuate if you're afraid," he said. "The Persians will have no trouble finding me." He lumbered off stiff as a tree trunk with his head bowed and dark robe pulled about him.

That night, torches burned for the evacuation, and delirious dogs ran about, infected with their owners' fright. All the next day, the people of Eleusis loaded boats to Salamis. Trunks, furniture, carpets, sacks of grain from Demeter's own storeroom, goats, sheep, chickens, all shipped to another shore.

Time came when Melaina and her mother were to leave also, their boat waiting patiently at the dock all day. Melaina delayed loading her dowry until the last moment, and in the end decided, over her mother's objections, to leave it behind. "I trust grandfather," she said. "The Persians won't pillage Eleusis." Finally, Myrrhine gave up and walked away from her headstrong daughter.

Late afternoon, a familiar boat appeared at dockside, one

carrying the dark muscular form of the Dadouchos. Kallias had come from Salamis with foreboding news. "Pray come, Myrrhine, bring your daughter," he said. They retired to the temple to consult the Hierophant, whom they found sitting on a stone outside the Gates of Hades, head bowed.

Melaina felt at sea surrounded by all these adults, a little frightened. She tagged along behind her mother but wished to be with Agido and Anaktoria. Are all my dreams of being a poetess and teacher simply a defense against becoming an adult? she wondered.

The Hierophant rose and bid them follow him home through the streets. "This is no place to talk," he said.

Kallias also sent word for Aeschylus.

Once there, the Hierophant offered prayer before the hearth of Hestia as Aeschylus stomped into the chamber, tired and dirty from working the evacuation. "This better be important," Aeschylus said.

Kallias spoke but lacked confidence. Melaina had never seen him so unsure of himself. "On Salamis, a debate rages in the War Council," he said. "Themistocles, the Athenian, and Eurybiades, the Spartan, are at each other's throats over war strategy. Eurybiades has convinced the council to abandon Salamis and forge the last line of defense at the Isthmus. But still, Themistocles argues."

"They couldn't agree on it being daylight or dark," said Aeschylus. "If Hellas' fate depends on harmony between those two, all is lost."

Kallias seemed devastated by Aeschylus' observation, but continued. "Several months ago, we consulted Delphi twice to learn our proper course. The first oracle spoke only doom for Hellas, but when the Athenian convoy returned wearing the sacred laurel of suppliants and begging some word of hope, the Pythia gave this." He held up a scrap of papyrus and read directly from it:

Not wholly can Pallas win the heart
of Olympian Zeus, though she prays him

with many prayers and all her subtlety.
Yet will I speak to you this other word,
as firm as adamant. Though all else
shall be taken within the bound of Kekrops
and the fastness of the holy mountain of Kithaeron,
Zeus the all-seeing grants Athena's prayer
that the wooden wall only shall not fall
but help you and your children.
Await not the host of horse and foot
coming from Asia, nor be still,
but turn your back and withdraw.
Truly a day will come when you will meet him
face to face. Divine Salamis, you will bring death
to women's sons when the corn is scattered,
or the harvest gathered in.

"See!" Aeschylus shouted at the Hierophant, "even Athena knew we should evacuate." Then he turned on Kallias. "I can't believe you've called me here for this. What good am I at interpreting oracles?"

"Patience," assured Kallias. "Though they've had Apollo's words all these months, the War Council is still in heavy disagreement over their meaning. The 'wooden wall' is the crux of the matter, it would seem. Where are we to regroup our forces? Some believe it's the wall being built across the Isthmus, others the wall of wooden ships Themistocles plans to sail against the Persians at Salamis, if he can convince the rest not to retreat further west. Help us. All Hellas weighs in the balance of this one choice."

Melaina had always known men to be decisive, ever ready with an answer. They didn't have any trouble telling women what to do. Knowing the generals were so uncertain about this oracle was frightening. Why did they have to resort to an oracle, anyway? Didn't they know how best to fight the enemy? And she wondered why Kallias wanted her and her mother there. They knew the ways of women but not where to fight a war. It made her mad to think these men floundered so. If her father were alive, he wouldn't put up with it. She could barely stay silent.

The Hierophant turned his back and addressed the fire, praying in an ancient tongue. Melaina loved the deep resonance of her grandfather's voice. Silence fell about the house and even the dogs no longer wailed. He spoke. "The problem goes deeper than the mere interpretation of this oblique oracle, Kallias. I've been concerned about the Mysteries ever since we heard Xerxes had crossed the Hellespont. If we don't hold the ceremony that provides the link between mortals and immortals, allow it to be severed, the human race will lose divine guidance and return to a witless existence."

Myrrhine stirred. "But we can initiate no one into the Mysteries with all Attica evacuated. We have no initiates. And besides, with the exception of us, the sacred officials have left Eleusis."

Aeschylus threw up his hands. "I'm not listening to a bunch of conjurors mumble trivialities while the real work of evacuation goes undone." He turned to walk out, pushed past Kallias.

Kallias grabbed Aeschylus' arm with one hand and took hold of his coat with the other. "No, Aeschylus," Kallias said. "We can't let you leave. The argument won't go the same without you. Stay, please. And though you may argue against us, still I'll feel the better for it. I like your contrariness. Keep us sensible."

Aeschylus turned back, though still reluctant. "Alright," he said, "but why not use the proven methods of determining divine will? Read entrails or flames of a sacrificial fire. In times long past, blind Teiresias was expert at reading bird flight. What's wrong with priests today? No talent for it?"

Kallias smiled sadly. "We've already tried that on Salamis. The results were inconclusive. Apollo, through this oracle," he held up the scroll, "has told us that Zeus will permit intervention on our behalf. Athena received that much from him. But from where the help will come and in what form are the questions."

"I haven't been initiated into your mysteries of Demeter," said Aeschylus, "but I know this. If we have a divine protector it'll be her. She alone values the individual. The goddess is behind this radical idea of putting power in the hands of the people. It's threatening to put into office any idiot who can raise a hand."

"This is no time to argue the finer points of politics, Aeschylus," said the Hierophant, "but your point is well taken. And, as you've stressed on numerous occasions, the stakes are higher than ever with the Persian invasion. Even the Trojan War was fought only for honor and glory. Here, freedom of the human spirit is at stake." He turned from Aeschylus and addressed Kallias. "Aeschylus is right. You've been looking to the wrong divine power for guidance."

"But how to approach Demeter?" said Kallias. "The Mysteries have been cancelled. She'd never listen to us the way we've abandoned her."

"Yes," the Hierophant responded, "you speak truly. It's a terrible dilemma." He fell silent and stared off into the distance, walked away from them. Then, he turned back. "Perhaps if we hold an abbreviated ceremony, enough for Demeter to maintain that bridge between this life and the next provided by the Mysteries, she might also send a sign to resolve the generals' dilemma."

"That's it!" exclaimed Kallias. "What do you have in mind?"

Melaina interrupted them. "But grandfather, why just Demeter? Perhaps we should appeal directly to the Mistress of the Underworld."

The Hierophant looked as if she'd struck him in the face. Greatly she wished she'd remained silent.

Yet, he seemed to taking her suggestion seriously. "Yes! How blind I've been," he said, turning to face Melaina. "You see what the rest of us can't. I've known for some time that you're close to Kore. Did not Theseus return from the dead to help us at Marathon?"

"A simple prayer to the unmentionable goddess then," said Aeschylus. "Done. Now back to the evacuation." He turned to walk out again.

"Not so," said the Hierophant. "Not a simple prayer but a

ceremony, a Mysteries ceremony for Kore."

"But how would we address those in the Underworld?" asked Melaina. "Most prayers are addressed to those on Olympus."

"You're versed in Homer. Remember Odysseus' descent into the Underworld to learn his way home?"

"He was instructed by the goddess Circe," Melaina said after a short pause, "and had to sail a ship without a helmsman to the crumbling homes of Death."

"What if we," and now the Hierophant's eyes glowed with fire light, "performed the epiphany ceremony while addressing those of the Underworld as did Odysseus. We'll not have to go so far as did he. A door to the Underworld lies nearby. The purest of us here would perform the rite." His eyes searched each of them, but fell on Melaina. "You are the one person who's demonstrated favor with the gods."

Melaina felt her mother grab her arm, fingers dig into her flesh. "No!" said Myrrhine. "You can't possibly do that to her, no matter the prophecies. She's not well. Everyone fears that Underworld entrance."

"What afflicts her?"

But Myrrhine looked down at her feet and mumbled. "She's just not well."

The Hierophant looked at Melaina. "Are you sick?"

"I still suffer from the trauma I experience at Brauron."

"Are you able to do this? You know what I'm asking?"

Melaina stirred, avoided his eyes and focused on the fire. "You're asking me to be the priestess of Kore?"

"I hadn't thought of it that way, but yes. Here on earth, you'll be the living representative of the goddess of the Underworld."

Melaina wondered how she could do this. She'd never been a priestess. "Will I go inside the grotto and sacrifice as did Odysseus?"

"The gods have already shown you the way. This is indeed encouraging!"

Myrrhine was still upset. "You can't possibly put the weight of this on Melaina."

"At Brauron, Artemis sacrificed her own priestess for Melaina," said the Hierophant. "I'm convinced she's the crucial link. She gave Melaina a second fate for a reason. No one has been so favored by the gods in my lifetime."

Myrrhine pleaded, "Don't do this... The Gates of Hades are a danger beyond telling."

Melaina knew her mother was withholding something. Why did she fall silent?

"I need to know if we're all in agreement. Aeschylus?" The Hierophant's fact was stern. "You have a vote."

"As if I could cast one for this ritual of the spirits."

The Hierophant turned to Melaina. "We'll go inside the grotto with you for the first sacrifice," he said, "but you'll be the one to enter the Underworld and address Kore. Before you do, we'll retire to our places at the Anaktoron and start the Mysteries ritual with the Hiera. Perhaps that'll help open the pathway to the Underworld. You'll be alone. Are you up to it?"

"But, grandfather, I won't know what to do."

"Nor would I. Think back to your initiation. Perhaps you'll find guidance there. Will you do it?"

She raised her hands above the fire, lowered them until she felt the flames lick her fingers. Melaina remembered the argument with her mother just a few days before when she'd set her mind against becoming a priestess. But she'd always felt close to Kore, the divine Maiden, though she was the most feared of any god or goddess. Perhaps if she performed this one rite, they'd let her go her own way. At least she'd have a strong argument for it. She'd been infected with the desire to determine her own future.

"For everyone's freedom. Even my own," she said. "Yes!"

Her mother voiced a last protest. "But you don't understand the risk."

"She does, better than any of us," replied the Hierophant. Melaina saw the depression lift that had gripped her grandfather for days. "Aeschylus, it's time for you to leave."

CHAPTER 8: ENTERING THE UNDERWORLD

Melaina had only seen the sacred grotto, the Gates of Hades, from outside. Even her mother had never been inside. This was where Earth had yawned a thousand years before, allowing Hades to surface, kidnap Kore, and take her to the Underworld where he married her, thereby making her Mistress of the Dead.

The slaves who'd stayed behind to help load the mother's and daughter's belongings were brought in to assist in the ritual, and they trembled on the sidelines. The Hierophant bid one, a trusted old man with a propensity for worrying, to retrieve a black ewe and a black ram from the sacred holding pen. "The finest we have," the Hierophant said.

"Lord Zeus, help me!" the old man replied, hurrying off.

The gates to the Underworld, set deeply into the east side of the mountain, were already shrouded in shadow. In the orange glow of sunset, the Hierophant said a prayer in the ancient tongue, inserted the large temple key, turned it, and swung aside the grotto doors, while the slaves whispered and cowered in the background. Myrrhine, now in the long robe of the priestess of Demeter and carrying a basket, entered after the Hierophant and was followed by Kallias, who'd donned the raiment of the Dadouchos. He carried the torch and led the black ram. Melaina came last, carrying the temple key and leading the black ewe.

Melaina had complained to her grandfather after seeing the ewe the slave had selected. "I raised her," she'd said. "Please don't make me slaughter her. She's pregnant."

"We always sacrifice the most precious when asking for divine gifts," he told her. "We give so that they give in return."

Inside, a small moss-eaten altar drank torchlight. Dark stone lining the walls of the cave held back the crumbling mountain-side. At the far end in the darkest corner, Melaina saw a small door that was barely visible in the dim light, looking even more ancient than the stone walls. The Dadouchos placed the torch in a holder just inside the entrance and brought the ram forward to the altar, where the Hierophant had already assumed his position and taken the basket from Myrrhine. From within it, the Hierophant drew forth a long bronze blade that glinted in the torchlight. Just outside the door, the slaves made ready the fire.

The Hierophant accepted the black ram and placed its front feet at the edge of the blood drain that emptied into a hole. The other three joined him, supplicating themselves, then rising to circle the altar. The Hierophant sprinkled the ram with chilled holy water, and, after it trembled its assent, he prayed.

"O Unseen One, lord of the blurred and breathless dead, imperious Hades, whose heart knows no mercy, I summon you on a matter of great urgency. All Hellas overflows with the arrogance of Xerxes, who calls himself King of Kings and blasphemes against the gods. His dark forces swarm our fields and burn your temples. We respect your solitude and ask only council with the dark goddess of your house. Call her from the misty depths of Tartarus."

As he spoke the last words, he slit the black ram's throat with a single swift stroke, and the women screamed as was the custom. The ram labored on the altar and stumbled while the Hierophant guided the blood-gushing neck to the hole. Melaina looked away as the ram's life drained in red runnels.

The Hierophant chanted, then carved the carcass and set the white thighbones, covered with glistening fat, to roast for the gods on the roaring flames. He cut and served a crisp portion to each of them. Until now, Melaina hadn't realized she was so hungry. After the ritual repast, the Hierophant poured red wine over the flames and turned to Melaina, his demeanor now formal.

"Granddaughter of tender years," he said, "now guised in the raiment of the priestess of Kore, your turn has come. The rest of us must retire to the Telesterion: the Dadouchos to spread the purifying Fleece of Zeus and prepare the pathway for the great light, the priestess of Demeter to summon the goddess to mourning for her kidnapped daughter, and myself to the Anaktoron, where I will summon Kore for her return to earth. When I summon her," he said to Melaina, "you must converse with her for a sign. No one has ever done what you are attempting, so your inexperience is no disadvantage. But be precise in executing the few instructions I do give you. The fate of us all may weigh in the balance.

He took a smaller temple key from the wall and handed it to her. "My instructions are these," he said. "Use the key to open the door at the back of the cave, which has not been entered even in my father's lifetime. You must open it and lead the ewe inside. Word from the ancients tells us little about what lies beyond. As far as I know, only dark sacrificial earth. You are to take the basket with you. Once inside, use the tip of the bronze blade to cut a gaping wound in Earth and pour libations from each of the cups. Then say a prayer to Kore and sacrifice the ewe, allowing its blood to flow into Earth's wound."

Melaina remembered Kynthia's death a Brauron and the uncertain fate of her friends. "No," she whispered, "after Brauron, I cannot take a life, particularly these two lives I've nurtured."

"I told you, Melaina hasn't recovered," said Myrrhine.

The old Hierophant dropped to one knee before Melaina, his eyes sparkling with excitement. "We must perform the grim rituals for the gods," he said, "even when they bring pain and take loved ones from us. If I had a choice, I would not leave you alone to perform this terrible rite. Be brave, little one, and reap great reward from it."

Melaina said nothing. Somehow, it seemed a step beyond what she could withstand right now. She felt her mother hug her, and then they left, flames outside casting a faint flickering light against the door she was to enter.

Melaina took a deep breath and approached the door, her footsteps echoing on the stones as if she were already inside a great chamber. Darkness enveloped her. She paused, thinking what a mistake she'd made to believe she could perform a ritual involving the dead. But then she scolded herself. If Odysseus could sail to the ends of the world to find his way home, surely she could perform a ritual just inside this small door to save all Greece.

She inserted the bronze temple key, a round bar as long as her forearm but with two crooks, forced a partial rotation and heard the grating of metal on metal. She clutched the cold handle and pulled, but nothing happened. She tried again, but it still would not budge. She was about to call the Hierophant to tell him she couldn't do it, when she thought perhaps a few words to the lord of this chamber would be appropriate. She didn't like the name Hades and decided to use his other, more agreeable name.

"Plouton, host of many and bringer of bountiful wealth, release the latch on the door to your realm so I may enter."

She tried the door again, gave it a jerk. It groaned and gradually swung open, setting free a gust of cold, musty air. At first, she thought it wasn't dark inside at all, but then realized she wasn't seeing blackness. She was peering into nothingness. She sat the basket on the ground before the void and, taking the bronze blade from the basket, she raised it high over her head and with both hands clasped about the hilt, drove it deep into Earth. She then pulled it toward her to cut the votive pit. She poured libations from the cups one by one around it: sweet milk, honey, wine and clear water. Then she scattered barley in a circle, encompassing all.

She brought the ewe forward, but still resented her grandfather's order. She'd raised the ewe from a lamb, had seen it frolic in the field and had looked forward to watching it bear her own lambs. Now as it reached the threshold of motherhood, she was to take its life. Already the ewe's sides swelled with pregnancy. She would be taking two lives. Tears of fear and anger welled up within her. She spoke to ease her escalating terror. "Grim daughter of Zeus, giver of life and death to drudging mortals, come forth from within the womb of Earth to hear my plea."

She put her arm around the ewe's neck and held it to her

bosom, running her fingers along the furry face and down until she found the loose-skinned throat. She brushed aside the tears and raised the deadly blade to her fingertips, found the ewe's most vulnerable spot and drew the sharp edge quickly across. She screamed. The ewe bolted but Melaina held on tight so that the black blood could find Earth's wound. The life-holding broth poured from one laceration into the other. She squeezed the ewe to her so its death might seep deep into her own living flesh. She bowed her head and cried painful tears into her dying companion's soft fleece. She was so lost in grief she didn't realize she was again praying. The dark goddess' forbidden name escaped her lips unbidden and unnoticed, and thus without fear.

"O dear mother of the Netherworld, Persephone, dark one who lights the Elysian Fields, take this beloved soul into your warm embrace and grant the sign needed so badly for our own earthly salvation. Grant this request that we might work a great redemption. Send us word, O Dark One."

Dread filled her as she felt the fading life release the limbs of the ewe, her only companion in that dark chamber. The two of them slumped to the ground together, and Melaina felt as though she had fallen into a deep sleep. She saw a dark shore round which the river Styx flowed nine times, and where the grumpy ferryman, Charon, ferried dead to the Underworld.

A great sadness overcame her, and she saw an apparition of a man coming toward her, one she didn't recognize. Some dreaded god, she thought. "Not so," the shape told her. "Simply a long-dead father, come to gaze one last time upon his beloved daughter." She reached out, longing for her father, but her hand went sifting through him. Ethereal as a shadow, he was. "Remember your promise," he said, "and don't fear even the most fearful. Also remember that not all burdens are a curse and that a short life is the more glorious." She wished to question him about this, but he vanished as quickly as he'd come.

A delicately featured maiden, hardly older than Melaina, now stood in his place, amidst a dazzling light. She wore a peplos drawn over a white chiton. A stephane woven of autumn pickings from the fields wound about her head, and her long hair fell in masses over her shoulders. In her right hand she held two torches, and in her left, several ears of grain. Melaina was buoyed by the feeling of love and friendliness radiating from this divine presence, expressed by just the suggestion of a smile.

The lady turned, and with a sweep of her arm flung the two torches into the darkness, unveiling a bronze fence beyond, crowned above by roots of dark Earth. Two iron gates slowly swung open to expose a new blackness: grim, dank, and loathsome. From within issued thousands of spirits led by gentle, clever Hermes. Fell, they were, spirits of murder and madness. They squeaked like bats wakened from a cavern wall, flitting about, their gibbering punctuated with faint cries of "Iakchos, Iakchos." They trailed after the guiding, lighthearted bringer of dreams.

★

Melaina woke screaming. She was no longer in the cave, but lying on the stone floor outside the Anaktoron in her mother's arms. She spit out a cloth her mother had placed between her teeth. She realized that her tongue was sore and bleeding. Blinding flashes of light split the night, accompanied by clashes of thunder. Great flames rose through a hole, the lantern in the ceiling of the Telesterion. Between thundering crashes, the booming voice of the Hierophant raged throughout the temple. The Dadouchos stood on a platform above the Anaktoron, torch in hand. Every time he lowered the fire, another detonation threatened to blast the walls from the temple. A vast chorus of ghostly voices erupted in a rhythm of pounding fury.

★

The group feasted on the top of the hill overlooking the bay. The light of Persian fires dotted the darkness east toward Athens and gradually merged with the sparkling starlight. So far, Eleusis was safe, but the doom of Persian drums rumbled in the distance.

Melaina's eyes followed her mother and the Hierophant. They'd not spoken to each other since leaving Melaina in the cave, and she hoped this was not something that would permanently stand between them. But Melaina was too hungry to let their quarrel slow her sopping and chewing. The old Hierophant stared approvingly at Melaina. He smiled, gray beard streaked with meat juices. They were eating the flesh of the two sacrificial animals, the black ram and ewe. Melaina rarely tasted roast meat and had never gorged herself solely on flesh. Her sadness at sacrificing had now been converted to ravenous hunger, and she consumed the body of the beast, ingesting the holy nourishment in tribute to its gift, while trying to protect her sore tongue.

The slaves' behind them were a constant chatter, their voices echoing far-off Scythia and Thrace, home of Boreas the north wind, from where they'd been kidnapped years before. Kallias had already left for Salamis, convinced he'd received not only the sought-for sign from the goddess, but also hope of divine intervention to save their fledgling people's republic. Themistocles would be hard-pressed to convince the others, but Greece must be defended at Salamis, where the cloud of souls had gone, behind the "wooden wall" of ships and not at the Isthmus.

Her grandfather was struggling to explain what had happened. They'd received so much more from the immortals than anticipated. "According to a myth more ancient than Kronos himself," he told Melaina, "Tartarus holds many dead, those not initiated into the Mysteries and thus never allowed into the Elysian Fields. They were suicides and murderers banished to Tartarus before Herakles taught us the purification ceremony we now hold annually at Agrai. They clamor for redemption, but Zeus never listens. Perhaps our ceremony provided a means for their rehabilitation, and an initiation for them."

"But what can they do for us, grandfather?" asked Melaina.

"Only time will tell, little one."

Melaina didn't reveal all she'd witnessed. She held back the one piece of news that would have softened her mother's heart toward the Hierophant. She would savor it as her own until tomorrow. She'd seen her father in the Underworld.

CHAPTER 9: A CLOUD OF SPIRITS

That same evening, two Greek exiles serving with Xerxes stood on a hill north of Athens overlooking Eleusis and the bay. While a blood-red sun plunged into the sea to the west, they discussed the impending battle. Behind them lay the abandoned hills and valleys of Attica, now being looted by Persians. Demaratus was the deposed king of Sparta, who'd lost the throne because of questions concerning his parentage. He hoped to be reinstated after a Xerxes victory. His companion was Dicaeus, a well-to-do Athenian of some repute and a man well-versed in the Mysteries. What the two were about to witness, Dicaeus would tell those who would listen all the rest of his life.

As twilight deepened, Demaratus raised his arm and pointed to a large cloud rising from the vicinity of the Telesterion at Eleusis. The sight visibly shook Dicaeus, and Demaratus questioned him about it.

Dicaeus said, "Listen."

The two cupped their ears into the wind, the better to hear the wisp of voices it carried. Gradually the sound swelled and Demaratus remarked that it sounded as though it seemed to come from a chorus of thirty thousand. Dicaeus recognized the song.

"But who could it be?" asked Demaratus. "All Attica is evacuated and Eleusis has yet to be occupied by the Persians."

"Sir," Dicaeus answered, "the king's fleet is about to fall to disaster. The voices we hear are clearly divine. They sing of Iakchos."

As they watched, the cloud drifted south and descended on the Greek fleet harbored at Salamis.

"And Iakchos?" asked Demaratus.

"Every fall, Athenians celebrate a festival in honor of the divine Mother and Maid. Anyone who wishes may be initiated into the Mysteries. People come from all over the world, even as far as Egypt. The initiates always sing the Iakchos song. I can't tell you of Iakchos. That is the great secret. To divulge it is punished by death."

Demaratus was quiet for several minutes. Finally he spoke, "Keep your secret of the Mysteries, but keep another also. Say nothing of the cloud and voices to Xerxes. If you do, you will lose your head and no one in the world could save you."

CHAPTER 10: EVACUATION TO SALAMIS

At the first hint of dawn, the small troop—mother, daughter and a handful of maids—descended the hill to the dock where the ship lingered in its slip. Although Melaina had lived by the sea all her life, she'd never been aboard a boat, and the one awaiting them swarmed with men, another forbidden quantity. Just forward of the bow oars, the bulwark broke to leave a narrow entry onto which Melaina stepped, the twenty-oared galley shifting a little under her weight, something she hadn't expected. She noticed a plaque on which the boat's name had been carved, *The Eleutheria, The Freedom.* But the whole affair felt unstable, wobbling about like some restless sea monster. A line of pale, sun-starved city women stretched along the boat's centerline, each stepping between two bronzed oarsmen, smelly men with grizzled beards and stern countenance. Bright-eyed in the presence of this feminine cargo, they breathed laboriously, as though they'd just recently wetted their oars.

The rest of the ship's company, dressed in drab, knee-length tunics, was cunningly arranged so as to afford efficient boat operation. The captain sat aft on a fixed stool before the small cabin; the bow officer, who maintained a proper outlook, stood forward; the helmsman sat at the steering oar; and the aulete took up his position at the center mast to synchronize the oarsmen.

With a single shout from the helmsman, they pushed off. Once through the slip, the yard groaned at the base of the mast, straightened and rose, deploying the square sail that billowed as it caught the breeze. The ship's aulete, the flautist, began his beat to sync the oarsmen, and the broad flat blades splashed, then creaked against the tholepins. A grand magic took hold the ship and propelled it forward under influence of both sail and oar.

They passed over the bay, with dawn's pink glow tingeing the water's ripples, and shortly came alongside Salamis. Skirting the east shore southward, they saw across to Athens, thin trails of smoke still frozen above it. The tweetle of the aulete's twin-fluted instrument caught Melaina's fancy, and remembering the choruses of girls she'd led at Brauron, she hummed along. Anaktoria and little Agido, who in the past were forever urging her to lead them in song, joined in, and it wasn't long before the other girls did likewise. The monotonous tootling of the ship's aulete turned divine ditty, and the mood of the finely tuned troop lifted, a promiscuous smile crossing every face. Melaina noticed that even her mother was caught up in this girlish delirium, though she uttered, "Shameful," loud enough for Melaina to hear.

They coursed the coast of Salamis that, as far inland as the eye could see, had become one large city of refugee tents, bleak peaks rising between buildings and around trees. They entered the cove, and a horde of hidden warships that lined shore came into view. Triremes were stacked six deep. At the docks, damaged vessels crowded together, frantic workmen hard at repairing them, their shouts and thuds of mallets a great din in the cove.

Word of the group's sunrise arrival preceded them, Kallias having dropped some not-too-subtle hints about the young priestess descending to the Underworld, as had Herakles and Odysseus of old. Several island priests and a crowd of the curious met them. Melaina noticed their looks of desperation and futility. A murmur arose when Melaina stepped from the boat, and the first rays of sunlight shot forth. Hearing whispers of "Kore" and "Underworld," she tried to hide behind her mother.

A great shout startled Melaina, and she turned to see a crowd standing before the beach, urging on a laboring dog who'd made the swim from Attica. His snout was blowing bubbles, and he barely stayed afloat. He made shore, but staggered and then fell onto the sand. A boy of ten with an unusually shaped head, a tall head as if he wore a helmet, ran to the dog as the crowd cheered him on. One man asked the boy's father, "Xanthippus, did your dog swim to Salamis for love of freedom or love of his master's bondage?" Melaina recognized the father as a general. She'd seen him at Kleito's on the way back from Brauron. The big-headed boy gathered the animal into his arms as his father responded. "For companionship. The simple beast has lost its life, dying just now in my son's arms. It knew nothing of the contrivances for which a man will give his life."

Melaina was caught up in the plight of the dying dog until Aeschylus, with young Sophocles at his side, stepped forward to take charge of the mother and daughter. She watched as Agido and Anaktoria were taken in a different direction. She'd be kept separate from them. Agido cast back a longing look. Melaina watched Sophocles from the corner of her eye, detecting a smile. Their arrival had been all the more symbolic as they were the only dignitaries from Eleusis. The old Hierophant had steadfastly refused to board the boat. This had brought Melaina and her mother to tears as they wondered if they'd see him alive again. "If everyone's going to die anyway," he'd said, "what's the difference if I die on Salamis or at home here in Eleusis?"

As they walked along the docks to a waiting wagon, a fog of unease settled upon the countryside. Birds circled overhead screeching, and Melaina saw several flashes of light, as a mirror will when it catches the sun. Dogs became irritable and turned on each other. Cats screeched and ran for cover. She saw ripples in the distance, like the distortion of heat waves on a landscape, flowing rapidly toward them. The soft sea breeze fell still, and she heard a rumbling, like the far-off thunder of horses' hooves.

The earth began to shake, sending people scattering and screaming in panic as waves rose up to capsize boats in the cove, smash fishing boats against the dock, jostle warships, and threaten to consume Persian and Greek alike. Stones toppled from buildings, roofs fell in, and the earth itself split open.

Melaina was knocked from her feet, and while still in the sitting position, having never experienced an earthquake, uttered words of prayer as a simple reflex. "Lord Poseidon, Earthshaker and deep-roaring ruler of the sea, don't destroy us in our moment of vulnerability. The Persians have already taken our cities. Don't deepen our grief by putting them beneath dark Earth."

As Melaina's words dissipated in the morning air, hardly more than a whisper, so the earth's rumbling crust ceased shivering, and the waves in the bay calmed. As she regained her feet, a murmur spread through the crowd, and old women rushed to touch Melaina's garments. Melaina withdrew further, hid her face behind her peplos and sunk inside herself.

She heard a woman scream. Melaina and her mother rushed to a nearby stone building that had been turned to rubble by the trembling earth. "Oh, my baby, my baby!" the peasant shouted, casting loose stones aside in a frantic search. Melaina stepped into the ruins, rummaged through scattered debris, and tried to raise a section of collapsed roof. She thought she heard a faint cry and asked Aeschylus to help. As if by magic, she raised the baby from the rubble, its bright eyes flashing. The mother was struck dumb, her mouth falling open as she dropped to her knees before Melaina who delivered the baby into her arms.

Whereas the flurry of activity when they stepped off the boat had only embarrassed Melaina, the extreme reaction of the mother, over seeing her child unharmed, along with the crowd's tempest, frightened her. She sought the safety of her uncle, and seeing his dark bull-like form brush aside the crowd, ran to him.

"I've heard of your antics," Aeschylus said, "but wouldn't have believed this if I hadn't seen it myself."

Melaina couldn't understand why even her own contrary uncle saw something extraordinary in her simple act.

Aeschylus and Sophocles ushered the two women away from the gathering crowd and to the home of Mnesarchides and Kleito, who'd offered refuge in Phlya after Melaina's escape from Brauron. From their home on a hillside overlooking the strait, Melaina could see the distant walls of Athens, now in the hands of Persians.

Kleito, a huge woman and an herbalist, decorated her home with wild thyme, frankincense, and myrrh. Clusters of exotic plants dried in the corners, and large jars of medicinal oils stood like dumb children in the various rooms. Kleito's huge bulk trudged about shouting orders at the slaves to prepare a room for Myrrhine and Melaina, all the time complaining about the shortage of space.

An aftershock sent women screaming, and Kleito ran to hold Myrrhine's hands for a moment, then lumbered off once again shouting at the slaves and search for bedding. Kleito scolded herself. "Why complain on the eve of doom? All will belong to Persia tomorrow."

Melaina looked for Sophocles, but he'd vanished soon after they'd arrived, and she heard his family was housed nearby, though his father, Sophillus, was chronically ill. Aeschylus and sour-faced Philokleia stayed in the chamber next to that of Melaina and her mother.

By mid-afternoon, Melaina's eyes drooped from lack of sleep. She was so shaken by the earthquake and threatening rush of the devout that she welcomed the chance to simply be her mother's daughter again and slinked into Myrrhine's arms on the soft bed. The sweet smell of wild thyme lofted about Melaina as she curled into the fetal position within her mother's arms. But sleep didn't come.

"Mother," she asked, "how did father die?"

"Aeschylus says he died from the blow of an ax." Her mother's voice was small and plaintive next to Melaina's ear.

"Is it possible to see the dead?"

"For those chosen by the gods, all things are possible."

"I saw father while in the cave of Hades," she said. "In my dream he was missing his right hand." She wondered how her mother would take this, but she didn't respond immediately, and Melaina wondered if she'd fallen asleep.

Her mother let out a deep breath. "Your father lost his hand reaching for the stern ornament of a ship. A Persian ax severed it, and he bled to death."

Melaina remembered her promise to her father, that she'd avenge his death, but chose not to tell her mother. It seemed something just between him and her. She snuggled against her mother's breast. Sleep still would not come. Her father had also mentioned something about a short life being the more glorious. She'd thought he'd meant his own. But now his comment sounded more ominous. Somehow, she felt he was talking about her.

★

Melaina woke with little Euripides standing over her. She hadn't seen him since her short stay at Phlya at the foot of Mt. Hymettos. He peered down at her, his eyes dark berries beneath his black hair.

"Someone wants you," he whispered.

She slipped from her mother's arms, and the little boy took her by the finger, leading her out back and up the hillside to a cave.

"This is my secret place," he told her. "When the Persians come, I'll close it up and hide until I'm grown." His deep eyes darted about. He took her into the shallow cave where he'd stashed broken arrows, spears and damaged armor of tarnished bronze.

"Who am I to see?" she asked. She remembered Salamis was sacred to Aphrodite, its skyline, as seen from Eleusis, resembling the profile of a woman on her back with knees raised and spread. She looked east where the Greek fleet harbored, and a warmth flowed through her when she saw Sophocles' slim form coming up the slope. She spoke first.

"The mountain in back of Athens, is that Mt. Hymettos?"

"The same. On the way back from Brauron, we stopped at the home of Mnesarchides at Hymettos' foot. But look farther south," he said, turning a little as he came up beside her, lowering his voice. "The Persian fleet makes ready for the sea battle."

"Yes, I've seen them. A giant school of sea fishes." She thought, Sophocles has the speech of a man but still the bearing of a boy.

Such an odd fellow to be so comfortable with himself. And to treat me as if I'm a woman. "Will you man a ship?"

He looked deflated. "Yes, but only to pickup survivors cast into the brink." He wrinkled his brow. "Shouldn't see battle myself. I've come to say good-bye for the present, wish you divine protection should all not go well tomorrow." He looked at the ground. "The island is abuzz with word of your descent into the Underworld last night and the remarkable way you held yourself during the earthquake. The gods are much closer to you than me. I only want to wish you well."

"Your good wishes are greatly appreciated, Sophocles, not at all brash. I'm not immune to Persian swords. And as for the rumors of desperate peasants...." She smiled.

He looked off into the distance again. "Hellene generals still argue the merits of abandoning the island in favor of the Isthmus. We are an antagonistic lot."

"Think they'll do it?"

He shook his head. "Kallias' tale of the sign from Demeter has given most the courage to make a stand here."

Melaina took a step toward Sophocles, luxuriating in the banquet of his body's smells. She saw an uncertainty, a fright in his eyes that was not there a few days ago, and realized this was his first venture into battle. "If the cheap gossip of peasants was true, and I do have influence with the immortals, certainly young Sophocles will return unharmed," she said, "for truly, how could the gods allow such a fine dancer and poet to be taken from us?"

Sophocles blushed, his face framed by chestnut hair. Searching for words where none existed, he bowed, handed her a small roll of papyrus, and walked back down the hill.

Melaina watched him go, tightly clutching the papyrus to her breast. Little Euripides, who'd been standing quietly inside the mouth of his cave, came to her side. She unrolled the papyrus and saw familiar letters neatly formed of lampblack. Her heart raced as she realized Sophocles had given her one of his own poems.

O sunlight in this war-drenched darkness,
my eyes now feast on you
the final time! For I am perhaps
setting off to conceal in Hades
the finish of my life. Most cherished friend,
in prosperity remember me
and you and your kinsmen
be fortunate in all time to come.

Melaina's eyes puddled. He'd written this just for her. She'd been in his thoughts just as he'd been in hers. Poets together we are, she thought. *Most cherished friend!* Oh Aphrodite, goddess of love and mistress of well-built Salamis, show a little restraint with me!

She felt a tug on her arm and pulled Euripides' thin frame close.

"Is Sophocles afraid to fight the Persians?" he asked.

"Sophocles is of stout heart. He'll overcome any fear."

As Melaina and Euripides descended through the olive trees, the sun cast long mountain shadows over the stone buildings, and she saw her mother waiting in the courtyard.

"Hurry," said Myrrhine, "the generals have summoned us."

"Mother," complained Melaina, "they want you. Keep me out of it."

"You were requested by name."

Melaina hung her head, and her mother wrapped an arm about her shoulders as they walked back together. "I know," her mother said. "Believe me; I understand your reluctance better than you think."

★

Early evening, Melaina stood beside her mother before the temple of Athena, a small stone building on a rise overlooking the crowded streets of the agora, which were banked with magazines and statues of long-dead heroes. The air was thick with the smoke of torches lighting the square and with the rumble of worried voices. Across the strait, Persian fires lined the shore of Attica.

The temple where she stood had a new addition. The ancient olivewood statue of Athena, which had fallen to earth centuries before and was usually housed in the Erechtheion on the Akropolis, had recently been removed and transported to Salamis. The statue was unveiled for the festivities, and they all now stood before it.

A shout went up as twelve bullocks, restrained by thick ropes, were led into the agora, a garland crowning each curly head. A wide-shouldered warrior hefted a sledgehammer and dealt a bullock a mighty blow between the eyes. It stumbled on the altar. A dark shape dressed in brilliant white stepped forward to make incisions at each jugular. Steady streams of black blood poured forth. The man's large mane of black hair was nearly invisible in the darkness.

"Kallias," Melaina whispered.

A fire in the square's center flamed, grew, and raged, the roar and crackle sending sparks in streaming trails to the heavens. The first sacrifice was for Hestia, goddess of the hearth, followed by one for Zeus, father of gods and mortals. They sacrificed to all twelve Olympian gods, each given pulsing blood from one bullock and the bones and fat carefully laid upon the frantic fire: Hera, Poseidon, Demeter, Apollo, Artemis, Ares, Aphrodite, Hermes, Athena, Hephaestus.

Kallias shared the officiating with the priest of Apollo from the island of Delos, their white robes streaked with blood. Their voices roared above the crowd's babble, calling to Apollo, god of light and order; Ares, god of war; Athena, protectress of cities and benefactress of Athens. From each they pleaded the salvation of Greece and that their warriors find courage to stand their ground, ships find favorable seas, and weapons find their marks.

It was a great sacrifice and a great feast followed. Red meat was filleted and roasted over the fire. Hot smoking wedges of dripping flesh disappeared into the crowd. Melaina was given a chunk without plate or knife and greedily devoured it. The succulent juice ran down her arm and trickled off her elbow.

As the feast ended, a cry went up for one last prayer. A lull followed, as it seemed each priest expected the other to step forward. A lightning bolt struck a nearby hilltop, followed immediately by a crash of thunder. Melaina heard someone shout, "The maid! The maid!" She felt a tingle flash across her cheeks.

Her mother nudged Melaina forward. "They want you," she said.

The call to prayer was irresistible. Melaina elevated herself onto a platform beside the statue of Athena alongside that of Ajax, legendary hero of Salamis. She was surprised at the excitement her presence sent through the crowd and felt a grip of fear as all eyes fell upon her.

She knew instantly what her prayer would be, and it came as a fully formed gift. She recognized the need of those going into battle tomorrow for leadership from long-dead heroes. She'd heard the words of Homer sung in the halls of Eleusis, and the legend of the great warrior Ajax in the Trojan War hundreds of years earlier. Ajax's father had been king of Salamis. She lifted her arms as she'd seen her mother. Her words started low, and the crowd bunched forward, the better to hear her, but gradually she found the resonance within her breast, and though some would later say she only spoke her words, others say she sang.

"O troubled warrior of ancient times, frenzied man of arms whose bloodthirst remains unquenched. Ajax! Lord of divine Salamis, warrior of incurable rage, put aside your eternal anger at Odysseus over Achilles' arms and hear our plea. Son of Telamon, namesake of eagles, your motherland calls through seven centuries for you to walk amongst us again. Lead these warriors into battle against the evil forces that would strip us of our freedom. Rise up from the Underworld to protect those who still love you. When you took your own life, you deprived us of your wise council and stout heart. We still suffer your neglect. Come to us now. Turn your heart's high passion to savagery. Lead our warriors to victory on the morrow. Bring that madness you unleashed when you butchered wretched beasts, turn it now upon Persia. Seek out Hermes, guide of ghosts in the Undergloom, bid him bring you hither. Help us, dear Ajax! Your countrymen command your help."

As she finished, all stayed silent, shocked by the power and depth of her prayer. Light rain swept over them and a song erupted. Many more were present than Melaina had thought. From her vantage point, she saw the crowd spilling out of the courtyard into streets and alleyways, heard a chorus of voices burst forth with such volume it frightened her.

Melaina felt a bear-like arm squeeze her about the shoulders. Aeschylus. "Well done," he said. "Well done indeed. If Hellas doesn't survive, it certainly won't be because of a broken spirit. I've never seen them so eager for battle."

CHAPTER 11: THE BATTLE OF SALAMIS

During the night, a noise woke Melaina. She realized her mother was no longer with her. Eyelids still heavy with sleep, she stumbled from the chamber and followed the sound of arguing voices. Just as she was to enter a room off the courtyard, where it appeared a fight was about to break out, an arm pulled her aside, and a soft but firm hand covered her mouth. It was her mother, who'd been crouched in secrecy behind a stone couch near the door. She whispered in Melaina's ear.

"Back to bed with you. If the men catch us, we'll be flogged."

Melaina's first taste of disobeying her mother while back at Eleusis had infected her with contrariness, and this business of spying on men far too exciting to walk away from. "I have to hear," she whispered, settling back into her mother's hideaway. They struggled physically a moment, and Melaina, realizing that her strength matched her mother's, simply held her ground and wore her mother down. The two listened as violent words emanated from the doorway.

Melaina recognized the voices of Kallias and Aeschylus, but a third voice eluded her until her mother whispered, "Themistocles, the Athenian general." Gradually Melaina put it together. Unbelievably, the War Council had again argued, some still set on withdrawing to the Isthmus behind the great wall being built there, others wishing to flee even farther to the coast of Italy. Themistocles, desperate to do something, had pulled together this select group of coconspirators, shunning even his closest advisors.

Again, Aeschylus was the enraged one. "If Eurybiades, in his incredible folly, is not willing to stand and fight, smash his head with a stone! Let vultures have him. The fleet will follow you!"

"No!" said Themistocles. "Murder is not the answer. We must remove retreat as an option."

"You do that," said Kallias, "and if Xerxes decides not to attack, he can starve us out without losing a man."

"That concerns me too," said Themistocles. "It was the great weakness of my plan to evacuate to Salamis all along. We must block our own retreat and force Xerxes to attack."

"Then all's lost," said Aeschylus. "We're a pack of fools!" He fell quiet for a moment. "Unless.... Let's not be rash. Perhaps you can accomplish both at a single stroke. Send word to Xerxes of the general's plan to escape Salamis. He'll block the retreat and be forced into action."

"That's no solution," put in Kallias. "You'd never convince Xerxes."

Silence filled the room for so long that Melaina wondered if the men had left.

"I think it might work," said Themistocles, finally. "Can you imagine any words sweeter to Xerxes than that the Hellenes have turned coward and plan to slip away during the night?"

Aeschylus laughed. "What fool would tell Xerxes?"

The words were barely out of his mouth when a new voice rose. "I'm your fool," it said. "I've been behind Xerxes' lines before and came away unharmed."

"Sicinnus," her mother whispered into Melaina's ear, "Themistocles' slave."

But Melaina already remembered the voice as belonging to one of the men who'd been with them when they charged the Persian camp on the way back from Brauron.

"If you do this thing," said Themistocles, "by all that's divine and with these good Hellenes as witness, I'll give you freedom and make you a rich man. Take Xerxes the message. Tell him the Hellene generals are at dagger tips with each other and will turn on one another when pressed."

Kallias added, "Say that many wish for a Persian victory and will fight for him when the tide turns. His own vanity will make him believe it."

With that, Melaina and Myrrhine, fearing they'd be discovered, slipped quietly back to their chamber. Neither could sleep, so they whiled away the silence standing before a second-floor window overlooking the eastern half of the island and the dark waters of the strait. As the sky turned pale, the stone halls echoed with the clank of armor. Women wept as husbands strapped on swords, hefted spears. Children cried, running after their fathers. Melaina heard a noise at the entryway, then saw a dark shape.

Myrrhine said, "Aeschylus! I thought you'd have assumed your command by now."

"You must not stay on Salamis," he said, entering the room. "By afternoon, it'll be overrun." He turned to Melaina. "A young virgin like you would be raped unmercifully. The aristocracy of Eleusis must survive. I've ordered you two evacuated to the west coast of Salamis where you'll be rowed across to Megara and taken by land to Patras. You'll sail for Siris, a colony in south Italy. An oracle has foretold that Athenians will live there some day. Perhaps the time has come."

"But Uncle," Melaina protested, "we're not really Athenians, and anyway, just this evening you saw how the soldiers depend on our presence to bolster their spirits. We can't abandon them." She wanted to add that she had great confidence in Themistocles' plan to fool Xerxes but thought better of it.

"Melaina," and his face filled with sadness, "we'll not win the sea battle."

Melaina dropped her eyes. "Grandfather believes we will. The gods will intercede."

"The gods are at odds over our fate, as they were at Troy. You're young, idealistic. Think of the smoke clouds over Athens. The gods didn't protect the Akropolis. You're a woman, still a girl really. These are men's decisions. Run now or you'll be at their mercy."

"Your uncle is right," said her mother. "We must get you to

safety."

Melaina shook her head and backed away from both of them. She spoke directly to her uncle, looked him directly in the eye as no woman should. "If you knew what happened at Eleusis two nights ago, you wouldn't be so impressed with Persian might. Even my father, your brother Kynegeiros, will stand beside you on the battlefield."

Mention of Aeschylus' long-dead brother gave Aeschylus pause. She went to him and threw her arms about his waist, her forehead reaching but to this powerful man's tangled forest of beard. She leaned back, looked up into his dark eyes. "I saw him in the Underworld, dear uncle. He was well and strong. He watches over me, over us all. He gave no warning but said to be fearless."

The sadness seemed to lift from Aeschylus' eyes. His back straightened. "Great Zeus! Perhaps it's my age catching up with me. I'm not the man I was at Marathon. Watching Kynegeiros sacrifice himself instilled fear in my heart. Ashamed am I of myself when I see your courage." He turned quickly from her and vanished.

Melaina heard his heavy footsteps loud on the stone courtyard, followed by shouting and the sounds of horses' hooves galloping into the distance. Melaina turned to her mother. "I'm going too," she said. "If all Hellas perishes in flame, I'll go up with it." Melaina had grabbed her robe and heard her mother call after her.

"You'll be in the way. You'll get trampled. You'll distract them from the business of war."

Melaina shouted back as she left, "I'll have to be bound hand and foot," and was out the door. In the courtyard, she flagged down Kallias, who was just mounting his chariot, his four midnight stallions snorting and pawing the earth. "Take me! I must watch the sea battle," she said.

Kallias was a man possessed, his arms working needless motions with the reins and whip, eyes vacant as if he'd already given up his soul to dark Hades. He hesitated but an instant, then grabbed her arm and pulled her aboard as he put the lash to the horses. Melaina heard her mother's frantic cry as they shot forward.

As they approached the shore, Melaina saw the dark shapes of heavily armed hoplites boarding the battleships. Seagulls shrieked and dogs ran circles barking and growling. Kallias shoved Melaina off the chariot and dismounted himself, handed the reins to a slave and ran to join his men.

Melaina dodged a wagon pulled by a frantic pair of saw-voiced donkeys, their frantic master lashing out with his whip and cursing them forward. She was lucky not to be trampled. She saw the triremes put to sea, their oars churning the surf. To the east of the cove, she saw more ships making ready. There, the beach ended and the landmass turned north, forming a promontory with a hill overlooking the strait. Just the spot to view the battle, she thought.

She pulled her chiton to her ankles and ran through sand, then up the hillside, dry grass crunching beneath her sandals. She stopped at the edge of the cliff where the headland abruptly ended. She stood overlooking dark water, peered down into the surf. Across the narrow strait, she saw Athens shrouded in murky morning light, the smoke-streaked sky above. She looked to the south, beyond the cove, where the Athenians had finished boarding their boats and sat quietly in the harbor treading water. In the distance, she saw the tip of Psyttaleia Island. She turned north, saw the dark shore of Eleusis where her ancient grandfather haunted the halls of the Telesterion, worried over him.

The eastern sky lightened, and directly across the narrows, on a hill in the midst of the gathering Persian land forces, Melaina saw the faint speck of a man emerge from amongst the multitude to mount a golden throne. He could only be Xerxes, King of Kings, come to watch his mighty fleet destroy the Greek navy.

Melaina looked south again, toward the Piraeus, and her heart sank. Now she understood Aeschylus' staunch belief that all would perish before Persia. Had she sent her uncle to his grave? The sea itself was made of Persian ships, dark shapes filling the channel and spreading into the distance.

The sun's golden chariot crested the horizon, its first bright rays falling on Melaina. She'd discarded her robe and stood on the hill overlooking the narrow waterway, her white himation flowing in the breeze, glowing. Some would later say a goddess taller than a tree stood on the hilltop, a bright light emanating from her as she protected the Greek fleet.

To the north, the Corinthian triremes foamed the sea with oars, emerged, and sailed north toward Eleusis with square sails set as if in retreat. This was the signal that would fill Xerxes with hope, if Sicinnus' mission had gone well.

Melaina held her breath and watched the Persian ships for any sign. Finally, she realized they moved. "Yes! Yes!" she screamed. Persians ships bolted north into the strait in hot pursuit of the Corinthian vessels, unaware that the heart of the Greek fleet lay in wait in the cove ready to charge their flank.

Her years of living at the edge of the sea had taught Melaina of the morning swell brought by southerly winds. Now she realized that Themistocles must be holding his ships in check, waiting to put the Persian ships at a further disadvantage. Then oars splashed as Greeks charged into the narrows. Trumpets blared and warriors raised a chorus to Apollo. Melaina was jolted as the paean metamorphosed into a song for Ajax. They chanted her prayer from the night before. She heard the crunch of the triremes' bronze beaks against Persian hulls, screams. Persian ships foundered leaving their cursing crews floating helplessly in the drink.

Melaina saw a flash of light, as if from another earthquake, then felt the sudden surge of her own power and a flood of internal warmth and peace. The fleet's trumpets again sounded, and she heard a splitting shriek, like the bugle of a great beast, and her vision shifted. She no longer saw killing, men spilling from gored vessels to be butchered like tunnies, beaten by club and oar. She saw shades, the tens of thousands from the Underworld, sending the Persians into panic. She glimpsed souls of the newly dead milling about, and quick-witted Hermes herding them into flocks. She heard Apollo's lyre, rhythmic music, misery set to some grand syncopation, elegant, beautiful. She felt unbearable pain, splitting agony, terror extinguished by darkness.

CHAPTER 12: EPILEPSY

Myrrhine saw her daughter fall as if struck by an arrow loosed from some angry god's bow. She was quickly at the scene, hiding her daughter within the confines of her own cloak, shoving a corner of it between Melaina's teeth to prevent her tongue from suffering more damage. Already the foamy phlegm was shaded crimson.

Kleito was at Myrrhine's side, helping shield the bundle of quaking limbs from the eyes of the curious. Little Euripides came with her, bounding about, shouting, "Is she dead, mamma? Is she dead?"

When Melaina's spasms stopped, the two of them, along with a couple of handmaids, hailed a wagon and took Melaina back to Kleito's home, which was now deserted and hauntingly quiet. Such were the numbers who'd gone to the beach to witness the sea battle.

The two women put Melaina to bed, covered her with warm blankets, and stood over her, both afraid to speak. Euripides darted to and fro, now on this side, now that. His mother kept a constant vigil restraining him.

Finally, Kleito broke the silence. "It's the sacred sickness."

Myrrhine responded slowly, her voice crushed by heavy sobs. "It's rarely called 'sacred,' mostly known as the 'falling sickness.'"

"Why didn't you tell me?"

"The stigma. Even Melaina doesn't know. She had it after her father died, but it seemed to cure itself. Her recent attacks came while sleeping. She's never had one while awake."

"Do you want help? I can cure her."

"Oh, could you Kleito? The uncertainty fills me with such terror."

"Come! I know a plant, hellebore. It can help."

"You have it?"

"It's dangerous. Can't keep it in the house with little Euripides into everything. For a child, it can be fatal. We'll have to go up the mountain."

"Will it be safe?"

"Certainly. I use it frequently to evacuate the bowels."

"She might wake while we're gone."

"She's resting peacefully. Leave her with the handmaids. I'll need you to help with the harvest." She turned to the two girls standing by the door. "Remain with the little priestess, and tell no one what you've seen. If you do, I'll slit both your throats and throw you to the dogs." Then she turned to Euripides. "Stay with the girls. We'll return shortly. While the men are off killing each other, we'll restore a life."

With that, Kleito grabbed a basket into which she placed a many-cloved garlic bulb, a cup of olive oil, another of thick wine, and a small two-edged sword. "I gather hellebore in the daylight for curing seizures; otherwise it's gathered at night." The two exited through the backyard, which was overgrown with cultivated plants, both medicinal and dietary, but trudged beyond, up the rocky slope and then down into a shrub-covered ravine.

Myrrhine wondered what the marvelous plant would look like that would save her daughter from the dreaded seizures. She asked, "How dangerous is it, the plant I mean."

Kleito stopped and looked at her directly. "Do you trust me?"

Myrrhine realized that this was the heart of the matter. Did she trust her friend with her daughter's life?

"You don't," said Kleito. "Your hesitation tells all. We haven't time to argue this. She should receive the treatment as soon as she wakes from the stupor. I'll harvest the plant and prepare the posset. If you trust me enough to allow me to administer it, I will. Otherwise, I'll dilute it for the goats. I haven't purged them in a while."

Kleito glanced back over the bay. "Look!"

In her concern for her daughter, Myrrhine had all but forgotten the sea battle raging in the distant strip of water separating them from Attica. From their vantage point on the slope, she saw the narrows littered with wreckage and corpses drifting away from the dense body of engaged ships, but she had no way of telling the sway of battle. A shudder went through her. If they lost, how little the hellebore would matter. The Persians would be upon them before the plant was broth.

"Look for a leaf with long, broad divisions," said Kleito. "It creeps along the ground. Grows everywhere. I have to pull it from the grapes or the wine becomes a purge." No sooner had she spoken than she stooped at a plant with pale-pink flowers and lobed deep-green leaves. "Black hellebore," she said. "Stand back!"

She took the two-edged sword from the basket, drew a circle round the plant and shoved the blade into the ground next to it. She motioned to Myrrhine, "Further, to the windward side. Put the basket on the ground."

Myrrhine did as requested and wondered at all the precautions for harvesting a plant the essence of which Melaina would have to drink.

Kleito took the garlic bulb from the basket and broke off several cloves, peeled and shoved them into her mouth, and handed two to Myrrhine. "Eat," Kleito said.

Myrrhine chewed the crunchy pulp, her mouth hot and eyes watering.

Kleito took a draught of wine and handed the small bottle to Myrrhine. "Chew it well and wash it down." She poured a puddle of olive oil into her own palm and handed the cup to Myrrhine. "I need the oil because I'll handle the plant. You may also if you wish, otherwise, stand upwind or your body will swell." Kleito anointed her face and arms, then bent to the task of digging up the plant with the sword while standing on its east side. "Say a prayer while I unearth it."

Myrrhine was caught off guard but quickly formulated a prayer.

Before the words came, Kleito spoke again. "Keep watch both right and left. Danger to Melaina's life will be revealed by the flight of an eagle."

Myrrhine prayed, "Wide-bosomed Earth, ever-sure foundation of all, old one who nourishes all things…"

"No, no, no!" said Kleito. "Asklepios, god of herbal craft. I need his guidance. Earth has already done her work. I could say it myself but figured since I had an expert with me…"

Myrrhine's mind raced, wondering if she'd actually let Kleito administer the concoction to her daughter. She prayed. "O mortal one turned immortal by your father Phoebus Apollon, Lord Paian, healer of sick and injured, blessed spirit of growth and blossoming, bring your divine guidance to Kleito that she may work your wonders on my sick offspring, as you would your own daughter, Hygieia, health herself, your blameless consort. Deliver this small hellebore into our hands that we might end this savagery afflicting Melaina. Ever we'll sacrifice mighty roosters in your name."

"That's better," said Kleito. "You start slow but redeem yourself well."

Myrrhine kept watch, not just left and right, but in all directions, turning rapidly lest she miss the winged creature that would foretell Melaina's doom.

Once the plant was fully exposed and lifted free, Kleito, skin glistening with oil, cleaned the dark earth from it and, cutting the slender lower roots from its base, stuffed the irregular nodular pieces in a leather bag, cinched it tight. Then she replanted the remaining foliage, said a few words in defense of her actions, and that she'd wished the plant no harm.

Back down the hill they went, Myrrhine keeping her eyes glued to the battle still raging in the channel. She noticed ships moving south, away from the action. Had the Persians already defeated the Greeks and were now sending ships in search of new prey? Myrrhine, though appreciative of Kleito's efforts, had made up her mind. None of the concoction would ever touch Melaina's lips.

Inside, they found her resting peacefully, though little Euripides maintained a vigil so closely bent over Melaina it was a wonder she could breathe. Kleito immediately fell to work at her craft in the next room, telling everyone to stay out. Soon she returned with a half cup of steaming liquid. She handed it to Myrrhine saying, "Your choice."

Myrrhine raised the cup to her nose. A faint odor, not immediately recognizable, lofted about the cup. She touched it to her lips. A bitter and slightly acrid taste spread to the back of her tongue. She'd expected a thick rich brew, perhaps with bits of root making it hard to swallow. This thin bitter-flavored decoction looked harmless enough. She wouldn't mind having some herself. And if it could cure Melaina...

"I've used two ingredients," advised Kleito, walking around straightening first the sofa, then Melaina's covers, as if disinterested in the whole affair. "The hellebore, of course, but also a little poppy called Herakleia, an emetic. The hellebore purges downwards, Herakleia upwards. The phlegm is the problem. We have to rid her of it."

Myrrhine thought how silly she'd been. Surely this simple mixture couldn't be a threat to Melaina, no matter Kleito's histrionics during harvesting.

Melaina stirred. They waited until she was on the verge of waking. Myrrhine then sat on the edge of her daughter's bed and, with Kleito's help, raised Melaina's head. Her eyelids opened a little, not enough to indicate awareness. Myrrhine put the cup to her daughter's lips and Melaina reflexively emptied it, smacked twice, then settled back to sleep.

"No!" said Kleito. "Get her up, keep her moving. Rest kills the action of hellebore." Then she quickly left the room to investigate a flurry of activity in the courtyard, which escalated from a clamor to screams.

Myrrhine scanned the voices for those of the barbarians. She

helped her daughter from bed, as Melaina regained consciousness, asking, "What happened to me? Why am I back here? What's
happened to the fleet?"

A series of shouts and screams from the courtyard sent Myrrhine scurrying from the room and into the courtyard. What
stretched before her appeared to be the battlefield itself. The injured and dying lined the courtyard walls, and more were being
carried in. The groans of the injured were eclipsed only by the
shrieks of women as they found their husbands and sons among
the casualties, some having gone hysterical before the body of a
loved one.

Kleito wasn't among them.

Myrrhine stood before a man shot through by an arrow, a
young woman bent over him. The arrow had thrust squarely in
his chest beside the nipple, piercing him through the lung. The
bronze point issued by the shoulder blade. Another spear, having
passed through, opened his midsection. He tenderly held his own
entrails in his hands as though cradling a child, breathing his last
breaths as the mists of death seeped across his eyes. The young
woman spoke to him. "Oh Attikus, most dear to me. How griev-
ous that you've returned dying. Woe be the day you left my side!
Now evil will follow evil for our three sons." He was a large man,
a great smooth-trunked poplar felled among the forest where he
lay now like a timber.

Myrrhine passed through the gate to peer into the channel at
the battle, but found it hidden by a eucalyptus grove. Through the
trees came a shouting woman and two men dragging a third. The
woman was Kleito, the man dragged, Mnesarchides.

Through the gate they came, Kleito in hot control of the situation, through the courtyard and into their home, Kleito shouting
orders to slave women to prepare a pallet where she could tend
her husband. Myrrhine ran to gather rags, a bowl of steaming
water.

With all the dead and injured, Myrrhine had forgotten Melaina. When she'd left to find Kleito, Melaina seemed fine, cloudy

headed but walking. Now she'd slumped on the bed, eyes bugged with urgency.

"Vomit!" Melaina said.

Myrrhine retrieved one of the two pots placed at her daughter's bedside, and quickly Melaina emptied stomach bile, a sour stench hovering about them. No sooner had the forceful stomach cramps subsided than she sounded another alarm.

"Toilet!"

Myrrhine found the other pot, and Melaina quickly emptied her bowels accompanied by great flatulence and many groans. She never left the sitting position, although a handmaid quickly replaced the pot. Melaina cradled a bowl in her lap and continued filling it with black stomach contents, issuing great belches. The stench grew, and Myrrhine recognized the greatly magnified smell of bitter hellebore.

Throughout the afternoon the din in the courtyard increased, and along with it, the sounds of Melaina's evacuation of the body from both ends. Just when Myrrhine thought the poor girl was really in danger, all stopped. Melaina settled back on the bed, slept a while, and toward evening ingested a little gruel, then began to tend the injured herself.

Myrrhine assisted Kleito with Mnesarchides. A spear point had pierced his left arm, leaving it inert, and a sword had sliced the muscle of his right leg. Once the bleeding stopped, his life out of danger, Kleito calmed, though she wouldn't leave his side. Myrrhine tended others in the courtyard where earth ran black with blood.

As a pink glow settled into the horizon, the halls of Kleito's home turned dark. The truth of the matter began to dawn on them: no Persians were coming. A great chorus erupted from shore with the fleet's return, while a full moon rose in the east over smoldering Athens. The strait was littered with war wreckage. Moonlight set an eerie glow to the landscape as the Queen of the Dark World illuminated Hermes' labor of shepherding shades to her bosom.

Myrrhine was inside talking to Melaina about her seizure, trying to explain the inexplicable, that she'd had the illness since she was a child, when the men returned. Sophocles stood in the doorway, a startled look on his face, speechless. Aeschylus came charging past Sophocles as a great lion might, eyes flashing, roaring his words. "Brace yourself for the miraculous!" he said. "We've held our own. Never in my life have I seen anything like it! I knew we could win at Marathon on land, but this battle was at sea. The strait runs red with Persian blood, the waves a soup of Asian bodies."

Myrrhine slinked back. Aeschylus was drunk with death, murder seemingly still at the edge of his actions. Men went for each other like wolves, whirling upon one another with ferocious hugging.

"Hellas is still alive!" Aeschylus shouted. "Tomorrow we'll finish the job." He brandished a magnificent Persian sword, jewels sparkling along the hilt.

Sophocles, a great terror still in his eyes, turned and vanished.

CHAPTER 13: XERXES' LAMENT

At the opposite shore, high atop his golden throne on a knoll overlooking the strait, Xerxes watched the sea battle unfold, a golden umbrella shading him from the sun. Great was the power of his Persian ships entering the narrows, greater still Xerxes' pride that he'd conquer Greece where even his father, Darius the Great, had failed. But the fleet's advantage became its doom. The great number of ships quickly clogged the channel, oars fouling one another. They were unable to maneuver when Greek war vessels bore down. Xerxes heard the thud and grind of bronze beaks as the rams of Greek triremes sunk deep into Persian hulls. His front line panicked and tried to turn tail, only to run afoul of those astern pressing forward to show their valor. Oarless hulls capsized, corpses floated, and soon reef and beach were strewn with dead.

The first blow to Xerxes' own confidence arrived with the body of his brother. He remembered how their father had doted upon Ariabignes, and now heard his father's great booming voice cry from the grave. "Your hot youth hath unleashed a spring of evils upon Persia, my son." Xerxes watched in quiet disbelief as even those flung into the waters drowned, while Greeks who ended up in the drink swam ashore.

When a group of Phoenician commanders docked and came to him making excuses, Xerxes could no longer restrain his anger. "Cowards!" he cried, then called forth the hooded messenger of death, and ordered the commanders' heads laid upon the chopping block.

Having turned on his own men, Xerxes felt cut off and alone

The Mysteries

in Europe and felt anxiety over his supply lines being spread across a continent. He'd just lost control of the seas. The Greeks had now but to cut the cables of his bridges across the Hellespont to trap him in a hostile land where the gods were against him.

CHAPTER 14: THE FUNERAL PYRE

Melaina woke tired, grumpy. Shouts of those leaving to join the fleet echoed again in the courtyard. Her chamber was dark, her mother gone. Memory of the previous day was one long blur punctuated by a recollection of nausea and vomiting. The world was a different place this morning. Every sound, sight, and smell was now tainted with the horror of epilepsy. She felt none of yesterday's eagerness to see the fleet disembark.

Her mother had tried to console Melaina; after all, Kleito had given her the hellebore. Kleito had told Melaina that epilepsy was caused when phlegm from the head stopped life-giving air from flowing into the veins. But Melaina wasn't so sure. She'd momentarily seen the world as the gods see it, remembered gentle Hermes herding the souls of the freshly dead, the exquisite euphoria. Mortals had seemed but actors in some great tragedy written by the gods. She had been a quasi-divine power viewing the battle as might a spectator in the theatre. The logic behind it all had been revealed to her. Just a blink of that divine world was worth her whole existence, a gift no one else would understand. She wondered if epilepsy was what her father had meant when he'd told her that not all burdens are a curse. Yet she was terrorized by the memory of the pain just before she collapsed.

Melaina walked from the women's quarters to the courtyard. Since the chaos of war had forced women into the open, they tended campfires, rushed back and forth looking for missing children, and lined the streets preparing their dead for burial while bracing themselves for a new wave of casualties. In the distance, Melaina saw the men laboring to get damaged triremes seaworthy, heard shouts and mallets pounding in the cove.

She worried about Sophocles. He'd made that short appearance after the battle, then disappeared. Had he suffered some terrible personal defeat? At least, she knew he'd survived.

Melaina found her mother with an old woman who was trying to decide whether to simply bury her husband and son or have them cremated and bury the bones. As priestess of Demeter, Myrrhine was much in demand. When Melaina appeared at her side, the woman turned to her, saying, "Kore, Kore," with respect and childlike desperation as she groped for Melaina, took her by the hand to a beloved corpse, raised her voice in anguish, and ripped fistfuls of hair from her own head. The woman lacerated her cheeks with her fingernails until little rivulets of blood streaked her face. With that, Melaina stopped her. "No more unseemly mourning," she said. "Limit your grief. Please, do not destroy yourself."

Particularly desperate were those whose loved ones had never been initiated into the Mysteries. Their souls were destined for a shade's existence on the Plain of Asphodel where they drank from the river Lethe, forgot the past, and forever retained a clouded mind. Those who'd been initiated resided in the Elysian Fields, the Isle of the Blessed, where they lived a carefree existence with the gods.

Even women whose loved ones had been initiated needed reassuring. These came to Melaina begging to be told of Kore and what Kore did with the dead after taking them from Hermes. They needed to know that Kore was gentle, understanding. The more jealous wanted the specifics about with whom their deceased husbands would be allowed to socialize. One woman demanded to know how she might keep Aphrodite from her husband, tears turning to jealous rage.

By mid-morning, boats of the Greek fleet began filtering back to the docks, but it wasn't until Aeschylus returned that Melaina and her mother found out what'd happened. Aeschylus looked strangely out of sorts, depressed, a pensive shadow of thoughtfulness invading his disposition.

"We manned the triremes with new resolve this morning," he said quietly, "anticipating a new wave of Persian ships, but when Helios first shed light on Phaleron, none were in sight. They'd fled during the night." A look of confusion, even disbelief, swept across his massive brow. "We've won the battle for the seas."

"Sophocles," asked Melaina, "is he well?"

"Well, but suffering from his first battle anguish."

Melaina had pondered Sophocles' sudden appearance and departure. What is the nature of his suffering? she wondered.

With the return of the fleet, mourning for the dead gathered strength. Wails passed wave-on-wave over the island as grieving women washed corpses in seawater, anointed them with olive oil, cleansed and bandaged wounds. They wrapped each corpse in a white shroud, carefully anointed the hair, closed the eyes, and laid it on the bier. Moaning, they covered the feet with laurel branches and placed a linen chin-strap around the head to prevent the jaw from sagging open. As a show of sanctity, they placed a crown of myrtle upon each head. Last of all, they inserted a one-obol coin between the lips as payment to grumpy Charon for the ferry ride across the Styx and on to the dark shore of the Underworld.

Women performed all these acts. Women had brought the men into the world, women must see to their departure.

That evening, Aeschylus called Melaina and Myrrhine into the banquet hall before the hearth of Hestia. This was the first time since arriving at Salamis that Melaina had seen Aeschylus' wife, Philokleia, and his two children. Thank goodness Philokleia hasn't heard of my epilepsy, Melaina thought. All Salamis would know by now. Melaina held little Euripides in her arms as he clung fiercely to her neck. Mnesarchides hobbled in, pale as death and leaning heavily on bulky Kleito.

Aeschylus spoke over the thud of axes felling trees for funeral pyres. "What I'm about to say," he began, "should not be retold. We know little for certain, although all our spies tell much the same story. We know for sure that the Persian fleet has fled east into the Aegean. Xerxes is in a panic that we might cut his bridges across the Hellespont, trapping him in Hellas. This may force his hand on the ground. He could make a land assault on the Isthmus and the Spartan's great wall. If he does, Eleusis is in danger. Let us remain optimistic, toning down our fear. It would be sacrilege to forget the dead before their interment. I've sent a scout to Eleusis. My concern now is for the Hierophant. The old fool should never have stayed behind."

Yes, Melaina thought, and I should not have left my dowry.

That night, Melaina lay awake listening to the wail of mourners mixed with the heavy whack-on-whack of axes, sounds all blown about by night breezes. She worried over the plight of her grandfather and her dowry, longed to once again run her fingers through the hidden compartment's ancient coins.

She felt humiliated by her epilepsy, felt fragile and stalked by a frenzied madness. Her mother had shut tight the jar of gossip that could have rippled through the families of Eleusis. The isolation here at Kleito's had been fortuitous. Thank goodness Agido and Anaktoria hadn't seen me, she thought. Even Uncle Aeschylus didn't know. If Kleito's cure worked, this would be the end of it, but Melaina wasn't optimistic. She'd been allowed to dip into the divine. Surely the gods permitted that for a reason, one not as yet revealed. Close to her breast, she held fast the blacksmith's broach, the golden eagle, symbol of Prometheus' punishment. To think you are divine, or even above other mortals, she knew was the great arrogance.

★

Her mother woke Melaina long before sunup. The procession of the dead had begun. They stepped outside into starlight and saw a cortege of horse-drawn hearses stretching through the streets. A torchbearer went before each, followed by men carrying weapons in one hand and pounding their heads with the other in the customary display of grief. Then came the hearse, followed by wailing women ripping their hair and clothes. An aulos player, his two-fluted instrument piping a mournful tune learned on some foreign shore, brought up the rear.

Melaina walked with her mother beside the train and through the dark until the procession reached the sea. Here the night's tree felling had produced timber now piled high along the beach. The restless surf gently tossed about the mustered battleships.

Melaina said, "I've never understood why we cremate the bodies, then bury the bones."

Her mother said nothing at first, then replied, "When Demeter came to Eleusis, she nurtured Metaneira's infant son, Demophoon, and while doing so placed him in the hearth to burn away his mortality. If Metaneira hadn't foolishly stopped Demeter, she'd have made him immortal."

"Fire can do that?"

"It nurtures the soul. This world's tribulations are the 'fires of life' given by the gods to make ready the soul for the Afterlife. If we don't experience the spiritual fires, we'll be stillborn in the next world. Demeter was simply accelerating the process. At the end of earthly life, we finish it off with literal fire, cremation."

"We are the beaten metal in the smithy of the gods."

"Well put, Melaina. Fire is the gateway between this world and the next."

"Palaemon's words," she said, "spoken to me but a few days ago."

"The smith is wise man. If he wasn't, I wouldn't put up with you visiting him."

"But why bury the bones?"

"Burial is the impregnation of Earth. We must be conceived within Earth's womb to be reborn in the Elysian Fields. Bones are symbolic of the soul's seed."

"As in the initiation?"

"Shhh. Don't speak of such things in public. The uninitiated might hear."

"But some don't cremate."

"Not everyone believes the same. Many want the body whole when left in Earth's charge."

Melaina looked north toward Eleusis, dreading that she might see a red glow, telltale sign of Persian fire. She added Palaemon to her list of worries should the Persians mount a land assault.

Along shore before the docked triremes, stacks of timber stretched into darkness. Each corpse was unloaded from its hearse and laid gently on the mound of limbs. When the funeral pyres were piled high with the dead, the male relatives stepped forward, cut dark locks of hair from their own heads and laid them across the corpses. The men dug deep pits, slaughtered a great number of beasts: cows, sheep, goats, pigs, and let the black blood flow into the earth. Bones, fat, and entrails they laid beside each corpse. The glistening red flesh they set aside for the feast to follow.

Two priests stepped forward, each carrying two torches, and approached Myrrhine and Melaina. They offered the two priestesses the flaming timbers.

Melaina realized then that she and her mother were to have the honor of lighting the pyres. Following victory over the Persians, rumors had spread that Ajax had been seen on the helm of the lead ship. Her prayer the night before battle was still on everyone's lips. As Melaina wrapped her fists about the rough stem of the two torches, she felt a wave of goose bumps. She remembered her vision of Kore from the night they performed the Mysteries, after seeing her father's apparition. Kore had carried two torches.

The women touched torches to the fresh-cut timber, but though they lingered with flames licking the gnarled bark, the fire would not light. Her mother stood back from the pyre, faced north, and motioned for the crowd's holy silence. Then the two priestesses held high the torches, so that they spread flickering light upon them all and the restless triremes afloat nearby. Myrrhine prayed aloud:

"O strong-hearted brothers: cold Boreas, god of north wind, and warm-whispering Zephyrus, god of brightening west wind, children of air, light-winged ones of the far reaches. Blow a lofty, quivering breeze upon these broken boughs; ignite our pyre so we may send these cold corpses to their rightful place in the Underworld."

Mother and daughter walked off in opposite directions along the beach, the flames now greedily enveloping the fallen limbs. The pyre was soon borne aloft by the roaring of a mighty internal wind carrying with it the chorus of wails. The stench of burning flesh filled the air with the rewards of war.

The igniting ritual complete, mother and daughter reunited to watch the women caretake the fire, nursing their loved ones into the Afterlife. The women's wailing mixed with the flames to form the confluence of two mighty skyward-flowing streams, one of sound, the other fire, wherein marks the entrance to Hades.

Soon the glowing skeleton of embers stood as one mighty deceased beast. Gradually the glow faded as pink-shrouded dawn broke to eclipse all but the brightest embers. When all was reduced to ashes, the women retrieved the bones of their beloved, and families who lived there on Salamis retired to their own cemeteries for the burials. The refugees of Attica collected the bones of their loved ones in urns, but the burials would wait until they could return home.

Before anyone left, several generals stepped forward; among them were Eurybiades, commander-in-chief from Sparta; Kimon; Xanthippus; Themistocles, commander of the Athenian fleet and engineer of the victory; and many others Melaina didn't recognize. The generals stood on a rise before the assembled crowd. Themistocles spoke with a new confidence, perhaps puffed up a little by arrogance. His voice boomed over the crowd so that even those in ships offshore could hear.

"By taking my advice and engaging Xerxes here at Salamis, the War Council has saved Hellas, gained a great victory, and preserved the Peloponnese. Already Xerxes prepares his land forces for evacuation. Although the full extent of his retreat is unknown, this bodes well for all. Soon we'll return home. Athens has been liberated!"

Before he finished, Aeschylus pulled Melaina and Myrrhine from the crowd. His eyes flashed excitement. "I've word from

Eleusis," he said. "The Persians never made it that far west. The entire town escaped unharmed, and even the old Hierophant is in good spirits. Already I have a boat waiting at the dock. Soon as you collect your things, you can return."

Grandfather was right after all, Melaina thought but did not say, biting her tongue just in time. That was close, she realized.

CHAPTER 15: THE ISTHMUS OF CORINTH

When Melaina, Myrrhine and the rest of the women from Eleusis reached the dock for the boat ride home, Aeschylus and Kallias came to them again. The men were dressed in fresh white chitons with their himations draped over their shoulders leaving the torso bare, ends thrown back over the shoulder. Kallias had restrained his mass of black hair with a bright-green strophion.

Aeschylus told mother and daughter, "The War Council will hold an awards ceremony at the Isthmus. You two are requested to participate in the women's chorus."

Melaina was sorely disappointed. She'd spent so little time at Eleusis during the last year and felt like an exile, forever on the run. The epilepsy had escalated her growing sense of insecurity. She wanted to see her grandfather and hear the ring of the blacksmith's hammer.

Aeschylus added, "We're to award prizes for valor in battle."

Melaina laughed. "What better way to contaminate victory than with jealousy and malice." No sooner had she spoken than she regretted it, would have swatted the winged words from the air like mosquitoes, but they were already out biting ears.

Aeschylus' powerful, hair-framed face turned red. Melaina saw him struggle, lips working to voice some deadly admonition against her, but he fell silent. He turned to Kallias, "Why bother with insolent youth."

Melaina breathed a sigh of relief. She'd better watch her tongue. Never had she known her words to come so quickly, so thoughtlessly. Perhaps it was the epilepsy.

The men led the two women to a great battleship, a trireme standing before the docks like a sleek leviathan riding proudly above the waterline. It was so long, seemed to Melaina it stretched on forever. Her first excursion, aboard the boat to Salamis, had whetted her appetite for the sea. That'd been a merchant ship and, although a crew sat at the oars, was chiefly powered by sail. The trireme was a warship and propelled through the rough Aegean by one hundred and seventy oars. It rarely unfurled a sail. A raised deck ran the length of the ship, leaving the sides open for near-naked oarsmen on cushioned benches. Down the center, ten hoplite warriors wearing breastplates, helmets, and greaves, took up position, some standing while others knelt. They had swords strapped to their belts and carried spears and axes. Four Cretan archers with long bows and arrow-stuffed quivers stood alongside them. Seeing the deck stained black from battle blood, Melaina took a deep breath and forgot about returning to Eleusis.

Standing amongst the warriors was Xanthippus, the quiet man she'd seen at Phlya on the way back from Brauron, the man Kimon hated. Though she understood Kimon's anger, Xanthippus' short, stout frame and quiet but firm bearing, gave her a sense of security she gained from no other.

Xanthippus noticed the women and came forward.

Melaina dropped her eyes.

"Welcome," he said to both women, but turned to Melaina. "Never have I heard such a prayer as you gave the night before battle." He returned to his station by the helm.

Melaina overlooked this scene from her position on the elevated stern, the poop deck, glowing from Xanthippus' compliment. She felt at one with these men and met the eyes of warriors and oarsmen alike as they followed her every move. At a shout from Xanthippus, they pushed off and the aulete stamped his foot thrice, tooted on his twin pipes to sync the oarsmen. Melaina realized Xanthippus was the commander of this magnificent vessel, the captain.

Melaina loved the trireme immediately, loved the creak and

groan of straining timbers, loved the sweaty smell of laboring men, their mumbles, light curses. Melaina felt the warship's wild energy, the power that could disembowel any vessel afloat. She heard the incessant grating of oars on tholepins, the threshing of seawater. What a mass of masculinity was housed within the motherly hull. She was reminded of her father and felt closer to him. He'd died a hoplite. She remembered her vision of him, his severed hand, and thought once more of her promise to him.

As oars foamed saltwater, Melaina and her mother stood astern with Aeschylus and Kallias by the huge steering paddles that swung at the vessel's sides. The helmsman touched now on one, then the other, to correct course. But her mother shrunk back behind Aeschylus and cast her eyes downward upon deck. She spoke to him, "Why have you brought us aboard a war vessel? Surely our presence here is forbidden."

"Rumors of Persian patrols," he said. "Xanthippus arranged it. Travel by land to the Isthmus is no longer possible. The Scironian Road was destroyed to keep Persians out of the Peloponnese."

At the forecastle standing alongside the bow officer, Melaina saw a thin form gazing off into the emerald water swiftly flowing toward them. This was young Sophocles, pensive, brooding. She wondered anew about his agony.

Melaina talked her uncle into taking her forward, "to see the deadly ram." Aeschylus balked, obviously concerned at parading her amongst the men, but her mother protested also, and that seemed to change his mind. Melaina wondered about this. She'd noticed a growing discontent between the two of them. Her mother always kept her distance when they spoke.

As Melaina and her uncle walked amongst the warriors to the prow, each armed man rose, gave ground. Melaina couldn't help smiling. When they reached the forecastle, fenced in by a solid parapet, Sophocles became aware of their presence and turned away, but not before Melaina caught a glimpse of his sad face, tear-filled eyes. He's suffered a tragedy, she thought, and wondered if someone close to him had fallen in battle.

A fine spray of saltwater chilled her cheeks as she peered over the edge at the great, two-pronged bronze ram protruding from the massive bow. The ram peeled the sea aside in thin transparent sheets. She wondered how many enemy hulls the ram had penetrated, how many men it had sent to their deaths? She understood why they named ships after goddesses, for this was indeed a divine being.

Melaina remained silent, and returned to the poop deck, not wanting to overextend her liberty. On the way, she noticed her mother standing at the railing next to Kallias—again witnessed her mother's interest in him—and thought what a striking couple they made. Kallias himself was as yet unmarried, and at thirty, highly ripe for it.

Because of the strong headwind, they'd not arrive until evening. The crew rowed eagerly over the depths of sea, the bay on the left, craggy shoreline to the right, passed the southern tip of Salamis, and sailed due east for the Isthmus of Corinth. Mid-afternoon, some of the men stowed their oars and broke out rations. As the sweet smell of yeast and honey swept past, Melaina watched them eating garlic, olives, grapes, barley biscuits. The boatswain brought Melaina and her mother a basket of wheat loaves, goat cheese, and chopped asphodel to eat with figs. They passed a wineskin around, and Melaina thirsted greedily at it. Soon, she felt a great urge to mix amongst the men, but restrained herself.

Her mother dragged Melaina below deck to a small compartment, where they spent their time stumbling among anchors and mooring lines. The trireme wasn't equipped for passengers. From this vantage point, Melaina watched the three banks of tireless oarsmen above while snacking on poppy-seed bread. The creak of ship's timbers seemed an ancient tongue. The men sweated streams from their brows and backs. Their eyes rolled askance while breaths came in hot gasps. All afternoon they toiled, stroke after stroke, dragging the oars through the sea.

That evening as they approached the harbor, distant shouts

brought mother and daughter topside again. Melaina pointed into the dark toward a line of torches stretching away from shore.

"Diolkos," said her mother. She'd been at the Isthmus several times. "We've arrived."

"What are they doing?"

"It's a great commercial center. Ships from all over the Aegean come here, unload their cargo into cars to be pulled across the Isthmus along a stone-paved portage, the diolkos, to the waters of the Corinthian Gulf. There the cargo is reloaded into ships headed for Delphi, Patras, or towns as far away as Brentesion in Italy."

"What's that?" asked Melaina, pointing to another line of torches running parallel up the slope west of the diolkos.

"I've never seen it before. Must be the defensive wall the Spartans built. That's where we're headed, just beyond to the temple of Poseidon."

The ship glided through smooth water and into the cove, where other vessels crowded to the docks serving the diolkos. They slipped into a space left open for the trireme, then stilled and secured the oars. Melaina and Myrrhine were the first to leave the ship, escorted by Xanthippus, with Aeschylus and Kallias close behind. Sophocles trudged past and on up the slope by himself, a lonely looking soul with his arms pulled about his body.

On land, they were met by a group of men and welcomed by Kimon, Kallias' friend whom they'd met on the road back from Brauron. Melaina had seen Kimon at Phlya in Kleito's home. He was younger than Kallias and handsome as any man Melaina had ever seen, tall and large, thick curly hair falling to his shoulders. He gave Xanthippus a wide berth, but when he saw the two women, he roared with laughter, sending up great clouds of wine-smelling breath. He was so infatuated with Melaina that he kept pawing her.

Kallias pushed him away. "Control yourself, Kimon," he implored. "Be civilized!"

"But she's Kynegeiros' daughter! I remember him when I was a child. My poor dead father spoke well of him at Marathon.

How can I not be in love with her?" Melaina's father, as well as the rest of the men she was with, had served under Miltiades, Kimon's father.

"Your affection is infested with Bacchus' spirit and will turn to regret tomorrow. Your problem is you drink frog-fashion, never eating anything. She's a priestess, not a flute girl."

Kimon looked greatly ashamed. "Acting a fool among sacred company, am I? You take them then, Kallias, and you also Aeschylus. I'll walk with someone who can make me behave myself." He spoke in great gusts of breath that filled the space around them with wine fog.

His pawing, the monstrous hot hands, gentle and kind on her arm, didn't offend Melaina, but she did resent Kallias assuming the role of her protector. What affection she couldn't deflect, her Uncle Aeschylus could save her from.

They walked the slope to the sacred glen, entered the temple of Poseidon through a line of stately pines, and passed statues of the Isthmian Games victors. The temple precinct was small and surrounded by stone, the northern side forming part of the now-infamous military wall, a great makeshift structure of sand, brick and timber, reinforced by strategically spaced towers. It swarmed with warriors. Poseidon's columned temple was no taller than the trees, and two Poseidons stood out front alongside a statue of the sea goddess Amphitrite, Poseidon's divine wife. The god's children were worked on the plinth, since they, too, were saviors of ships and men at sea. A rowdy horde of warriors packed a nearby theatre and an adjacent white-stoned stadium.

The men joined the feast, while the two women were taken inside the temple. Melaina and her mother stopped before a great marble basin resting on a ring and supported by four stone women, each standing on a lion's back. Female servants brought pitchers and tipped holy water for their hands into a silver bowl. Others filled the wine bowls and poured a fresh cup for each. A larder mistress brought a tray of honeyed loaves for their bedtime repast. Against a far wall, a hearth-fire burned, and Melaina and her mother sent a shower of wine over the flames, crumbled a loaf into the coals, drank deep, and spoke a prayer to the great bearded god in whose temple they would spend the night.

The priestesses and servants disappeared down an echoing hall to their quarters. Handmaids brought blankets and deep-piled rugs, and they went to bed wondering what morning would bring.

★

A commotion in the hall woke Melaina well before daybreak. Shouts of angry women's voices and the howl of a beast followed. Melaina heard her name spoken in desperation just before a great white wolf strode into the chamber, followed by a tall woman dressed in sacred raiment. The servants tried vainly to restrain her. The oil lamp in her hand cast a pale light and flickered nervously. The beast moved to the center of the room and stood at attention, surveying all within his realm.

"Where's the maid from Eleusis?" the woman asked, scanning the chamber. She was the tallest woman Melaina had ever seen, standing goddess-like among the servants.

Heart pounding, Melaina raised her head from the pillow. Her mother responded.

"Back off, woman! If you won't let us sleep, at least let us make ourselves decent before accosting us. And remove that demon! His eyes have stalked me since he entered."

The woman motioned the wolf back to the door. "Forgive me! I must know if the maid was at Brauron during the Persian siege. Please!"

"Leave her be," Melaina said to those trying to restrain the woman. "Let me learn her mission before she's banished." She turned to the woman. "Perhaps your rudeness is not without purpose. I was at Brauron."

"Ah! At last!" But inexplicably the woman turned her back and hid her face. "I'm terrified to speak with you." She fell at the foot of Melaina's bed, cried, prayed. "Oh divine Artemis, august goddess on Olympus, be gentle with me, that this tender maid's storehouse of memories might not hold my doom."

Melaina watched as her mother left her bed and went to the woman, shook her by the shoulders. "Stop this!" Myrrhine said. "You've frightened us all quite enough. State your business."

The woman suppressed her sobs. "I'm Keladeine, priestess of Artemis at Kenchreai nearby, but more importantly, sister of Kynthia, priestess of Artemis at Brauron."

Melaina felt a chill ripple through her and her grief reawaken. She knew she was about to cause Keladeine a great heartache. She slipped from her covers and, though still in her sleeping gown, took both Keladeine's cold hands in hers. "I saw the Persians strike flames to Artemis' temple at Brauron." Though a sizeable woman, her face was gorgeous, with large intelligent eyes that reflected the lamplight.

Keladeine spoke again. "I've heard nothing but rumors and wrung my hands with uncertainty. Withhold nothing. The kindest words be those of complete truth though they slay me in the hearing."

The woman's icy hands were the largest Melaina had ever held. "I can only offer a cruel recital indeed for the sister of my dear mistress." Melaina stopped to let her words soak in. She took Keladeine, a young woman barely more than her own age, into her arms, let her weep. She seemed a huge child.

Myrrhine turned to the servants. "Prepare a place here on the floor, and do something about the chill. These walls leach cold." She lowered her voice. "And be quiet about it. No sense waking the entire temple."

With that Melaina and her mother donned their house robes as befitted modesty, and the women serving them brought a plate of glowing coals from Hestia's hearth to break the room's chill. Myrrhine, Melaina and Keladeine gathered round the radiating heat, each sitting on a small pillow, as those in service hovered in darkness about them. The wolf quietly maintained his guard at the door.

Melaina told Keladeine of the events at Brauron that had

sealed her sister's fate. She was gentle with the description of Kynthia's death, revealing nothing of the gore, so she might deny Keladeine the gruesome image, but was emphatic about the result. Kynthia had passed to the Underworld. Melaina omitted that the Persian was trying to get to her when Kynthia stepped between them. She couldn't bring herself to say it.

Keladeine cried hard tears, and Melaina and her mother had to restrain her from lacerating her cheeks. Melaina told Keladeine of her own affection for Kynthia, the long hours they'd spent together beyond that required for her training at Brauron. Eventually, she came around to expressing her own interest in following Artemis. Melaina finished by telling Keladeine of her own plans to start a school for girls at Eleusis.

Keladeine recovered a little. Her eyes, set in wet cheeks, met hers for the first time. "You must come to Artemis' temple, my temple, just off the road between here and Kenchreai. You can't return to Eleusis without seeing it."

Myrrhine spoke, "Melaina won't have time. We leave after the celebration tomorrow."

"Then we must go now," said Keladeine. "We could be there and back by the time the men are up. We've an ancient wooden statue of Artemis. Some say it's the oldest in Hellas, that Manto, the daughter of the great seer Teiresias, carved it at the request of Apollo to honor his divine sister."

Melaina was struck with Keladeine, the wide-spaced eyes, her openness. Her chiton fell barely to her brown knees, and her shoulders were bare and golden from long hours in the sun. Though large, she was agile as a cat. Her hair glowed yellow, a striking contrast to her sun-darkened skin. She controlled the wolf standing watch at the door with a glance, the lift of a finger.

"Mother, I must go," cried Melaina. "We have no such temple at Eleusis. Give this one moment apart from you. I'll return promptly. Quick Hermes will see to it."

"No! For many reasons, no."

"Why do you imprison me so by your constant presence?"

The question was direct, stinging. Melaina saw hurt in her mother's eyes and regretted it immensely. But this young woman, Keladeine, exuded such excitement. Melaina realized that her mother was concerned that the epilepsy might return. "I feel great, mother. Don't worry."

Melaina could tell that her cutting remark had hurt her mother immeasurably. Myrrhine didn't resist further, and Melaina left with Keladeine, but not without a growing guilt at how she'd won this moment away. Outside they climbed aboard a small, two-wheeled cart pulled by a single donkey. Keladeine spoke once to the wolf, "Lykos!" He jumped inside. Though Keladeine had two male slaves with her, the girls took seats in front, and Keladeine took the reins.

The pink sunrise made the road easy to follow, and they heard a chorus of roosters the entire route. Shortly, a dirt trail left the main road and ran up the forested hill away from shore. Melaina viewed Keladeine anew in the glow of morning light. Never had she seen such radiant beauty, a messenger of the gods she seemed.

At the top of the hill the trees parted, and they stopped before a modest temple. Keladeine left the cart and donkey with the servants. A single palm stood before the temple. She touched it as they passed. "I brought this tree from Delos. It's an offshoot of the palm marking the spot where Leto gave birth to Artemis and Apollo. It's but one of my treasures. The palm bears only female flowers, and, since it's the only palm in the area, forever virgin."

"You've been to Delos?"

"Once."

"Oh, Keladeine! What I wouldn't give to see the sacred isle."

A herd of deer grazed in a meadow nearby, and clouds of sparrows fussed among the trees. Keladeine swung aside the double doors and spoke in hushed tones. "This was modeled after the great temple of Artemis at Ephesus but doesn't approach its magnificence. The simplicity serves Artemis well."

"Kynthia used to tell me of Ephesus. I do so hope to get there some day," said Melaina.

"We have close connections with them, both being near commercial ports. Their temple is truly a marvel."

"You speak as if you've been there too."

"I have."

"In Ionia? Is there any place you haven't been? I'd give my life to see Ephesus."

"Oh, Melaina, you do love Artemis, don't you?"

"Kynthia was very persuasive."

"Then I've found a sister in you!" And then she started to cry. "I've known in my heart Kynthia had been taken from me but wouldn't admit it. Artemis has sent you with the crushing news to cushion my grief."

"Kynthia said that in Ionia, Artemis is worshiped as the great mother goddess."

"Even Zeus has no temple to compare with hers at Ephesus."

Keladeine led Melaina through the columns and into a darkened hall, stopping before a door to a small chamber. Melaina peered inside and saw children sleeping in rows upon blankets laid directly on the dirt floor. One little boy cried in his sleep.

"War orphans mostly," said Keladeine. "Some from unwed mothers. We take those who'd be exposed on Kithaeron."

"How do you care for them?"

"They'll gradually be absorbed into the surrounding communities. Merchants who come to cross the Isthmus at the diolkos will adopt some. We also take in orphaned animals, birds, deer, bear cubs. One young mountain lion."

"Then it's not just a temple of worship. It's a refuge."

"All that are lost come here."

Melaina thought if she became an outcast because of her epilepsy, she might end up here. Artemis' temple at Brauron had been dedicated to educating girls in their rite of passage from girlhood to womanhood. But here the unfortunate, the vulnerable sought refuge. If she could combine the two at Eleusis, provide not only for girls' training but also a shelter for the abandoned, her life would have even more purpose than she'd imagined. Perhaps that was why Artemis had saved her from the Persian assassin. Melaina again felt the guilt of not telling Keladeine the full story. Would Keladeine hate her if she knew the complete truth?

Keladeine led Melaina into a large chamber with a vaulted ceiling, at the far end of which stood an adytum and a dimly lit altar. A small statue of no greater height than Melaina herself appeared faint in the light of oil lamps. A circular depression before the altar contained ashes mixed with charred animal bones. Beside it stood a slaughter stone, discolored by black blood.

"I'll tend the children," said Keladeine, leaving Melaina alone.

Melaina allowed her eyes to adjust to the dim light. The age of the statue was evident in the wood grain revealed through the paled paint. The goddess was clad in a short sleeveless chiton that left her right breast bare and hardly reached her knees. It was bound at the waist by a scarf drawn across and tied. She wore buskins laced halfway to the knees and was in half stride. She held a torch in her left hand and in her right the tiny hooves of a fawn that had just sprung up to greet her. Her strung bow was strapped to her back along with a shut quiver. Her maidenly character showed in her clear bright face and dimpled chin. Her hair was pulled back severely and secured in a long plait. Her gaze was fixed upon the distance. Melaina imagined Artemis returning home through the woods in the early evening after a day of hunting, her way lit by the torch.

Melaina's eyes feasted on the icon. She'd often heard of Artemis the huntress, and ironically, protectress of animals, but she'd never felt the liberty inherent in this one image. She'd sensed Keladeine's self-determination, but the image of the goddess, the perfect unfettered being, struck her soul on fire. Never had she truly known what the word "freedom" meant. No wonder men willingly gave their lives for it. This statue of the maiden goddess, the embodiment of the woodland secluded life, made Melaina want to run off into the woods herself, walk alone through meadows, wade knee-deep streams, and sleep staring up at the stars.

Melaina realized she was committing a sacrilege. She remembered Palaemon's warning. She'd been allowed to see Artemis' freedom and now envisioned it for herself. A mortal could never, should never, strive for that reserved for the gods. To do so was insufferable arrogance. She took a deep breath, straightened her back proudly before Artemis, and raised her arms.

"O divine Artemis! Modest maid of thick-shaded forests, who loves Earth's wild beasts and brings quick death by the bow, I pray your indulgence in this personal matter. Not long ago, I came to you seeking to keep my virginity, not yet realizing the full bounty that worship of you brings. Keladeine, your temple priestess, and your likeness here before the altar, have shown me more than a state of existence, a path more precious than life itself. Give me that measure of freedom befitting a temperate mortal maiden and strike from my heart the infectious arrogance corrupting my thoughts. Fair-faced Bringer of Light, give me this life, and I'll always burn fat thighs pieces upon your sacrificial fires."

As she finished, Melaina realized she must make everything right with Keladeine. If she didn't tell her the full truth of how Kynthia died, it would always come between them. She found Keladeine among the children suckling a baby at a goatskin bladder.

"I must return," Melaina told her. "I've been gone too long."

Shortly they were back in the donkey-drawn cart on the road to the temple of Poseidon. Melaina became quiet. She felt that her friendship with Keladeine was about to end. She'd known her such a short time, but already loved her as the sister she'd never had.

"I've something to tell you, Keladeine." Melaina held back tears. "When Kynthia fell to the Persian assassin, she wasn't his target. He'd come for me. Kynthia stepped between us, offering herself up for sacrifice without hope, so I might live. But for me, Kynthia would be here with you today, and I would be in my rightful place in the Undergloom. I'm terribly sorry." There, she'd said it and would now have to suffer the consequences. She could hear Keladeine also crying and wondered when her new grief would turn to anger.

Instead Keladeine said, "Your every statement is a gift. My one unspoken doubt in Artemis was that Kynthia's life had been taken for nothing. I wondered how the goddess could let that happen. But you come forth humbly with word that Artemis is not arbitrary, that she in her infinite wisdom used Kynthia as your springboard to womanhood. Though you may not realize it, this demonstrates without doubt that the threads of your life are entwined with those of the gods. My life is here at my small temple on the Isthmus, but yours is mingled with the divine. I envy you, but still must pass along a warning. Mortals are never more than dust caught up in the whirlwind of the gods. Those closest them inherit nothing but grief."

The sun was well above the horizon when the cart pulled up in front of the temple of Poseidon. Melaina saw her mother standing in the doorway and quickly said goodbye to Keladeine. "Will I ever see you again?"

"Only the will of the gods can keep us apart."

"Have you been initiated into the Mysteries?"

"No."

"Oh, Keladeine, you must be initiated. We must be together in the Elysian Fields."

Keladeine shook the reins against the donkey's back, and the cart moved off down the dirt road. When Melaina reached the temple of Poseidon, her mother was on her at once, grabbing her by the hand and holding it until Melaina's fingers ached.

"Please don't leave like that again," Myrrhine said. Melaina saw her mother's quiet desperation.

Looking toward shore, Melaina saw a crowd of men: generals, warriors and priests. She and her mother watched as the men led out nine sacrificial bulls, an offering to the blue-maned god who made the islands tremble. Taking the sweet entrails to eat themselves, the priests stacked high the flaming altar with fat-wrapped thighbones for the god, while those around them skewered red beef and held it scorching in the flames.

★

All morning and into the afternoon spectators assembled: warriors, merchants, refugees poured in from the north, and the curious from nearby Corinth. Festive shouts erupted when Themistocles was recognized, and again when a captured Phoenician warship powered into port for dedication to Poseidon.

Melaina heard a tumult from the assembly of generals. Word came that the voting had not gone well. The civic award for valor had gone to Aegina, Athens being narrowly defeated due to Spartan jealousy. The generals could give no individual award because every commander had voted for himself. A many-sided tie resulted, although each had given second place to Themistocles, who bellowed insults and accusations of cowardice. The assembly broke up, but groups of men lingered about, shouting at each other and bickering about bravery.

Melaina saw scuffling, a fist fight, and wished she'd been wrong, hoped her uncle wouldn't remember her callous comment about awards ceremonies. She realized that the men were still caught up in war's afterglow. The forces of anarchy still controlled them. War had created internal chaos, and the coming celebration must restore each person's innate accord. They'd sing and dance to lofty-spirited, harmonious Apollo, god of light and order. Women would join in to help reweave the fabric of civilized life.

When the ruckus subsided, the men came to Poseidon's temple: magistrates, ambassadors, and purple-robed priests. A murmur spread through the crowd as it parted. Shouts and hurrahs followed, as a man of renown stepped forward. It was Pindar, poet from much-hated Thebes. Pindar had expressed no allegiance to his native city since it had gone over to Persia and had sat out the sea battle on Aegina.

Melaina and her mother ran to get close enough to hear the famous poet. Beside him stood his own lyre player, and Pindar let the instrument start first and lead him into song once he felt the beat. Pindar's light, speedy rhythms were known to be unrivaled. At first Melaina couldn't catch his words, but then held her breath

as they flowed to her. They were severe, beautiful, and seemed
to her that they came from the distant past, as if Pindar had just
stepped out of Homer:

> ...therefore, I also, though stricken sorely at heart,
> am bidden to invoke the golden Muse. Now
> that we are set free from mighty woes, let us not
> fall into brooding over our sorrows. If we cease
> to dwell on unavailing ills, we shall be delighted
> with some strain of sweetness, even after toil;
> but, for me, the passing away of terror hath caused
> stern care to cease; yet is it better to look
> at that which lieth before one's foot, for man
> is entangled in a treacherous time that maketh
> crooked the path of life. Even this may be healed
> for mortals, if only they have freedom.

Melaina recognized his rhythm as Dorian, the tone epic,
though less adorned than Homer, strong and grave, grand. She
was struck by the personal content of his ode, and that it had
obviously been written since the battle of Salamis. She counted
herself blessed to be in his presence, and mentally shuffled the
words of her own troublesome lyrics with his insights. She was
sorry to see him step back into the crowd.

The men's and women's choruses assembled. What a glorious
sight: men and women all in congregation, voices intertwined,
peaceful, and standing in camaraderie. Melaina stood with other
girls her age, listening to the mature voices lofting from the temple out over the bay.

She heard a shrill note from their own aulos player and ran
with the rest of the girls to start the procession. Melaina's chorus
was composed of two groups of nine, one representing the Muses, the other divine Artemis. Melaina took the lead as Artemis'
proxy: tall, stately. She marched to the aulete's festive beat. The
girls entered Poseidon's outdoor altar on a promontory before the

beach. They sang a hymn to the gods, their voices undulating to the aulete's thin tune, inviting the all-powerful to bridge the gulf separating mortals and immortals and join the festivities.

The boys' chorus came alongside the girls', and Melaina caught sight of Sophocles. His eyes were no longer red, and he looked as though the festivities had lightened his heart. All stood on a white stone floor among trellises of grapevines, plump, purple fruit in bunches glistening in sunlight. The most-cherished girls danced in soft-linen gowns and garlands. They touched wrists, twirled, while handsome young men with a sheen of olive oil and dressed in well-knit chitons, pounded a solid rhythm. The beat quickened, the pat of fast feet reaching a frenzy as the girls whirled and circled with ease, the way a weaver at her wheel will give it a spin between fingertips, then let it run. In lines first, then ranks, the boys and girls moved on one another, interlacing ranks to weave feminine and masculine motifs of a single fabric. Magical dancing, manic, the aulos piping shrill accompaniment.

The crowd stood quietly, ready for the solo dancing.

Melaina tried not to feel the eyes on her as she stepped forward, spun, felt the hair loft from her shoulders, her breasts bob. She felt the soft beat of her lightning feet tingle her toes. When her frantic pace could quicken no further, Sophocles charged on stage. He startled her by flinging aside his chiton. Naked he was, anointed with oil, as he struck a pose beside twirling Melaina. With lyre in hand, he harped sweetly, stroking with a plectrum, stepped high and gracefully around her, magnificent, as if the god of order and light himself had entered, sublime Apollo. Many poses he committed, this way and that, enacting divine order and expressing a stately profile of perfection. Around him, Melaina twisted, turned, each revolution gravitating closer to twine round him.

Freedom-coveting Melaina felt a great stirring. For Artemis' sake, she'd buried, she thought forever, all thoughts of male attraction. Whether it was sublime love or low-based lust bleeding into her now, she felt was quite easily told. Sophocles' small, unfettered penis and plump, tightly grouped testicles, glistening fruit, was an image virginity-loving Melaina could never purge.

"Aphrodite," she whispered, "you've come for me again?"

★

That evening they feasted outdoors, the sacrifice attended by both men and women. Melaina and her mother stayed out of sight, the daughter afraid she'd reveal her favor toward Sophocles, or at last suffer her uncle's wrath over her misspoken words about awards. But nothing was said of it, and Aeschylus kept his distance, directing his attention to young Sophocles. Slaves swept the floor, washed cups, and garlanded each in attendance. One brought round a perfume dish of holy frankincense.

Melaina watched the two of them from a distance: Aeschylus at his meal, Sophocles by the fire pouring a wine libation. Aeschylus asked, "Do you wish me to drink with pleasure?" And when Sophocles answered, "Of course," Aeschylus responded, "Then hand the cup and don't rush away." Sophocles blushed, and Aeschylus said to a man next to him, "His scarlet cheeks shine with love's light." He asked Sophocles if he was cleaning a scrap from the cup with his little finger. "Yes," said Sophocles. Aeschylus then said, "Blow it away, for I shouldn't want your finger wet." As Sophocles brought his face to the cup, Aeschylus drew it near his own lips so their heads might touch, and kissed him in the corner of the mouth. The men erupted with laughter and shouting, celebrating Aeschylus' clever strategy.

Melaina had watched the action unfold, anticipating the outcome but was shocked at the sexual affection shown her young friend. She knew the older men lusted after the younger ones and never thought much of it. But this was Sophocles. Shortly the two of them retired, Sophocles tucked neatly under the arm of Aeschylus, seemingly delighted at being fondled. Melaina felt her cheeks flush again. She experienced a new feeling, hatred for her uncle.

Sophocles can never have me, she thought, for I'm committed to Artemis, but I'll make him wish he could.

★

As they poured the final libations to the gods, Themistocles stepped before the throng and requested quiet. Renewed weight rested upon his broad shoulders. His voice was weakened and weary.

"Scouts have just returned from Boeotia with news of Xerxes. He's taken most of his troops and retreated to Persia, as we expected."

Shouts and cheers erupted.

Themistocles raised his hand. "But he's left his cousin Mardonius with half a million infantrymen to winter in Thessaly. They'll renew their assault in the spring."

Silence fell over the crowd.

Oh no, not Mardonius, thought Melaina. The general grandfather fears most.

CHAPTER 16: HALCYON DAYS AT ELEUSIS

As Melaina stepped off the boat at Eleusis, she saw the silhouetted shape of her grandfather disappear over the hilltop on his way back to the temple like an old bear returning to his lair, his dark robe pulled tight about him. I must confront him soon, she thought. I've fulfilled my role as priestess. Do I have the courage to ask for my freedom?

Melaina's excitement that first day home was fueled by the voices of her friends shouting just to hear the old stone halls echo. Melaina found her chamber unmolested, but not quite as she remembered. A quick check of her dowry chest revealed nothing missing, although it did seem disturbed. She became lost again in luxurious ancient fabrics, gold-threaded robes, coins locked away in secret. One mantle was her favorite. It had a wide trim interlaced with woven gold and was made to be worn about the back with ends pulled over one arm and thrown over the shoulder.

The Hierophant gathered all the officials of the Mysteries in the Telesterion, the ancient many-columned auditorium where the initiates congregated during the yearly ceremony, including Melaina and her mother. Melaina had never attended an assembly but was well known to all, related to many, and now the subject of whispers and finger pointing. The Hierophantides, the Hierophant's assistants, were Eumolpids, Myrrhine's distant cousins and also the mothers of Agido and Anaktoria. The mothers avoided Melaina and Myrrhine, still upset over Melaina dragging their daughters out in public. The All-Holy Ones were virgin priestesses also known as the "bees." They avoided contact with men and lived secluded lives outside the sanctuary. Melaina used to visit them with her mother from time to time. Melaina loved their stories and ancient ways. The Herald of the Mysteries was from the family of Kerykes, Kallias' family, and a descendant of Hermes the divine herald. He spent most of his time in Athens but still kept a home in Eleusis. The lesser officials maintained the temple: the Phaethyntes cleaned statues; the Neokoros cleaned and decorated the sanctuary; and the Hydranos were two priests in charge of the holy water used for purification during the Mysteries.

All were present at the assembly, having been called to the Telesterion by the Hierophant. They sat on the steps inside the columned chamber where the initiates sat during the Mysteries. The Hierophant stood before them, though leaning on his staff and in obvious pain. Melaina wondered if he was ill. He didn't hold them long, but spoke of the religious rites to the Mother and Maid, the practices for choral groups, and said a few words about the remaining construction work on the sanctuary. He also talked about the destruction of crops around Eleusis and urged food rationing. He reminded them to stay close within city walls with the Persian menace still lurking to the north.

The Hierophant then paused in his instructions and looked at Melaina. He seemed to be weighing some worrisome question. Here it comes, she thought, my elevation to priestess of Kore. Her breathing stopped. This could be the end of her quest for freedom. But he looked away and dismissed the group back to their homes. Her sigh of relief echoed off the forest of columns. Melaina then knew she needed to have it out with her grandfather. She didn't know why he hadn't made the announcement, but Melaina did know that if she didn't do something quick, the act was inevitable and possibly irrevocable.

Everyone who'd evacuated had returned, although they realized that the Persians would renew their threat next spring. The noise created by all these people and their families brought Eleusis back to life. Melaina spent her time in the weaving room close to the hearthstone, where a great fire blazed, scenting the air with cedar. She loved the weavers' song, the highs and lows of their sweet voices as the shuttles slipped to and fro. Melaina stood before a tall vertical loom where warp threads hung from a horizontal beam. Her hands were lightning with a shuttle. The woman next to her packed the woof with a wooden rod.

The room buzzed with the gossip of a dozen women, some stretching wool and combing it, others dying the tow-yarn. One spun it about a distaff, drawing the dampened thread from the spinning wheel, shaping it between her fingers and cutting it with her teeth when the trundle was full. She dropped the soft fleece into a wicker basket.

The women were working on Melaina's marriage wardrobe, a disconcerting prospect for a young woman not wanting marriage. She'd been laboring over the wardrobe the last two years and had carpets, wall coverings, and embroideries for tabletops. Melaina envisioned herself as one of the Fates, weaving an unwanted life. She repeated poetry to buoy her courage and focused on building the case she'd present to the Hierophant.

Finally, Melaina could stand it no longer. She passed the shuttle off to one of the slave girls and went next door where women prepared the newly sheared wool. They washed it in hot root-of-soapwart water, while others prepared it for dyeing by soaking it in wine, olive oil, and pig's fat. Melaina tried to busy herself carding the combed wool, but found she had no interest in this either. The slave girls laughed at her absentmindedness.

It was fate that bothered her. Was it possible to determine the future? Do the gods really fix our fate? she wondered. Or are women really the pawns of men? And what about this "second fate" business her grandfather had mentioned?

Finally, she went to see her mother.

Myrrhine was before the ovens. Great steam clouds of yeast and honey from the glowing ovens filled the room as she and a slave girl retrieved groat loaves made of rice-wheat and then pushed bulging pans of dough, soft and white as baby bottoms, into the inferno.

"Please. Come with me to see the Hierophant," Melaina said.

"I must know if I'll be allowed to follow Artemis."

"So it's come down to it now, has it." Myrrhine looked very dissatisfied. "I petitioned your grandfather to hold off the announcement of you officially becoming a priestess. I didn't tell him the real reason, only that I wanted you fully recovered from your ordeal at Brauron before we added this new pressure to your duties. Can't say he was pleased."

"But mother, if I don't tell him now, he'll make the decision public without weighing my objection."

Her mother took Melaina out of the others' hearing. "Okay. I'll go with you. But don't get your hopes up. He's been looking forward to you becoming a priestess for many years. Oh," she stopped and became stern again. "The epilepsy, don't mention it."

"Why?"

"You're cured."

"Grandfather should know I had it. I thought I might use it as an argument in my favor."

Her mother took Melaina's hands in both hers. "No, Melaina. No one should know you ever had it."

"But why?"

"The stigma. Some would view you as polluted even if cured. They could stop you from becoming a priestess or running a school for girls."

Melaina became irritated. "But mother, you don't understand. It isn't all bad. If you only knew what I felt and saw just before I fell. Something miraculous happened. Grandfather might value it."

"What? Tell me about it."

Melaina fell silent. Words didn't exist to describe it. "It is a union. I'm as one with the gods."

"To view yourself as a goddess is the great arrogance."

"I don't mean that. But I do understand what it's like to be a goddess, only as can one who has been with them."

"You've been with the gods?"

"On the promontory overlooking the sea battle. Just before I fell, I saw Hermes guiding the souls of the dead."

"Tell no one!"

"Why?"

"Men are not tolerant of aberrations in women. They want us predictable and trustworthy."

"But grandfather knows how the gods cherish me."

"This is a step beyond what even he will understand. Trust me in this."

"Okay! If I say nothing of my vision or the epilepsy, you'll help?"

"I'll go with you. Nothing more." Myrrhine hesitated. "I've noticed you've stopped averting your eyes or lowering your head, as is customary when women address men. It's particularly important with your grandfather. He is the Hierophant."

Melaina flushed and wild anger welled up inside her. She said nothing and forced back words of defiance.

"And be gentle with him," her mother added, "I've become concerned with his health lately."

They left to find him, Melaina mumbling under her breath and now uneasy about her mother's presence. Perhaps I should have gone alone after all, she thought.

The Hierophant was in his library humped over a scroll and grumbling to himself about "painful old age." He rose from his table bowed over his staff, and crept about anxiously. Melaina noticed that his limbs trembled, but apparently not from weakness. He looked strong enough. From time to time he grunted as though he'd suffered a blow. He drew his tunic about him as if to ward off a chill.

Melaina caught herself staring at his eyes, trying to read his mood. She remembered her mother's caution and forced her eyes to the floor.

When he had taken a seat again, he spoke. "What grave task has brought you before me, child? You look as if you've committed a crime."

Melaina knelt before him, took his knees in her arms and

kissed his hands. "I've come as would a slave to ask for the freedom to determine my own destiny," she said, bracing herself for the blow to fall.

Out of the corner of her eye, she saw his brows jerk up toward her mother.

"Grandfather... To some being a priestess would be all life could offer, but the Muses have given me song that I might write poetry, and a soft heart for babies and little girls that I might see to their entry into the world and teach them to be good wives and mothers. I wish to remain virgin and follow Artemis."

He placed both hands on her head, his cold fingers touching her ears. "Would you agree you've shown considerable talent as priestess?"

Melaina tried to resist the impulse, but her head leaned back and her eyes found his. She saw the worry there, and the suffering. "Yes, grandfather, more than I would like to admit." She looked down again.

He nodded and looked away. "You were voted on and passed by the Sacred Officials some months ago." He paused. "And you realize how much we need a male child to carry on in my footsteps as Hierophant?"

"Yes," she said reluctantly and sank back from him, eyes still lowered. "And the need for a priestess of Demeter to follow my mother," she said reluctantly.

"The line of Hierophants from the Eumolpids extends back a thousand years. One of your cousins may bear a son, and the Kerkyes are anxious to have a hierophant named from their clan, but you're the only one in the direct line of descent."

"I know, grandfather. Yet it's what's in my heart. What of my second fate?"

He stayed silent, and, unable to resist, she raised her eyes again, let them roam his wrinkled face. His mass of hair had lost its luster. His beard was streaked with gray. "If it were anyone else," he said, "I'd refuse flatly, but the gods have interfered in your life. Before birth, we're all allowed to select the life we'll lead and its inherent end. But when Kynthia died in your place at Brauron, you were, as you say, allotted a second fate. What the Fates have woven, you must live through to the end. Nothing I say can affect it. The spindle of our lives ever turns on the knees of Necessity with Atropos weaving the web of irreversible destiny."

"And... I can remain virgin?"

"I admit that I've had my doubts about demanding you follow in your mother's footsteps. First, Artemis saves your life, and now you come to me wanting to follow her."

"Oh, no. I'd already decided to follower her."

"Then that act may have predisposed Artemis to you and saved your life."

"So... I can remain virgin?"

"I mean," he said, touching a finger to the tip of her nose, "I'm not the one to ask. I'm not even sure the gods have settled the matter, because Kynthia's sacrifice was not given willingly. She died struggling. The gods are warring over you."

"But, grandfather, what am I to do?" she asked, catching sight of her mother walking up behind him.

"I'll say nothing more one way or the other. Your fate will show itself soon enough." He pulled her toward him and kissed her on the forehead, something he hadn't done in a long time. "Now leave an old man to his misery."

But she couldn't. She had another request plaguing her. She tried to ignore her mother's eyes as they also looked down from behind him. Melaina looked at the floor as she spoke.

"Grandfather, could you build a temple for Artemis here at Eleusis? I've long thought it strange that we have none. We've neglected the virgin goddess, and she'd greatly appreciate it. No need for plans. I've a vision of how it's to be."

The Hierophant leaned back and laughed heartily. "You've long thought? What a treasure you are, my little one! Nothing in your sweet life has been long. And that you've had a vision, I don't doubt at all. Perhaps you're right. Is that why Artemis has you tormenting me so?"

★

As the days passed, the moon waned and renewed itself, the Pleiads set, and the weather turned. A cold, blustery wind blew from the north. But gradually the storms lifted, and warm days of sunshine returned, if only for a while. The rains had turned the fields and hillsides green.

Even as a child, Melaina's favorite place to be alone was in the courtyard beneath the pomegranate tree. She frequently fell asleep there, and her mother would find her and carry her indoors. Next to the pomegranate tree, Melaina's favorite haunt was the hill overlooking Eleusis and the bay. There she'd go with or without her companions and watch the activity of the entire area. Ships brought evacuated goods back into Eleusis, and to the northeast, teams of great oxen pulled carts to and from the verdant valley of the nearby Thriasian Plain, clouds of dust rising from the loose soil. Triptolemus, prince of Eleusis and the first to sow grain, had planted his field there centuries ago. Demeter had given him three laws: honor parents, harm no animal, and glorify the gods with earth's first fruits.

Eleusis, as the ancient abode of Demeter, received annual first fruits from all states, not just nearby farms, as it had for the last three hundred years, ever since a festival and sacrifice to Demeter had ended a great famine. The festival was repeated each year as the plowing and sowing began. Looking over the land, Melaina heard the ring of hammer and anvil as Palaemon forged plows for tilling. She knew how he enjoyed this time of year because of his love for green fields. The planting of wheat, barley, peas, beans and lentils had already begun.

South of Mt. Olympus, a half million Persians occupied Thessaly under Mardonius, the general Melaina's grandfather deathly feared. Yet, Eleusis developed a decidedly festive atmosphere. The grain fields left unburned by the Persians had been rapidly harvested and threshed. Figs, almonds, and chickpeas, picked before the invasion, had been pulled from storage and taken to Salamis. But the pears had rotted on the trees, and the grapes rapidly turned brown and wrinkled on the vines, although laborers had worked hard to salvage them.

To this perch on top of the Eleusinian world, Melaina came one afternoon, and this time brought her little troop: stately Anaktoria and smiling Agido, after some fast talking with their mothers; but also quiet Euphemia and ever-yapping Dorothea, sisters whose mother had practically thrown the girls at Melaina to be rid of them for the afternoon. Melaina was thrilled to have four in her group, and took along her lyre to sing from Sappho and recite her own poetry when she could squeeze it in, entwining it with soft rhythms and sweet melodies.

This had always been Melaina's way. As a child she took to wearing a stephane about her hair, sometimes of myrtle, glimmering olive at others. And always she was in the presence of children, telling a story, guiding them through a dance. Sometimes she even slumbered herself with the children asleep in her arms.

On this day, after having sung a few verses of her own poetry, Melaina was in the midst of questioning its rhythmic quality when her Uncle Aeschylus appeared, coming up the hill. She'd been trying to correct her attitude toward him since witnessing his affection for Sophocles, and once again realized that she was quite fond of him. Surely his appearance is a favorable sign, she thought. I can ask if he'll help improve my verse.

Aeschylus had taken to wearing the sparkling Persian sword he'd captured during the sea battle and looked very smart in it. But he pulled Melaina aside before she could speak and spoke quite sternly to her. "If you're going to do this, do it indoors, where you can't be seen. Don't make a spectacle of yourself."

Melaina took her reprimand gracefully but was secretly devastated. He acted as if they were at their toilet. She saw that he'd frightened the girls. But she was still determined to ask his help. She'd been concentrating on her eyes' arrogance and consciously lowered them. Were his knees far enough? Perhaps the feet?

He stood impatiently.

"I've decided to follow Artemis, become a poetess, and run a school for girls, in the tradition of Sappho. But I'll need training. I know you're the greatest poet in all the world and wonder if you'd mind helping me. I'm so clumsy at rhythm."

"Teach a girl?" He looked incredulous, walked away from her, then turned back. "Years ago, when I was but a boy of the fields caring for a vineyard, I fell asleep in the warm afternoon sun, and Dionysus came to me in a dream. He told me to write tragedies. I didn't have a particular inclination for the craft but didn't want to disobey a god, so I tried, and found that I was good at it. I suggest you spend less time indulging in your own desires and more searching for the will of the gods."

"I've been told I have the Muses' gift. If you'd just..." She held up a small scroll.

Her uncle had appeared disinterested until he saw the papyrus. Melaina knew his curiosity had been piqued. He held the unrolled sheet out from him, as the eyes require of those his age.

Melaina felt vulnerable. Her uncle was used to arguing the finer points of line construction with the best in Greece. How could she possibly measure up? He stared for a long while, eyes darting back and forth beneath his massive brows. Her fractured confidence faded further. Finally, he spoke with a thin voice, barely a murmur.

"I can't imagine the gods wasting such a gift on a girl."

"You like it?"

"The cohesion and smoothness is shocking for one so young. Nothing wrong with your meter. It's simply original. Though you could benefit from a little... Great Zeus! What metaphors."

"Then you'll teach me?"

"Find a poetess," he said, flinging back the roll. "Korinna perhaps. She defeated Pindar five times. Myrtis may be too old, though she taught Pindar and Korinna. Either would suffice."

Melaina stooped to pick up the scroll, indignant. "Those poets were both from hated Thebes." How could he suggest such a thing? she wondered. "Korinna is so... so parochial," she said, shocked at the outrage in her own voice, but her mouth kept going. "Her language and subject matter are inferior."

"You can't expect to be taught as a man. Understand your station."

"But I'm your brother's daughter. You won't help me?" She felt humiliated in front of her students.

"You seem more suited to Sparta where worshipping Artemis is required of girls, and they're educated the same as boys."

"But the Muses!" Anger flashed in her eyes as she stared him down.

He walked off, throwing a last remark over his shoulder. "When hastening to your own undoing, the gods take part with you."

She was confused, felt cheated, abused. She stamped her foot, and her cheeks again flushed, whether from rage or embarrassment at her own presumptuousness, she didn't know. She scanned her four bug-eyed students. Melaina had never been dismissed like this. She fought the urge to call him back.

★

Palaemon was just returning from the smelter, shuffling into his shop as Melaina entered. She stood watching as he and his two servants, Akmon and Damnameneus, stacked heavy ingots of bronze, iron, and lead in the storeroom. Smaller ones, of silver and gold, he stored in the chest within his living quarters. Melaina cornered him there.

"The brooch you gave me for use against arrogance is troubling," she said. She heard his two giant workmen singing wordless hymns, melodies strangely warbled as if by ancient Orpheus.

The smith laughed melodiously while tightening the strap securing his leather apron. "As it should be."

"Is not the love of freedom itself a great arrogance?"

"So some would say."

"Then is not all Hellas at risk?"

"Only the desire to be free of the gods' will is forbidden. To be free of another mortal's suppression, I think not. Thinking yourself better than your fellow mortals is an arrogance that corrects itself."

"I've noticed it infecting the great general Themistocles."

"Ah, it's easiest to detect in others, but obscure within."

"What about women?"

"I'm but a crippled smith, the legs of my arrogance broken in the womb. I'm not a philosopher and ill-suited for all these questions. I'm afraid you've outgrown me."

Melaina took a deep breath, looked down at her hands and so saw his withered legs. Never had she felt so close to him. They both had their defects. Few others would ever understand. "The gods marked me early also," she said, "but it didn't stifle my arrogance." She thought about what she was going to tell him, her mother's caution. But she'd never believed in Kleito's cure anyway. "I'm epileptic."

Palaemon stopped fidgeting with his metals. "How could this be, child? Are you sure?"

"Mother says I've had seizures since father died. They've always been during sleep, but recently they've waylaid me no matter the circumstance."

"The purest metal comes from the hottest fire."

Melaina thought this comment curious. "I experience a great euphoria with it, but can tell it's wearing on me. No one else at Eleusis knows this but my mother."

"Your secret is safe. I…" Something seemed to gripped him. He came toward her, staggered, seemed to stumble, or was it just his awkwardness? She was within his arms, and at first she thought he'd grabbed her while falling, then realized he was hugging her. He'd never touched her before. What a great comfort she felt in those sooty arms, prickly wool like rose thorns on his massive chest. She wondered if this was a father's love.

After they finished talking, Melaina stayed awhile, and he joined his two slaves at the bellows. Gigantic men they were, groaning, hovering over the crippled blacksmith and around a molten mass. She heard the din of anvils, and loved it, the great blast of the bellows. The men hefted heavy hammers far above their heads and smote rhythmic blows on glowing iron. The furnace fire in Palaemon's eyes gleamed like jewels.

★

Many days later, Melaina was in the temple with several others, overseeing the cleaning of the columns, when she overheard a loud conversation from the courtyard. Thinking she recognized the voices, she walked to the entrance and saw young Sophocles arguing with her Uncle Aeschylus. Although it wasn't a heated argument, she saw belligerence chiseled into Sophocles' face, and it wasn't over the finer points of poetry, as one might expect from a student and teacher. It was about politics, Sophocles taking the side of the radical democrats and her uncle that of the aristocratic conservatives.

Ever since she'd seen the two men locked in embrace at the Isthmus, Melaina had been stalking Sophocles. Now she walked straight to her chamber to carry forth her scheme.

First, she had to correct all her imagined physical flaws. She supposed she was too tall, and put on a thin slipper, planning to cock her head to one side while in conversation to decrease her altitude. I have no hips, she criticized, and warned herself to wear garments beneath her skirt. Her blond eyebrows were too light, and painted them with lamp-black, then, thinking they were too dark, plastered them over with white lead. She thought her teeth were pretty and wished to remember to laugh, but realized she wasn't much disposed toward mirth.

She searched through her wardrobe and selected a finely woven chiton buttoned along the top of the arm to form sleeves, leaving a little flesh showing, each button radiating rippling pleats. It had green stars within red circles, and a green edge at the neck with a wandering red motif. She adorned her left arm with a green spiral bracelet, wore a green necklace and earrings of red rosettes.

She gathered the front of her skirt in a vertical column to pull it in and up at the ankles. She didn't want to look like a country wench, though she wouldn't mind the sensuousness of a courtesan. As she fretted in the mirror, she felt dressed as one of those tuneful decoy-birds of the coin, Aphrodite's trained strumpets.

She fretted with her hair and finally contented herself with four tightly curled locks falling over each breast, and she adorned her forehead with a congregation of curls. Sixteen wavy locks fell at the back of her neck. She remembered a line from Sappho, something about blondes with torch-yellow hair needing fresh garlands and a fashionable headband, so she donned a green and bronze diadem with a red lotus and palmette.

She selected a fine Egyptian perfume, stolen from her mother's gold-inlaid box, with which she anointed her feet and legs. Her cheeks and nipples she touched with palm oil, arms with bergamot-mint, knee and neck with tufted thyme. She put a little marjoram between her breasts, where the heart is. For breath, she chewed two wine-flavored myrtle berries.

While perfuming, she kept repeating, "O Artemis, please forgive me," and "Aphrodite, stay your ground."

Wishing for something to do with her hands, she grabbed a basket, stuffed it with green cheese, slice of tripe, dried figs, and stole a honey-cake on the way out.

Down the alley, she twice caught sight of Kallias, and guilt caused her to wonder if he tracked her. Sophocles, she found outside the walls, a waxed writing tablet and stylus hanging from his belt. She motioned him to follow and headed for the sacred myrtle grove, realm of Aphrodite, where initiates wandered during the Mysteries.

As she'd earlier spun the thread, woven the intricate fabric at the loom, so now she twisted her plot among the bushes. Melaina laid Sophocles back beneath the tender stalks of myrtle onto beds of basil. Radiant and magnificent, Melaina's white skin shone, yet a blush moderated its color. Her long tresses tossed about in the humming breeze. The two youngsters nibbled the repast as Melaina noticed her own appetite of the flesh awaken. But Sophocles was still disturbed, his long face casting a shadow she'd have to dispel. She questioned him concerning it.

"A lingering effect of battle," he said, then told of being at sea but out of the action until going ashore on the island of Psyttaleia. "There we ringed the Persians round with warriors, and from our high vantage point, hurled stones, shot arrows, and battered them with clubs until all were dead. I sent a begging man to his grave." His talk brought more sadness. "I was caught up in Ares' murdering madness, but after committing the crime, my conscience wouldn't have it. The man's pleading face still haunts me. I can't believe I committed murder."

Such a frail man, she thought, so deliciously vulnerable.

"But that isn't the worst of it. After committing the murder, a Persian escaped our trap and came for me. I ran like a coward. And then later, I found out that two of my uncles died in the sea battle." The telling brought tears to his eyes. "Better to have never been born," he said.

Melaina held him, cradled his head in her lap and stroked away the pain. She wished to divert him from this worrisome discourse and placed her hands where she shouldn't. "Tell me again where you live, Sophocles," Melaina quizzed, making conversation while they traded gifts, each allowing the other entrance to private folds. His breath was short; his hands trembled.

"Kolonus," he replied with a quivering voice, "Earth's fairest home, where the nightingale trills her clear note even as she does now in this myrtle grove. It's the abode of great Demeter, her daughter, and Poseidon, Demeter's consort and divine lord of horses. Earth's great doorsill of brass is there, an entrance to the Underworld."

"You're a devotee of the two goddesses?"

"I follow Dionysus, god of indestructible life."

Since men wore no undergarments, this was her baptisia, her first view of that tiny unfettered member she'd seen dance at the Isthmus, only now turned rigid, obedient military marvel.

"Have you been initiated in the Mysteries?" she asked, fighting back her own desire.

"No," he said. "Not yet,"

Melaina's chiton slipped from her shoulder, leaving the left breast bared to the evening's eyes. Its color, so white, shone in shadowy darkness. She clasped the strong neck of her companion, brought him to her and kissed him, showing a glimpse of thigh from beneath its hold.

Melaina saw desire within his smile, and felt her own yearning blossom as she knew it mustn't. She found herself defenseless, caught within the weavings of her own romantic cloth. She wanted him. Forget life-long virginity, she thought. She found the swelled member, stroked it.

But from among the myrtle came a crack as from someone creeping, and sharp-edged fear pierced her. Kallias was her immediate thought. Or is it the divine huntress, Artemis, come to prevent my destruction?

Sophocles also stirred. Spooked, he lofted from the ground to standing.

Again, the rustle of bushes.

Each turned away from the other, took one look back.

Off they sped, each in a different direction. Out of the woods and through the alley went Melaina. She saw darkness encroaching, Erebos gathering the blackness of Hades, inking out stars. She panted through the gate, caught two dogs copulating in the alley, caught another glimpse of Kallias disappearing into the night and Palaemon peering from his smithy.

She slammed the door to her sanctum, but had never seen her chamber so dark. She stumbled about refusing to light an oil lamp, stripped and fell amongst the blankets, quilts and rugs. The coarse, pubic feel of animal fur, the sour smell.

Quick guilt plunged in upon her. What have I done? she wondered. She felt drained. She wished dark sleep to cover the memory.

Slowly night's black slumber crept at last, and she dreamt of that which hadn't been. Sophocles, firm, full, erect. Yes! His light touch, gusts of breath. Her dream was so deep and vivid, that she felt a presence was with her. Now, all was possible within her sanctuary. She woke realizing that someone really was with her. A man, full-bearded, powerful, yet ethereal, dream-like. Was it Sophocles? A buzz within her head seemed to singe her thoughts. No, she thought, no, no!

But he was no longer timid, his weight crushing down on her, separating, driving, matching her yearning. Instantly, she thought she knew him, his smell. His massive chest raised, lifted her pelvis to enter her more deeply. She sensed his full size as a sharp shaft of pain split the darkness in a blinding flash, heat threatening to consume her. She seemed in some strange twilight realm between life and death, heard a roar of great ecstasy, felt touched by fire.

CHAPTER 17: THE SEIZURE

That night, Myrrhine passed her daughter's chamber while walking the courtyard and heard a noise from within just as the Hierophant happened by. The two peered through the door, harsh hinges grating, oil lamp barely breaking the darkness. She saw a frightful thrashing under quilts accompanied by wild beastly sounds. Myrrhine thought, Some dumb animal has crawled in bed with Melaina and is killing her. But when she threw back the covers, Melaina was alone and in the clutches of a mighty seizure.

"How long has this been going on?" the Hierophant asked.

"Since she was a child."

CHAPTER 18: THE PHYSICIAN

The next morning, Melaina woke dull, irritable, and afraid. Her tongue was swollen and sore. When she opened her eyes, she saw her mother hovering over her, deep wrinkles chiseled into her forehead. How suffocating her mother's presence had become.

"Yes, mother, the epilepsy returned. Leave me alone." Melaina was surprised at the venom of her own words.

She drifted in and out of sleep. She felt somehow violated, ravaged. She had troubling flashes of the previous evening. Her visitor had seemed both ethereal and corporeal. Her experience during the Mysteries ceremony, when she'd dreamed of entering the Underworld, and the euphoric visions before each of her seizures, had blurred the fine line between illusion and reality. But the smell of *him* was still on her, replacing all the perfumes. Had it been Sophocles? Had he followed her home and presumed her risky, temptress role an invitation to enter her dark chamber? Or was it a dream?

She was sore between the thighs and wondered if she'd forfeited her maidenhood. She'd never really understood virginity. She'd known girls who'd taken lovers but were still married later as virgins.

That afternoon, as the sun's rays entered from the window high on the wall, she finally rose from bed, donned an old chiton, one to which her mother was especially partial, and went to her chamber. Melaina was surprised to see her mother there on her knees before the bed with her face buried in the covers.

"Don't mind me," her mother offered, rising to reveal tear-filled eyes, "I've been missing your father lately. You've matured considerably since you left for Brauron. Something in your manner reminds me of him."

"My irritability?" Melaina said, slumping to her knees beside her.

"Hardly."

"The seizures do it to me." Melaina hugged her, realizing how grouchy she'd been upon waking. "I've been thinking of my commitment to Artemis lately, and now I realize that what you told me before is true. I don't really understand virginity."

"If you won't marry, why worry?" Her mother looked smug.

"Curiosity."

Her mother smiled, took a deep breath, and shook her head. "Virginity is a purity of the heart defined by a maiden's relationship with the divine. That's why the Pythia at Delphi must be virgin. She's a conveyance for Apollo's prophecies, leaving his word untouched as it flows through her, a perfect rendering."

"But the Pythia is... Some have had children."

"Virginity can be restored. Hera restores hers every spring in Kanathos, the sacred fountain at Nafplion."

"How does a maiden lose her virginity?"

"When married, she dedicates her life to Hera, thus changing her relationship with the divine. When she's joined with her husband, the gods close her off spiritually for bearing children. A woman's body is like a leaky jar. When she becomes pregnant, the jar is sealed and set in its ideal condition. This stops the flow for it to nurture the child."

"The end of virginity is not first intercourse?"

"Definitely not. As I said before, it is similar to initiation into the Mysteries. In the uninitiated state, the soul sways from one life path to another, wandering in a great spiritual wilderness. The desires are insatiable, whether for money, power, sex, or food. After initiation, the soul closes, as an oyster in its shell, and is able to differentiate between what is seemly and what is not. It retains that which nurtures, expels the rest. The desires moderate. Life's tribulations become tolerable, enlightening."

"But what of deflowering? Isn't that loss of virginity?"

"Oh that!" Her mother slapped her leg, stood up. "Men invented that to satisfy their need to be first, to mark the woman as their conquest and bolster their weak opinion of themselves."

"What if a maiden lays with a man before marriage?"

"If an indiscretion occurs but is not made public, the question of virginity never arises. What's the harm?"

"But what of the relationship with the divine."

"If her status with the gods has changed, it will be revealed."

"And if it becomes public?"

"Banishment from the family. Sold as a slave."

Melaina tried hard not to let her mother see how this last pronouncement hurt. She heard a voice outside her mother's chamber that sent a chill through her. Kleito burst into the room and came for Melaina, her great bulk shaking the walls. Little Euripides, clasping her dress, was swept in her wake.

Melaina backed off, turned and flung herself against the wall. "No, Kleito!" she shouted. "No more hellebore!"

Her mother stepped between them and calmed Melaina, explaining that as soon as she realized the epilepsy had returned, she'd sent for Kleito. Melaina relaxed when assured hellebore was not what Kleito had in mind.

Melaina had just caught her breath and stooped to greet Euripides, who tugged at her chiton, when the Hierophant entered with a man and a young woman. The man carried a staff about which was coiled a live yellow snake.

"I've brought Podaleirius, a physician, to examine you," said her grandfather. "He's from the island of Kos, a man of great learning."

Melaina wasn't quite sure what "examine" meant and, if the snake was involved, not particularly anxious to find out. She'd never really been sick. Her constitution had always been sturdy, and good physicians were scarce in Eleusis. Yet trusting her grandfather, she averted her eyes. As the man approached, a pleasant whiff of spikenard preceded him.

The Hierophant addressed her mother. "A medical center has been established on Kos. The knowledge gathered there could one day change the lives of all Hellenes."

"I heard mention of hellebore upon entering," Podaleirius said, already intensely observing his patient. "Has someone administered to the maiden?"

Melaina noted the physician to be tastefully modest in dress, alert, and she liked him instantly.

"I did," said Kleito, "after a previous seizure."

The physician's face flooded with pain, eyes momentarily closed. He was tall, broad shouldered, bearded, a man of great dignity. He questioned Kleito about the hellebore while circling Melaina, his eyes scanning every detail of her anatomy. "Method of preparation, please."

Kleito bristled but gave him the rudiments of the harvest and extraction of the active ingredient, the steaming broth she'd administered.

"That's all?"

"Yes… Well…" She looked ready to lie but glanced sheepishly toward Myrrhine. "Also a little Herakleia," she admitted, a little girl's frightened look flashing her face.

"Administered?"

"In the broth."

"Simultaneously?" The physician's expression of disapproval returned. "Unfortunate. You could have killed her."

Kleito's face turned bright red. "Never would I do anything to harm the child!"

"For epilepsy, Herakleia should be used separately in a posset of mead, a fermented drink of water and honey, malt and yeast."

"I know how to prepare a posset," said Kleito, spitting out the words. "Her condition dictated a unique praxis."

"She survived. We certainly won't repeat it."

Kleito stepped toward the physician who flinched slightly then regained his posture. "I came to recommend they take her to Epidaurus," she said. "I've recently heard of cures for the sacred sickness there."

Melaina eyed the snake coiled about the staff. Slowly its head moved, slithered, scales flashing pale golds. A serpent, she thought, a dragon. She noticed that her grandfather was also distracted, as if suffering himself.

"Epilepsy is no more sacred than any other so-called divine disease," the physician said. "All diseases have a cosmic cause. Epilepsy not more so. Its origin lies in heredity." Melaina thought his speech was elegant, and that Podaleirius had a generally pleasant presence.

"Her father's death caused it," countered Myrrhine. "Neither her father nor I, nor any of our family, has ever had it. She had no sign of it before his death at Marathon."

"Still, she had the inclination. One of you gave her that. The brain overflows with phlegm, which rushes into the blood vessels. It's released by cold, wind, or sun."

As he examined Melaina, she noticed how his eyes at times looked upward into the distance, projecting great inner emotion, as might one who absorbs the suffering of his patient.

"Won't she outgrow it?" asked Myrrhine.

"Is it getting better or worse?"

"She had no seizures for years but started again recently, following her trauma at Brauron."

"I'd say not. Marking is the only chance of recovery."

"Marking?"

"Gnarling of a hand, drawing of the mouth. Some such paralysis or a distortion of the eye."

"Oh, by all that's divine, no!" said Myrrhine.

"Perhaps when she's married. Intercourse and pregnancy help."

"But she's given herself to Artemis and sworn to remain virgin."

"Does she become hysterical easily?"

"Never."

"Her womb is not overly dry then, no straying about the abdominal cavity seeking moisture from the liver, heart, or bladder. The animal within it desires bearing children, becomes discontent, angry, and wanders about the body. Does she suffer mental derangement, ramble or utter obscenities?"

"Outrageous!"

He handed the staff with the coiled snake to his assistant and approached Melaina directly. "Have you started the menses?"

"While in Brauron. I've had the flow six times."

"Ah, you've danced the Bear for Artemis. Is your flow regular?"

"Only a day's difference."

"How do you measure it? I'd have thought the south wind might make it unpredictable."

"The phase of the moon."

"Okay then," he said looking satisfied with his physical examination. "Yesterday was the winter solstice, which activated the seizure, I'm sure. The fit occurred in the evening, I assume, a general violence of the body including shaking of the limbs."

Melaina wondered why he didn't ask her what had happened rather than make these pronouncements, even though they were correct.

He took her chin in his palm, pushed his finger between her lips and pried apart her teeth. Melaina gagged. His finger was cold, musty, with a hint of mint.

He spoke to the young woman. "Hygieiadora."

His assistant had stayed silent and back from the group but now returned the staff with coiled snake, and she began testing Melaina's body. She took both hands in hers, squeezed, same with the forearms, biceps. She brought Melaina's arms out from her sides to test freedom of movement, felt the constriction of waist, the thighs, flair of hips, felt the newly ripened breasts.

Melaina giggled and pulled away.

Hygieiadora returned to Podaleirius and spoke quietly in his ear.

"She's in excellent health," he informed his attentive audience, "deformed less than most women from the male norm."

Melaina was greatly offended by this remark, but bit back her words.

"She's hotter than most females, less moist. Good signs but they don't help the epilepsy." He fell into thought, closed his eyes as if communicating with some apparition, then, with a start, resumed talking. "My guess would be that you've been suffering from melancholy, and are unusually devoted to the gods. Ill-tempered, perhaps even ill-mannered."

Her mother again defended Melaina. "Scandalous! Certainly not."

"This is the so-called diviner's disease. You may at times prophesy while experiencing wondrous visions and frequently lapse into the madness of the Muses. Last night, by all indications, you had gnawing of the tongue accompanied by copious froth. Afterward, you felt weak, pale, and lethargic, the head heavy."

"Yes," said Melaina. "Correct on all counts."

"A treatment frequently used in the east, in such a case, is to drill a hole in the head, drain excess fluids directly from the skull."

Myrrhine screamed and rushed to Melaina. "Enough!" she said, "No more of this outrage!"

"Not a treatment I'd recommend for this maiden," said the physician coldly.

"Mother, please." Melaina pushed her back. "I'll not suffer the skull drilling, but the diagnosis is accurate. He understands the euphoria. Not all burdens are a curse," she added, remembering her father's words. She turned to the physician. "Just before each seizure I exist in the presence of the gods."

"As do we all. You are only more intensely aware of them."

"Not true," said Melaina. "I see them."

The physician stared piercingly. "Visions?"

"Yes, same landscape but with the gods added, as if a veil has been lifted to reveal their presence." She remembered her experience last night but didn't dare say that one had lain with her.

"Astonishing! Your condition shouldn't be meddled with by a mortal. Physical sensations at onset?"

"It comes like a breeze, an aura. I also see visions in fire."

"Of the future, no doubt." He turned to Kleito, who'd slinked back out of sight. "I agree she should go to Epidaurus. Put her directly in the hands of Asklepios. I'm afraid to touch her myself, although I'm a follower of the god, one of the Asklepiadai." Melaina realized this intimated that he was a direct descendent of Asklepios.

Kleito stepped forward, her sour face cracked by a smile. "Precisely my thought."

Podaleirius again turned to Melaina. "I can provide you with some preventive measures. Stay indoors, avoid a south wind. Here at Eleusis, you're protected by the mountains to the north but subject to southern winds off the sea. The hill provides little protection." He trailed off for a moment, seemed to lose his train of thought. "Because of this," he continued, "inhabitants of Eleusis have heads clogged with phlegm, which aggravates the maiden's problem. It also disrupts other internal organs. Their constitution is flabby. They tolerate neither food nor drink. Women are susceptible to vaginal discharge and miscarriages. Men are sterile, suffer from dysentery and fevers; boys experience dropsy of the testicles."

Melaina noticed her mother flinch, catch her breath, when the physician mentioned miscarriages, and she wondered why he'd added the bit about male anatomy.

He again turned to Kleito. "Your simultaneous treatment of the maiden with hellebore and Herakleia was brutal but courageous. If she was to be cured at all by them that would have certainly done it."

Kleito smiled, beamed at this redemption.

Podaleirius turned to Melaina. "Until you go to Epidaurus, avoid sleeping on the ground. That's particularly bad for adolescents. Nor should you sleep on your back. Avoid whirling wheels. They can cause paroxysmos. I could bleed you, but that is better accomplished in the spring. Maintain a light diet. Eat the meat of young he-goats, lambs, pigs, and dogs. Avoid foods that produce constipation or flatulence. Absolutely no mushrooms. No wine. Instead dilute honey in a little vinegar." He searched his bag for a moment and produced a vial from which he poured a powder into a terracotta cup. "Sniff this to provoke sneezing before bed."

The physician closed his bag and prepared to leave. He spoke quietly to Hygieiadora before addressing the Hierophant whom he'd ignored throughout his examination. "Let us not forget, the gods are the real physicians. We but exercise their wisdom. Don't delay the trip to Epidaurus." He looked at Myrrhine. "Her life could depend on it."

With that, the physician and his assistant left the room, the Hierophant leading them, leaning heavily on his staff, and arguing the fee.

"Now, about my illness," the Hierophant said.

Little Euripides ran to Melaina, and she lifted him into her arms with a great sense of relief. Someone finally understood her condition. Once Euripides had hugged her neck, he struggled down and tore out of the room after the physician. "Snake!" he cried.

CHAPTER 19: PROPHECY ON THE ROAD

Melaina's flow was absent for the next two months, but she hid the fact from her mother by smearing her rags with goat blood. Simply an effect of the south wind, she told herself but broke out in a nervous sweat nonetheless. Sophocles seldom came to Eleusis anymore, and this both puzzled and troubled Melaina. When next she saw him, he'd had his shoulder-length hair cut, long blond locks now clipped in the short style of most men. She noticed the beginning of a beard. Melaina realized that Sophocles' father had given him a festival and initiated him into the deme of Kolonus. He had come of age. Her attempted encounters with Sophocles had ended before they began, were brief and confused. Melaina was guilt-ridden, angry, longed to see him more than ever.

Despite the physician's urging, wet winter weather did delay her trip to Epidaurus. Boreas' evil frost-breath unleashed its fury from the north, bringing rain and settling drought dust. Not to be outdone, his brother Zephyrus' stormy blast howled in from the west. Intermittent sunshine brought tender barley shoots to the fields and hillsides. Wildflowers lent fragrance to the air, iris and blooming honeysuckle.

Melaina brought her little troop indoors to the women's courtyard, as her Uncle Aeschylus had suggested and the weather demanded, and it swelled to ten. She'd turned down several as too young. They'll be sending them to me in swaddling clothes, she thought. Word that she had something special to teach was spreading. She'd composed her own songs on the lyre, as had Sappho on the sandy shores of Lesbos four generations before.

Melaina concentrated on local myths and customs of Eleusis. She taught the girls to write. They read poorly, and Melaina was appalled that most couldn't make their letters. She realized then how thorough her own mother's training had been. She started drawing the letters with a stylus herself before giving them the slate, and then told them to trace hers.

One night Melaina woke from a nightmare of being raped, and rather than dwell upon it, rose to write down some of her own lyrics, having noticed the epilepsy stealing bits of memory. She'd seen spider webs before her eyes and wondered if she was having small seizures while alone. She lit an oil lamp and retrieved waxed tablets, papyrus and lampblack from within an old chest where she stored miscellaneous items.

Thus, she was already up when the Hierophant came to wake her for the trip to Epidaurus. The weather had changed overnight and the prognosticators gave several days of moderate winds. She was to make ready for a trip of seven days. She ran quickly to her mother's chamber to ask what to bring, and found her sitting in the middle of her floor weeping and talking to her dead husband as if he were present. "Please forgive this longing for remarriage," Melaina heard her say.

"Mother, why are you crying? You're to marry?"

"Don't I wish," her mother said. "These are tears of relief. I've wanted to go to Epidaurus for years."

While they gathered the few things allowed, Melaina listened to her mother gush details of desires she'd kept secret. "After you were born, I had no more children," her mother said. "I've willed not to marry again out of love for your father, although no one would have me anyway because I'm barren. Epidaurus is a great center for curing this problem. Since you've refused to marry, I've been considering it again myself. Asklepios may be the answer." Then Myrrhine broke down completely, sobbing like a little girl. "I've felt so distraught because Demeter and Kore could send up blessings from beneath the earth, but they chose to leave me barren and unmarried."

Melaina took her mother into her own arms and let her heaving sobs take their course. It seemed to Melaina that her mother had become her child. She'd never realized how tormented her mother had been since her father's death. But Melaina also recognized a change in herself. While still short of fifteen, she felt that she was gaining an uncommon maturity. Melaina wondered if this was really true or arrogance's sly seduction.

★

It was still pitch dark when Melaina and her mother arrived at the dock with her grandfather. With them, they brought two slaves, a married man and woman, who used switches to goad along a small herd of sacrificial animals: goats, sheep and pigs. The man also dragged a wagon of caged cocks, all with legs tied to keep them from fighting. In the dim torchlight, Melaina could barely make out the ship's crew, hard at work hauling at the forestays to raise the mast from its crutch and set it in the tabernacle. This was a merchant sailing ship with rounded swooping lines, none of the linear sleekness of a trireme.

The crew pushed the ship away from dock with punting poles, and immediately Melaina missed the aulete's beat, the swish of oars. But she soon learned to appreciate the pop of white linen sails, the sing of twisted-papyrus halyards, the groan of the yard against the mast. Even in rough water, however, the galley was lethargic.

They sailed on in silence, dawn's pink glow gradually revealing the coastline of Salamis as they skirted west through the strait of Megara and broke out into the open water of the Saronic Gulf. The Hierophant's deep voice came alive to tell Melaina of Saron, the ancient king of Troezen, who hunted a hind into these waters, but became overcome by waves and met his fate in the deep. The gulf was named for the king. The Hierophant also told of Theseus being born and raised in Troezen, just south of Epidaurus. They'd not sail quite that far.

Conversation quickly lapsed as they passed the southern edge of Salamis and were more exposed to the winds that carved

great swells in the sea. The boat pitched violently, bow breaking
through wave after wave sending showers of seawater across the
deck. The animals' worried cries, bleats, oinks and baas were a
constant strain on Melaina's ears. She'd never been south farther
than Salamis nor seen the open sea. Now the expanse of the
Mediterranean stretched all the way to Egypt.

The Hierophant seemed to shed his years, along with the
pain he'd lately felt. He came alive, talking as Melaina had never
heard him, telling of how in his youth, he'd commanded a ship
himself. Before becoming Hierophant, he'd been a merchant and
sailed to far off lands: Crete, Cyprus, even Phoenicia. The Hierophant hummed ancient sea tunes long since forgotten by most,
and talked of Melaina's grandmother, how she'd died in childbirth. He was an old man when he'd married her, she just a girl.
Melaina, he said, reminded him so much of her. If she'd lived,
she'd be Aeschylus' age.

Melaina noticed her mother's saddened expression at the
mention of her mother. Melaina knew that she had never known
her and realized for the first time what a tragedy that must have
been.

Afternoon came and went, and just before sundown, they
made dock at a small headland jutting out into the gulf. The Hierophant pointed to a building on a rocky spur. "Hera's temple,"
he said. "We'll spend the night there."

"This isn't Asklepios' healing center?" Melaina asked.

"Half a day's journey inland. We'll be there midday tomorrow."

Melaina felt uneasy staying in Hera's temple. She'd avoided
the goddess of marriage since making the decision to follow Artemis. Tonight she'd have no escape.

The grain ship dropped them off at the dock and continued
on south. Melaina wondered why no one met their group, but the
Hierophant didn't seem to expect anyone and labored on up the
hill, each step torturing his bent frame. He leaned upon his staff
and poked at their small herd of animals to help the two slaves.

The goats, particularly excited about being off the boat, kicked up their heels.

The sanctuary was enclosed within a stone entry with large double doors. All was silent except for the wind whistling between stones and bowing trees. The Hierophant pounded on the doors with his staff, waited, then pounded again. Finally, they creaked open, and an old toothless man poked his head out. When he saw the Hierophant's purple cloak and gold-spiked staff, he fled. Soon an old, cow-eyed woman appeared, her matronly face partly shrouded by a veil, her dark hair falling freely to the middle of her back. She spoke little but showed great respect for the Hierophant. She ushered the group inside and slaves provided an abundant repast, then she showed them to their bedchambers. She left to show their slaves where to pen the animals and let the chickens loose to stretch their legs.

But Melaina had another errand to perform and stole quietly outside to Hera's temple. Inside, she found a beautiful ivory and gold statue of Hera seated on a throne. The goddess wore a gold diadem, as had the old crone who'd opened the gate, and a double-sleeved chiton exposing white arms. In one hand she held a pomegranate, a seed symbol linking her to the Mysteries of Eleusis, and in the other a sceptre. A cuckoo sat on top of the sceptre, a manifestation of the form Zeus took to court Hera. Hera's face had broad, handsome features, a high forehead, and a dark, somber mood revealed in the eyes. The corners of her mouth drooped. Zeus' wife was stormy, sullen, but glorious.

Melaina stood uneasily before the statue. "Dearest mother Hera, first of goddesses on Olympus, blessed queen of all and consort of almighty Zeus, who guards the keys of marriage. I've come to beg your forgiveness. I've neglected you since deciding to remain virgin and follow Artemis. I mean no disrespect…"

Melaina stopped. She heard a ringing in her ears and felt the presence of a great hostility. She tried to characterize it further but was lost. She continued. "Threefold goddess of the moon, though I myself will not marry, I'll forever be in your service, preparing young maidens for the celebration of your sacred marriage rites…"

Melaina sensed a growing threat, a hovering hatred. She backed away from the statue and returned to her chamber. But she didn't sleep well, tossed and turned, and lay awake most of the night. She heard her mother's deep breathing next to her and the Hierophant's groans in the adjoining room. Throughout her life she'd always sought solace in the presence of the divine, but here at Hera's temple, she was an outcast.

★

Next morning, Melaina and her mother were up before dawn and loaded into a four-wheel, mule-drawn carriage. They brought a second four-wheed cart for slaves, sheep, goats, and pigs and pulled the two-wheeled chicken wagon behind. The cold wind blew through Melaina's clothes and chilled her to the bone. The weather prognosticators had miscalculated the duration of fair weather. Four heavily armed horsemen—two in back, two in front—escorted their carriage. The men had to shout to be heard over the wind. Melaina's excitement had been dampened by a distemperate mood, and she wondered if she'd had another seizure during the night. Her tongue showed no sign of it.

The Hierophant told her that they needed the military escort as a precaution. Asklepios' sanctuary was not far from Argos. The Argives, perennial enemies of the Spartans, had remained neutral in the war against the Persians, had not participated in the battle of Salamis, and had lately entertained an envoy from Mardonius. The Hierophant's little entourage would probably not encounter open hostility, but roving bands of raiders were a possibility.

The two mules pulling the carriage were strong, quick-stepping beasts of great presence and confidence. The passenger carriage had a substantial roof supported by ornamental columns, and the sides were closed with draw curtains of gaily-decorated silk separating passengers from driver. Their compartment, although private, provided little comfort from the jostling of wood wheels wrapped with iron straps. Even being tossed about was tolerable, but the tortured shriek of the axles spooked the mules. Just when Melaina thought she would scream herself, one of the horsemen halted the carriage and applied dregs of animal fat to the spindles.

Farther from the coast, the forest became thicker, and a heavy rain hit, large drops pounding the roof. The wet road dropped into a deep wooded ravine and soon became a wash. Waterfalls brought down boulders that had to be pushed aside before proceeding. Melaina took every opportunity to peek outside the compartment and watched as the road again became steeper. The mules struggled up the mountainside, wheezing as the breast bands rode up against their throats. A lightning bolt struck a tree just in front of the carriage, followed immediately by a loud clap of thunder that echoed off the hillsides. The mules lost their confidence. The left one turned stubborn and crowded his companion into the rocky cliff. At a second thunderbolt, he stopped completely, sat on his rump with front legs stiff as posts, pointed his nose toward the zenith and brayed loudly.

A horsemen dismounted and covered the reluctant mule's face with a cloth, tied it behind the ears. The mule recovered, rose to all fours, and swished its bony tail. The man then grabbed the bridles of both mules and walked between them. But the day grew darker under the heavy clouds while bitter winds swirled among the trees. The carriage struggled up the flanks of the mountain as a dense fog engulfed them. Eerie noises emerged from the gloom, and Melaina heard distant shouts. The road descended from the mountainside onto a plain, and the fog thickened. The horseman removed the cloth from the mule's face, remounted his horse, and quickened the pace. Melaina lay back on the cushions and dozed.

Shouts woke Melaina from a painful sleep, her heart pounding. Myrrhine pushed the curtain aside to reveal a band of horsemen descending upon them, as if conjured from the fog. Men in strange dress surrounded the carriage, two with sparkling-white turbans. The four soldiers who were supposed to protect the Hierophant and priestesses stood at the ready, swords drawn, but were hopelessly out-manned.

Melaina felt a pounding in her ears, and her vision blurred. She couldn't seem to wake up. Harsh words were exchanged and their own four soldiers sheathed their swords. The entourage then pulled off the road and made for a grove of pine trees, leaving behind the slaves and their carts of sacrificial animals.

Melaina struggled to remain alert, realizing that they were now prisoners.

All were forced from the carriage at sword point, and Melaina's vision cleared although she lost her hearing. More soldiers were present than she'd thought, some mere phantoms. Someone spoke her name, and a helmeted warrior-woman appeared at her elbow. A stab of pain in her temple told her she was having a seizure. She heard her mother shout, "She's falling!" The Hierophant grabbed her.

★

Melaina regained consciousness lying on the wet ground, her head and shoulders in her mother's lap. She tried to speak but still lacked full control of her tongue. She gradually remembered where she was, and became aware of a whispering crowd gathered about her. Her mother argued with someone Melaina didn't recognize, then realized it was one of their captors. A painful mixture of fear and anger coursed through her. She struggled to her feet but immediately fell to her knees.

As soon as she could walk, the turbaned men led the Hierophant, Myrrhine, and Melaina before a large tent within the grove, where they were told to stand under the shelter of the trees. Their captors were dressed in tiaras, embroidered tunics with sleeves, coats of glistening mail, and baggy breeches. They carried javelins, light wicker shields, and quivers with cane arrows. Swords swung at their sides. Melaina heard her grandfather whisper, "Xerxes' so-called Immortals."

They were ushered into the tent where a man, who appeared Greek yet spoke with an accent, addressed them. Melaina's cloudy mind gradually cleared although she desperately wished to sleep. Her mother remained close.

"My name is Mys," said the seated man before them. "I'm a Carian of Euromus, sent by Mardonius to consult the oracles about the coming land war. We've visited the cave of Trophonius at Lebadia, the oracle of Ismenian Apollo at Thebes, and the oracle at Abae in Phokis. We'd go to Delphi if they'd accept us, but Apollo routed our forces there when we first entered Hellas a year ago."

Another man stepped forward, one with a clubfoot. "I'm Hegesistratus, Mardonius' diviner. We've heard rumors of one amongst you, a maiden, who has the falling sickness. She carries great weight with the gods, stopping earthquakes and enlisting the help of long-dead heroes in battle. Some say she's descended to the Underworld and can tell the future."

Hegesistratus was famous throughout Greece. His was a strange story, having been captured years before by Spartans who had planned to put him to death. They chained him to a post, but during the night, Hegesistratus carefully gauged the size of his foot, and amputated part of it to slip free. Melaina could see that his left foot was now made of gnarled wood.

Hegesistratus continued. "A word from that maid may be worth all the oracles of Hellas. Is she the one we seek?" He pointed at Melaina.

The Hierophant stepped forward. "Suppose she is. You expect her to commit treason?"

"No," replied Mys. "Revealing the future won't change it."

"But one who knows could shift the circumstance to advantage. Otherwise you'd not care to know it."

Hegesistratus responded. "I already know the future. We wish to influence the Hellene generals. Words from the mouth of one of their own seers might help them understand the futility of resisting."

Mys spoke again. "Hellas can never escape the long arm of Xerxes' superhuman forces. Mardonius now commands Xerxes' army, and Hellas will soon lie in ruins in its wake."

"And what god gave this privileged knowledge?" asked the

Hierophant.

"The gods of Intelligence and Reason."

Melaina's thoughts had cleared considerably, but she was left with the usual irritability. She spoke from behind the Hierophant's back. "More likely the Persian gods of Arrogance and Conceit."

One of the Immortals pushed her forward so Mys could get a better look at this insolent maiden. Another restrained the Hierophant by pushing him against the tent wall with his shield, dagger at the Hierophant's throat.

Melaina hadn't intended to endanger her grandfather, and she wondered if his life might now hinge on her words. Watching as Mys assessed her, she felt her anger boil again and had to bite her tongue.

Mys's words, initially charged with anger, softened as he spoke. "I've come to prevent a great catastrophe. Mardonius has no desire to destroy Hellas. The generals will find that he's offering excellent terms, but if they don't accept, Hellas will be reduced to a dark world of shades. If you do have insight into the future, reveal it, so your generals may see their folly."

Before meeting Keladeine at the Isthmus, Melaina might have believed him, but the breath of freedom she experienced on that outing taught her what was at stake. Her grandfather started to speak, but one of the Immortals shut him up with a blow to the midsection.

Melaina found courage in her anger. "The gods grant our earthly freedom, and it's not subject to any mortal's dominion. As long as a single Hellene remains alive, no peace with Persia is possible. Such is the love of freedom Zeus planted in our Hellenic hearts."

"Listen to reason!" Mys said, hot anger again thickening his voice. "I'm Hellene also. I come in good faith. I ask only that you consult the gods yourself. Let them reveal the future, so you may enlighten the generals."

Hegesistratus whispered into Mys's ear. Mys spoke again to Melaina. "If you perform your augury by sacrifice, we'll supply the victim."

Melaina stood her ground before both of these great men. She saw the sincerity in Mys's face, his desire for peace. She distrusted clubfooted Hegesistratus and spoke directly to him. "I have no need to filet a beast, spread its entrails upon the earth and examine the shapes and hues. When you came upon us just now, I had a seizure. At times before I fall, I'm allowed to view the world the way the gods see it." Then Melaina turned back to Mys. "This time, I saw great Ares, god of war himself, sitting on your right shoulder, goading you on."

"See! I told you as much," said Mys. "Surely with such a god on our side you must see the inevitability of Xerxes' victory."

Melaina didn't budge. "Such is the god of war's way that he prefers bloodshed to peace. Ares' affection for war makes him poor counsel. And he's no good in a skirmish. Remember Homer? Ares fought with the Trojans and even appeared on the battlefield to participate in the slaughter, but was wounded himself by Athena. He went whimpering to Zeus. Even the mortal Herakles injured him in one-to-one combat. Follow Ares to your ruin. Just now, however, I also saw Athena, Zeus' daughter and guardian of Athens, standing with us and offering her wise council."

Deep lines of concern crossed Mys's face, but he was silent. Hegesistratus stepped back from Melaina.

She continued. "Before I fell just now, the gods revealed the way before us as simultaneous paths to not one, as you envision, but to two great battles. Zeus himself doesn't know the outcome, also being subject to the Fates who have yet to weave the fabric of our future. But the gods revealed to me the death of one man, a Persian. He'll ride a great white horse on the battlefield and be toppled from it, his head crushed by a mighty stone."

Mys was visibly shaken. His face paled.

"You wanted my prophecy," she said. "Now you have it."

"So be it," he said. "You may return then, in all your stubbornness, to your own travels. May the gods be merciful with us all."

Shortly, the Hierophant's little troop was back on the road. A powerful shivering then seized Melaina. She shook so much that she feared another seizure. Myrrhine wrapped her in a blanket and held her close. Gradually, Melaina's shaking subsided. "It's just fear," she said. "I'll be all right."

The slaves along with sacrificial animals, were waiting for them back at the road, although the Persians had confiscated a pig and a goat. "Not a bad price for our lives," said the Hierophant.

Melaina's mother was quiet, eyes still glued on her daughter for any sign of further sickness. The Hierophant, seeing his grand-daughter's rapid recovery, was all smiles. "The gods must have let me live to this ripe old age just to witness the antics of this young one."

Hearing more voices, Melaina pulled aside the curtain. They'd arrived at the rain-drenched sanctuary of Asklepios.

CHAPTER 20: THE SEER OF EPIDAURUS

The Hierophant's troop approached from the north, halting at a rise to take in the view. Below them, Asklepios' sanctuary sat in a sacred glen crowded with pines and stone buildings and enclosed by rolling hills. The dark thunderheads parted, allowing sunlight to rain down on the holy site, while shadows shrouded all else.

"Helios honors Asklepios with his rays," said the Hierophant. "The sanctuary has grown considerably since I was here last." Then he pointed out three buildings in the center of the glen. The first was a tall rectangular structure with marble columns. "That's the temple of Asklepios," he said. "The Tholos next to it is new, definitely not here when last I came, but it's quite something. Perhaps we'll learn its significance. The long building is the Abaton, where patients incubate."

"Incubate?" asked Melaina.

"You'll learn soon enough."

Melaina was disappointed when they didn't enter the sanctuary immediately. After the Hierophant dismissed their escort to return to the temple of Hera, each of the three separated a goat from the animal cart, bidding the slave couple wait outside the sanctuary. Then, each leading their goat, they went on foot up a hill to the southeast, Mt. Kynortion, ascending along with several other travelers.

"We climb to this hilltop to first sacrifice to Apollo, Asklepios' father," said the Hierophant. "He was the original healing god, and his son heals in his name."

Melaina saw a father and three sons carrying a fourth brother with paralyzed legs, and then listened while her mother questioned an old woman, who said she came in place of a daughter too sick with dropsy to make the trip. Another woman complained of a worm in her belly. Melaina also saw a boy with an oozing growth on his neck, and a man, wounded in the lung by an arrow, who was spitting up pus, a bowl a day, he said.

Before sacrificing to the god, they cleansed themselves at a fountain house where priests collected holy water the god had sent up from the ground. Then the three, along with their goats, trudged on up the mountain. On the hilltop, the three approached a small, open-air sanctuary set on a stone terrace. The temple's considerable age was obvious from its two gnarled timber columns that supported the slanted, patchwork portico, which sheltered the slaughter stone and the two priests performing the sacrifices. The three crowded forward along with other rain-drenched supplicants.

As they stood before the butcher stone, the Hierophant explained the need for sacrificing to Apollo. "The two gods, Apollo, the bringer of plague, and Asklepios, the one who cures, are representations of the same universal force. Through Apollo's son, the power to kill becomes the skill to heal. Before we can experience the healing light of Asklepios, we must acknowledge Apollo's deadly darkness. Apollo has been worshiped here since far back in time. After murdering his mother, Agamemnon's son Orestes came here seeking refuge. The sanctuary of Asklepios didn't exist then, just this temple."

After the sacrifice, they started down the hill with the rest of the supplicants, but the Hierophant stepped off the footpath. "Spread your cloaks over the damp grass," he said, taking a seat under a large oak and stretching out as if ready for a nap.

"Why are you delaying us again, grandfather?" asked Melaina.

"Patience, little one," he said. "I want to rest my head on the soft grass, listen to the rustle of the old oak's leaves, and pretend I'm at Dodona decoding the words of Zeus. Dealing with near-death experiences may be refreshing to you, but it's tiring to an old man. I shook in my sandals after that Persian knocked the breath from me. I don't care much for my own life, but to see that of my only descendents snuffed out would be more than I could bear." He looked at Myrrhine. "Tell her of the life and death of Asklepios, so she won't be bored while I try to restore myself. Growing old is such a delight when you can spend it witnessing the bravery of your grandchildren."

"It wasn't bravery, grandfather. I'm always irritable after a seizure. My ill temper caused my brashness. I worry that I could have gotten us all killed."

Since she'd not been able to sleep following the seizure, Melaina still hadn't fully recovered. She worried about her performance before Mys, realizing how certain she'd sounded when she told him of her vision. Had she really seen Ares and Athena? Or simply made a convenient assumption to win her argument with Hegesistratus?

Her mother began telling the myth of Asklepios, but Melaina wished her grandfather had told it instead. She loved his deep, mystery-filled voice. Her mother's voice was smooth enough, though quiet, and Melaina feared she might fall asleep.

"Apollo, deity that he is, was unlucky in love," Myrrhine began, "and so he was with Koronis, Asklepios' mortal mother who took her name from her beauty. While she was pregnant with Apollo's child, she lay with a mortal, which enraged Apollo, and he killed her. Her body was put on the funeral pyre, but Apollo couldn't bear to see his son die with the wild flames of the fire god lapping about it, so he snatched the infant from his mother's burning corpse."

Melaina heard her grandfather snoring and realized that he hadn't slept much lately because of his unspoken illness. She lay back beside him, watching the mountains of fluffy clouds sail overhead while her mother continued.

"All mortals, who have a divine father, also have an earthly one. The mortal side of Asklepios' myth is that Koronis, who in this version was also named Aigla, the Luminous One, was the daughter of Phlegyas, the most courageous soldier alive. He didn't know that his daughter was pregnant when he brought her to Epidaurus, so when she gave birth to Asklepios, she abandoned the child, who was then suckled by a she-goat on Mt. Titthion. Aresthanas, a goatherd, saw the child, who was being protected by the dog guarding the goats, and went to get him, but was driven back by dazzling light as if from a divine epiphany."

Melaina's grandfather stopped snoring. "The hill we're on is Mt. Kynortion," he said, "and was named for the dog that watched over the child. Mt. Titthion," he pointed to another hill in the distance, "that one there, was named for the goat's teat from which he garnered nourishment."

Her mother continued her story. "Hermes took Asklepios to the Centaur, Cheiron, the wisest and most learned of all beings, who taught him the art of healing. Though a son of Apollo, Asklepios was mortal. He became famous for inventing medications, and was so effective at healing that he could resurrect the dead. Zeus thought he might make humankind immortal, so he killed Asklepios with a lightning bolt. Thus, Asklepios was born and died in flames. Apollo, saddened by the death of his son, made him immortal."

"What's wrong with resurrecting the dead?" Melaina asked.

Her grandfather answered. "Mortals are not meant to spend eternity here on earth. The body is a prison for the soul. Remember your training in the Orphic myths. To raise the dead in this world is no boon. We must pass to the next life."

"Is there a connection between resurrection and fire?"

Her mother answered, "Remember the funeral pyres on Salamis? Fire is the coinage for transport to the world of the immortals. To go to the Elysian Fields is a resurrection. That's why Asklepios is there. It's another statement of the Mysteries."

Some of the other supplicants drifted close by, and the Hierophant said, "We'd better stop speaking of sacred subjects in public. We could be overheard."

They roused themselves and rejoined the stream of visitors

descending the hill, but the Hierophant continued speaking of Asklepios. "The gods' temples are usually on mountaintops, as is this temple of Apollo, but Asklepios is a chthonian god and dwells below, so he may send up holy water and healing herbs. Thus, his sanctuary is in this sacred valley. In his worldly manifestation he lives both in the earth and atop it, traveling between worlds. The priests here will teach you about his method of communing with us: dreams."

The group reached a double stone wall, the two separated by a ditch that surrounded the entire cluster of sacred buildings. The Hierophant had the slaves take their sacrificial animals to a holding pen outside the sanctuary. There, inside a dormitory, the slaves were to remain and care for the animals until they were needed for sacrifice.

The Hierophant and two priestesses passed into the sanctuary through a gate and over a small bridge. They met a groaning old man as he left, writhing in pain and assisted by two young men. "Beware the cures," he said as he passed. "Immortals apportion two trials for every blessing." Melaina wanted to question him about this, but the others had continued on, so she followed, wondering if some hidden danger lurked within the sacred glen.

A priest met the stream of visitors as they entered the grounds. Several assistants stood at his side, and as he determined each person's reason for coming, bade one of the assistants walk that person to the appropriate facility.

They witnessed their first cure. A mute girl, who saw a snake just as she entered the sacred grounds, screamed and returned home healed, having yet to even meet the priest. But Melaina witnessed something she'd not imagined seeing at a healing center. The man in line before them was very ill and being carried on a couch by his five sons. In spite of his dire need, the priest would not allow them entry. "But he's dying!" cried the eldest son. "Precisely why he can't enter," replied the priest. "No one can die in the sanctuary." The argument continued until a small troop of soldiers appeared and forcefully removed the sick man and his family.

Melaina started after them and had to be pulled back by her mother. "They've given him a death sentence," Melaina argued.

After sizing up the three of them, the priest said to the Hierophant, "Ordinarily our patients are assigned a space in the dormitory, but for dignitaries, particularly those of your stature, we put them up in a residence." He turned to an assistant, an old man whose eyes were strangely sunken and kept shut. The priest spoke quietly in the man's ear, then turned back to them. "During your stay here remember one fact. Whosoever passes through the Propylon, under whatever auspices, leaves the profane world and enters the sanctified." He looked directly at the Hierophant. "Make sure all your actions are in keeping with that thought."

Melaina wondered if her grandfather had taken offense, when the priest grabbed her hand and placed it into that of the old, shut-eyed man. Melaina realized that she was to lead the man, who was in fact blind, his eyes sunken, wrinkled, and seeming to suck his entire face into the sockets.

"Point me along the path," the blind man said, "and we'll find your accommodations."

Was that possible? Melaina looked to her mother and grandfather.

"Yes, I'm blind," the man said, "but still quite useful as a guide. I'm called Udaeüs, named for the forefather of Teiresias, blind seer of Thebes." He walked with a cane of cornel wood that he banged against her to test her position.

"Careful of my shins," Melaina said, wincing. "We know of Thebes, traitor to Hellas and co-conspirator with the Persians."

Udaeüs ignored her cutting remark. "Tell me, have you any idea where we are?" he asked.

"A small temple is on our right. It's not very well kept," Melaina said.

"Ah, the temple of Themis. A little farther then. My family is from Kolophon in Ionia, a Hellene colony founded by Manto, Teiresias' daughter."

"Another Persian stronghold," said Melaina. "Are you a spy?"

Her mother grabbed her by the arm, her eyes casting daggers, but Melaina had taken an immediate disliking to the blind man.

Again Udaeüs ignored her. "Where are we now?" he asked. "What have we come to?"

"A long building stretching away from the path to the right, and beyond it, a temple."

"The long building is the Abaton. You'll get to know that well enough, I suppose. Guide me to the temple. It belongs to Asklepios." He pulled her by the hand. "Come. Guide me, guide me. We don't ordinarily allow patients into the temple even for prayer. To stay on temple grounds is a great honor."

Then Udaeüs asked Myrrhine and the Hierophant to remain just inside the temple entrance. "Into the hall," he told Melaina, forcing her forward. As they walked, he played with her hand, traced a sensual circle over her palm.

She hated him for it. "Don't molest me," she said.

Udaeüs chuckled. "The tender digits of a young woman are such a comfort to an old man."

She led him to the back where he spoke to an elderly priest, who was shorter than Melaina. The three then returned to the entryway to the Hierophant and Myrrhine, where Udaeüs took his leave, speaking directly to Melaina as if he could see, although she realized he meant his words for the three of them. "You'll be seeing more of me. I attend the fires at all the altars."

The tiny priest then addressed them, Hierophant first. "My name is Theognotus," he said, clasping his hands before him. "I seldom work with patients anymore, but having such an illustrious group from Eleusis is a rare pleasure. I'll hear your ailments and recommend treatment. We're terribly overcrowded, so you'll stay with me until your incubation, if that's required."

With that, he led them into the temple proper, where they stood before the gold and ivory statue of Asklepios. The god was seated upon a throne, a serpent in his right hand, his left resting on the head of a dog. The face of Asklepios projected calm, solemnity, and suffering. Melaina turned to her mother. "The physician from Kos," she said, "bears this likeness." She felt great affection for it.

Theognotus dropped to his knees before the altar and raised his arms. "Lord Asklepios, who dwells within dark Earth and heals the suffering of mortals, bring Health to these three holy suppliants, answer their pleas brought from far off Eleusis. Come to them in the days ahead, O savior! Grant your gift of vigorous existence, and they shall grace your sanctuary with an offering befitting your miracle."

Then Theognotus took them out behind the temple to a nearby stone building, his own home, where they entered a courtyard and talked amid dappled shadows of grapevine-covered trellises. "At this healing center," he said, "as with Eleusis, we serve the individual. Whosoever comes suffering the sores of nature, Asklepios delivers from diverse pain. Others, their limbs wounded by bright bronze or hurled stone, he tends with some kindly incantation or soothing julep, swathing limbs with simples. He restores some with the knife."

"Do you heal all who come?" asked Melaina.

"The rituals we priests prescribe only open the pathway for divine intervention. Asklepios provides treatment for each differently, refusing in some cases. So tell me your ailments. Perhaps Asklepios can relieve your suffering."

They then revealed their reasons for coming, first the two women in turn, but when it came to the Hierophant, he refused to speak before his daughter and granddaughter, pulling Theognotus to a far corner of the courtyard. They whispered quietly for a while, then returned, the Hierophant bracing himself with his staff.

Theognotus prescribed treatment. To Myrrhine, he said, "Many women come to us with barren wombs. Treatment requires a night of incubation in the Abaton, as does your daughter's epilepsy. But before you can incubate, you must fast for three days, nothing but clear barley broth, and bathe in the hot springs. Each morning our attendants will massage your flesh to relieve the physical toll your lives have placed there. Remember, Asklepios was first a mortal man. He died because of his sympathy for the human condition and was made a god so he might improve it. Sunrise is sacred here. The resurrecting light is anastasis of mortal life and reprises the luminous child. Our hope is that you experience the solemnity of Asklepios' sacred healing center and return home cured."

He rose and so did they. "Now, I'll get Udaeüs. He'll see you to your quarters."

Melaina stopped him. "Question, please. At the gate a sick man was turned away because he was dying. What good is a healing center unwilling to attend the most grievously ill?"

Her mother pinched her arm, but Theognotus was not fazed.

"Excellent question," he said. "I've been deficient in my orientation. Death is not permitted here, nor is birth. As a priestess you must be aware of the contamination of the passageway between this world and that of the immortals when life enters or exits. The purity of the facility must be preserved, even if it means refusing entry to those too hopeless for treatment. I regret that your first impression of the sanctuary was formed viewing this grim limitation."

His answer multiplied Melaina's questions, but another of her mother's pinches silenced her tongue. They turned to go then with Udaeüs in the lead, but the Hierophant seemed perplexed, perhaps a little exasperated.

"My condition?" the Hierophant asked, then swallowed deeply. "Can you fix it? Or am I doomed?"

"Oh, yes, we have a procedure," and for the first time Theognotus smiled, "but you won't get to dream your way through it. Afterward, however, dreams will blossom every night and won't stop though you will it with all your might."

★

Melaina had difficulty with the fast, finding the thin barley broth totally inadequate. She complained of nausea in the morning, but was refused anything to settle her stomach. She'd developed a ravenous appetite of late, possibly even put a little weight on her lanky frame. She started looking for a way around the fast, found the kitchen and snooped for leftovers until the servants caught her.

For a distraction, she dragged her mother out to the dormitories to visit other patients, many of whom had been injured during the battle of Salamis. The draining, festering wounds of some would not heal. That of one man emitted the putrid smell of gangrene, which helped rid Melaina of her appetite. She talked to a boy with no voice while he listened patiently. She visited with a man who had lost an eye, with only an empty socket remaining, and avoided another with a stone in his penis. She was patient while her mother consulted with several women who also had barren wombs. Melaina drew the line at a man who'd had a spear struck through both his eyes. He still carried the bronze tip within his face. She felt sorrow for his blindness, but witnessing his pain was more than she could bear.

The Hierophant went off to see Theognotus again but returned without satisfaction. "He told me I might undergo the procedure tomorrow. You have to stay after these priests, or they'll keep you here forever." His pain, as evidenced by a wincing restlessness while sitting and difficulty walking, had seemed to multiply daily. Melaina grew increasingly concerned about him, but neither he nor her mother would discuss it.

★

The following morning, Melaina decided that the light barley gruel, which at first she'd detested, gave off a delicious aroma and even asked, but was refused, seconds. Theognotus caught her with earth on her mouth and touching ashes from the sacrificial hearth to her tongue. He ejected her with a laugh. She particularly enjoyed the thermal spring that came from the depths of Earth, and bathed lavishly in the nude with her mother and other women. They were told that all the water at Epidaurus was sacred due to it being sent up from the ground by Asklepios himself. Afterward, large muscular women massaged and generously splashed the two priestesses with olive oil. Melaina felt rested but limp, even stumbled about, her legs so relaxed they refused to carry her weight.

To pass the time, the two women and Hierophant visited the inscriptions, left by grateful patients, just outside the Abaton. Melaina found them interesting. "Here's a curious one," she said standing before a large plastered plank with a detailed account of a cure scratched across its surface. She read aloud.

> Kleo was pregnant for five years. After the fifth
> year of pregnancy, she came as a supplicant to
> the god and slept in the Abaton. As soon as she
> had left it and was outside the sacred area, she
> gave birth to a son who, as soon as he was born,
> washed himself at the fountain and walked about
> with his mother. After this success...

Melaina was laughing so hard she broke off reading. "Why have you brought me here? This place is a sham!"

"Hush!" said her mother. "Shame on you! You're here but two days and ready to close the place. Until you can relieve suffering yourself, don't criticize the efforts of others."

"But mother...five years?"

Myrrhine pushed Melaina along. "Don't upset your grandfather with your insolence."

★

That night, Melaina couldn't sleep. She left her mother and crept through the dark into the temple to see Asklepios' solemn face. She'd fallen in love with the image. Such great sympathy, such suffering in the eyes. She stood before it, reaching to touch the bearded chin, when she heard a noise, perhaps a sigh. In a dark corner of the chamber lurked the outline of blind Udaeüs.

"The little priestess from Eleusis," he said.

"So you can see after all."

"Just good at reading the patter of footsteps. Rarely do I hear anyone so light on their feet."

"You eavesdrop here all night?"

"Tell me of the epilepsy," he said. "Do your seizures bring prophecy?"

His directness startled her. "So some believe. It's but my illness sending visions."

"Diviner's disease. I thought so. It's no boon to see the future. Fools, those who practice the soothsayer's art."

"I'd not choose it for myself. It comes unbidden."

"A gift, some would say. I say, a pity."

"Both, as is the gift of life."

"Ah, but seers are a useless lot."

"And I might question a guide who cannot lead. What good are you?"

He feigned great offense. "Sometimes I have luck with the weather."

"As can a peasant."

"Do you read entrails?"

"I've great interest in the future, having read grandfather's scrolls of Sibylline oracles. But I've no learning in animal innards," she said, "no real knowledge in any form of prophecy. One would have to go to Delphi."

"Follow me," he said, and felt his way along the wall to the door, banging with his cornel stick. "Take my hand," he said, and she led him out into the dark. "To the top of the hill," he ordered. When they were there, "Behold!" he said, "the heavens above and earth below. Point me northward."

Melaina turned him to face Arktos, the Great Bear.

"Both heaven and earth are quartered," he said, stretching out his arms to feel the wind. "Events occurring on the left are calamitous, on the right propitious."

They labored there on the hilltop for some time, Udaeüs explaining each quarter, dividing the quarters again and further dividing, marking segments for the meticulous observation of lightning. "Each of the gods has a direction." He also revealed which of the crook-taloned and ravening birds the gods marked as auspicious, which sinister omens of bird-flight.

"I thought you were to teach me entrails," she said. "It's a great mystery I've often wondered about."

"As you wish," Udaeüs said and had her lead him down the slope through the dark to a sacred holding pen. There he cornered a lamb, put it under his arm, and they stumbled back to the temple. He stood before Asklepios, said a solemn prayer and slit the lamb's throat over the slaughter stone. Melaina screamed spontaneously for the sacrifice. After blood darkened the altar, the blind man laid the lamb on the stone floor, slit the abdomen up to the breastbone, scarred it, laid aside the knife, and broke open the chest cavity. All this he did by feeling, his fingers doing the work for his eyes.

Udaeüs called her to him, had Melaina take hold the slippery vitals, cut loose the liver. "Hold it so the gall points down, large lobe away. Note the division across the middle?"

She said she did.

"That marks the division of north and south. Now turn it over, keeping the large lobe away. All that is visible there is but a reflection of the vault of heaven," he said. "The celestial divisions I taught you on the hilltop are reflected in the liver. All quarterings have the same import."

Then he taught her liver scrutiny as one with authority, as one who knows how to read shape, dappled smoothness, gall-hues that mark the god's pleasure, the speckled symmetry of the liver lobe.

"How can you know these things?" she asked. "Being blind."

"I was a seer before I lost my sight," he said. "I've suffered all the bitter woes of the seer trade."

"Teiresias was a seer *after* becoming blind."

"Ah, yes!" he said. "External blindness, internal sight. But Athena washed his ears in recompense, so he could understand the language of birds. We can't all be so blessed."

"I suppose Athena took your eyesight because you saw her naked, as she did Teiresias?"

"A Persian gouged them out with his thumb and exiled me from Kolophon for insolence against King Xerxes."

"I'm sorry. I've misjudged you. I've become overly sensitive and suspicious. The seizures make me quarrelsome."

"No matter. Again, view the liver."

Late into the night they bent over the animals as they brought sacrifice after sacrifice. Even as the glow of sunrise rose in the east, he sorted the diverse paths of prophecy, describing among dreams, which are fulfilled, which not. He taught her the reading of savor-wrapped thighbone and tapering chine, the face of flame.

Thus, Melaina came to know the art of prophecy, but as morning broke, so she worried, and knew she must return to her mother.

Udaeüs had a further word. He took her by the shoulder and spoke before her as if his dark empty sockets could see deep into her. "Remember this well, young lady. Prophecy is an unruly art. Zeus delivers utterances incomplete, reveals only half the truth.

Melaina interrupted him. "That explains it. On our way here, we were waylaid by a band of Persians. I had a seizure with a vision of great battles, but nothing of the outcome. Yet I saw Athena side with Hellas and Aries with Persia."

Udaeüs became quiet and seemed to look off into space with his eye sockets. "Do not encourage these beggars who desire to know the future. It'll bring nothing but trouble."

"Oh, but it's irresistible! And they crave knowledge of the visions as would a starving man for table dainties."

"Run from these people. Practice your gift only when cornered. What you know is burdensome. Teiresias thought it dreadful to have knowledge not benefiting the knower, for surely knowledge does not change the future once set by the Fates. It'll bring you fame but not love. If you should announce an adverse answer, you make yourself disliked by those who seek you. If from pity you deceive, you provoke Heaven. Apollo should be man's only prophet."

★

Melaina's head had barely touched the pillow when her mother woke her. She felt lightheaded and giddy. "If they don't feed me soon, I'll be hallucinating," she said.

Late that afternoon, following baths in the hot springs and olive-oil massages, Theognotus visited the trio again. "Today completes your fast," he told Melaina and her mother with his hands clasped before him as was his custom when addressing them. "We must prepare the two of you for tonight's incubation. The Hierophant," he looked at him out the corner of his eye, "will undergo his ordeal later."

The Hierophant's face turned sour at the prospect of another uneventful day. "My suffering means nothing to you," he said.

Theognotus, unperturbed, turned his attention to the women.

"Is dreaming necessary for a cure?" asked Melaina.

"But of course."

"I have troubled sleep of late, if I do at all," she said. "My dreams are frightening, horrid. Perhaps the cure will not work for me."

"A skeptic!" His impish face beamed approval. "Asklepios enjoys a challenge. Many with epilepsy, and the melancholy temperament accompanying it, have come to us. We've been quite successful, perhaps because sleep is a little like epilepsy. For many, the malady begins during sleep. Have you had seizures while slumbering?"

"I've wondered but never been sure."

"Yes, many," Myrrhine blurted out.

"Mother! Why didn't you tell me?"

"A good sign, for that will put the problem directly up against Asklepios. Provided, of course, we can get you to sleep at all," said Theognotus. He was silent for a moment, appearing more concerned than Melaina would have thought.

"Is my situation impossible?" she asked.

"Of course not," he said, "I've been talking to Udaeüs about his teachings to you last night. He's never taken such an interest in a patient. Claims you have an extraordinary gift."

"What's this you've done?" asked her mother. "Escaped while I was asleep?"

"Please, mother! You know of my insomnia. I need to fill the hours."

Theognotus continued, "Udaeüs is a great seer. He chooses not to practice his craft and instead only teach. Yet, rarely will he accept a student. I won't be able to help with your insomnia and troubled dreams, but he might. The nature of dreams is such that they're sometimes no more than memories of the day's activities, but these remnants can be directed to become the seed wherefrom Asklepios' presence blossoms. Dreaming is a descent into the dark world of Hermes, and we can give you an experience to sow dreams."

"How?" asked Melaina.

"The Tholos. We have secret rites there that I can't reveal," he looked up at her grandfather, "even to a Hierophant. You'll not participate in those rites, but Udaeüs will take you with him when he performs his weekly ritual inside the Tholos. He'll tell you about it."

The Hierophant said, "I've wondered its purpose. It wasn't here a few years ago."

Theognotus looked up at him. "The Tholos is Asklepios' tomb and represents his dual nature: the aboveground portion, his life here on earth; that below, his life as a god."

"Which aspect will concern Melaina, just the above or also the below?"

"Enough!" said Theognotus. "I can reveal no more. Your preliminary days here are over. Prepare for treatment."

CHAPTER 21: ENCOUNTER WITH ASKLEPIOS

With the sun casting long shadows, Melaina and Theognotus left for the large circular building, the one that'd captured the Hierophant's curiosity from the time they arrived. The Tholos was adjacent the Abaton where the women would later undergo incubation. But first, Melaina and Theognostus stopped before a small building to the east that smelled like a barn. Inside, Melaina saw blind Udaeüs within a fenced enclosure, crawling on all fours. When she peered over the waist-high wall, she realized he chased white mice. Unaccountably, Theognotus scooped Melaina into his arms and set her over the wall, which had no gate.

Mice were not Melaina's favorite animals, being considered a nuisance at Eleusis because they spoiled the grain.

"Help me," said Udaeüs. "We need three."

Melaina chased the mice into a corner, caught each by the tail, lowering it into a leather pouch that Udaeüs held open for her. He then pulled the drawstring, took her hand and wrapped her fingers about the pouch.

"Now," he said, "we're off to the Tholos."

She led him to the circular building, up a stone ramp, and through a ring of Doric columns to a stone wall with a door that opened into a paved portico. When the priest opened the door, the growl of the hinges echoed in the dimly lit chamber. Another circle was inside the circular wall, this time of Corinthian columns, set about a floor with alternating patches of black limestone and brilliant-white marble in a spiral pattern. Melaina felt irresistibly drawn to the center of the room.

She'd expected the room to be empty, but a girls' chorus, each girl carrying a terracotta oil lamp, ringed it just inside the columns. The tiny flames sparkled in the girls' eyes and reflected off the marble walls and ceiling. Except for the soft shuffle of feet, the chamber was quiet. Udaeüs slammed and bolted the door behind them and walked to the center of the chamber, footsteps echoing. The chorus then began a wordless hymn, something from the ancient poet Olen, a celestial sound, ephemeral, haunting.

Udaeüs fumbled for, found, and lifted a trapdoor, then again requested Melaina's hand. "Illness is descent toward death," he said. "All cures point toward resurrection. With your Mysteries of Demeter, resurrection is in the Isle of the Blessed; with Asklepios, it's back to life on earth. You'll not be cured here, since this is but preparation for the dream world. You'll descend to feed the god and render him predisposed toward you."

She stepped into the black hole. "We're headed into darkness. Won't we need a lamp?"

"For a blind man?" he laughed. "No light is allowed below ground. You're entering my world. In the Mysteries, as the initiate approaches the dread goddess of the Underworld, Asklepios receives him first. At Epidaurus we don't go as far as the Mistress of the Undergloom."

Melaina wondered at his in-depth knowledge of the Mysteries, but didn't ask because she worried what would happen next. She pictured the suffering, kindly face of the icon with which she'd fallen in love. "At Eleusis we ascend, not descend," she said. "You want me to go into Asklepios' grave to meet the god in person?"

"He's seldom seen. Even then, he takes an earthly form, a serpent."

"What!" she exclaimed, backing out of the hole. "In underground darkness, I'll encounter a snake?"

Udaeüs was astonished at her. "A friendly one. You don't know? Always at Epidaurus, the god appears as a serpent."

"You treat me as all-knowing, yet, I'm barely fifteen. The mice I hold in this pouch frighten me. Surely I'm not one to meet a dragon underground."

Udaeüs leaned back, pursed his lips. "True, your spirit projects a more mature woman to a blind man. We'll go now, while you still have some semblance of courage."

He took the lead, stepped down through the hole and pulled her behind him by the hand. The passage was much tighter than Melaina imagined. Wooden steps were set between concentric stone rings, descending below ground. As the dim lamplight faded to blackness, so the voiceless chorus faded from hearing.

Udaeüs said, "Watch your head," just as she bumped her brow, then he pulled her through an opening in the circular wall. Circumnavigating, they ran into a dead end but entered another stone ring through another doorway. Again, they circumnavigated and entered yet another doorway.

Melaina said, "I feel as though I'm Theseus descending into the Labyrinth."

"An apt comparison. But this is the last chamber," he said, as they again encountered a brick wall. He turned loose of her hand. "Take the stool."

She fumbled, found a seat against the wall at the narrow walkway's end. "The darkness is disturbing," she said. The chamber's walls dripped, and the smell of moist earth hung thick in the air.

"To be blind is to exist at the threshold of the gods."

"Theognotus said that are you the only one to feed Asklepios."

"No other has the lineage. Remember? I'm a descendant of Manto and her father, Teiresias. Teiresias' heritage was from the Sparti at Thebes, the sown-men. When Kadmos came to Thebes, he killed a sacred dragon and sowed its teeth in the ground as one would wheat. From those teeth sprang the Sparti, my ancestors." His breath came rapidly, as from excitement. "Also, I receive prophecy from Apollo, who took over the temple of Earth at Delphi by slaying the she-dragon, Python. I'm charged to fulfill a debt to both."

"I'm beginning to see again," she said. "A bright light, growing brilliant."

"Let's feed the god quickly and return. You're being seduced by the world of the divine."

"Just a moment. It's a child! I hear the chorus again, even down here."

"Please, young mistress. Now you're frightening me. The pouch, please. Witnessing the divine is deadly."

"A divine child bathed in flame, surrounded by a chorus of Nereïds." Melaina loosed the string of the leather pouch, placed it against the ground and pushed out the squirming bodies. "I can see the white mice," she said. "They scintillate."

"Quickly!" he said. "The god already has them. Ascend!"

★

"What did I see then," she asked, on the way to the fountain.

"It is said, 'I sing of the Divine Glorious Child and great light of mortals, Asklepios.' I can't say with certainty, but that would seem the gist of it."

"I'd thought it was Dionysus," she said, "as it was a child."

"That's only natural for one versed in the Mysteries. The rites of Asklepios and Demeter are closely linked. In the end, all deities merge to one. All within mortals' perception is ultimately Zeus. What surprises me is that you saw the divine and lived to tell about it. To gaze upon an immortal is fatal."

"I always see them just before a seizure. Remember?"

"Most would say you're blessed. I say what a shame."

It was almost as dark outside as in the Tholos. The stars had come out. The slaves had already delivered the piglets, with which Melaina and Myrrhine were to bathe and then sacrifice. The mother and daughter stood in torchlight at the sacred spring just north of the Abaton.

"Asklepios sends up this water so we might purify ourselves before incubation," said Theognotus. Again, the Hierophant was excluded but had to pay the healing fee demanded by the sanctuary. His disposition clouded further. "Intolerable!" he said.

They sacrificed both pigs and sheep in the temple before Asklepios, then burned the swine whole upon the blazing pyre, as sparks trailed skyward into the deep night. Each fleece was stripped from the sheep for the women to sleep on.

After the sacrifices, Theognotus took them to the Abaton. "We'll separate you and your mother, she to the east end of the building, you to the west. During incubation, you must withdraw from mankind and surrender to the force within, meet the god halfway for naked, immediate healing."

The open-air dormitory was one long room, the open front formed of columns, the floor separated into individual stalls for each patient. Melaina felt a breeze blowing through the building. Heretofore, they'd been separated from the other patients because of their lofty, priestess positions, but now they were included among the masses. Melaina's fresh fleece had been wiped clean of blood, but it was still slick and slippery on the straw bedding. She placed it, bloody skin down, in the straw within her walled stall and lay upon the soft fur.

Theognotus put Melaina down to sleep himself. "I've done all I can for you," he said. "Now it's up to you and the god."

"Don't be disappointed if I can't sleep. I thank you for helping."

The priest left her alone, and she lay back on the fleece listening to the muffled voices of those who couldn't keep their mouths shut despite the injunction against talking. She heard a baby cry. She watched the moon set and the Pleiads. It was the middle of the night and still she lay awake. I've come to the darkness of suffering to see the sun-like healer, she thought, and still can't get beyond myself.

★

Melaina woke the next morning, refreshed and encouraged. She smiled and rolled over on her back, excited to talk to Theognotus. All her fears had been unwarranted. But the priest didn't appear as early as promised, and she was dressed and waiting, rolled sheepskin at her feet, when he entered followed by the Hierophant and Myrrhine.

He'd already read Myrrhine's dreams, and her mother looked

devastated.

"Mother!" cried Melaina. "What happened?"

Myrrhine dropped to her knees before Melaina. "Continued disappointment," she said. "The god came to me but didn't cure my barrenness. He said I would have children, but not from my own womb, and that I would not raise them."

"I'm sorry. It's indeed a heartbreaking plight."

"Mine's an old complaint. The world has heard it too long. I'll get over it." She looked up at Melaina and managed a smile. "Now we must hear from you."

They gathered around, Theognotus' mood cloaked, expressionless.

Melaina's smile was irrepressible. "You were right!" she said. "I slept well, had only one dream."

"Aha!" he said.

"But," she added, holding his attention, "not what I expected."

"Just the dream," he encouraged, "I'll interpret. Make me earn your grandfather's drachmas." He clasped his hands before him.

"Well, the serpent came to me, as you said he might. He was going to touch me, black tongue flitting in and out, but someone stopped him. An intruder, not threatening to me or the serpent, but he interfered. He picked up the serpent just as it reached me."

The priest seemed at a loss. "The intruder, describe him."

"Oh, he was a fine young man, friendly, compassionate, hardly had a beard. His hair was in tresses, their masses falling upon the shoulders. He had a double row of locks on the forehead. The face was strong and broad, a stout chin. Strong, muscular, naked. He scooped the serpent into his arms lovingly. It coiled, writhed about his forearm."

"Anything further?"

Melaina thought, then remembered a last detail. "A stately stag stood behind him."

"Of course! Apollo, accompanied by his sister. The deer is an unmistakably sign of Artemis." He looked first at the Hierophant, then Myrrhine. "We've never had a patient visited by the father."

He turned back. "Anything you haven't told us?"

She looked away sheepishly. "He kissed me, then walked off."

The priest jumped to his feet. "Extraordinary! A clear sign of this young woman's importance to the gods." He paced about wringing his hands. "I only wonder why Artemis appeared as a deer instead of in human form. A rebuff, I'd guess."

"But why did Asklepios not cure me?"

"Perhaps he did. Asklepios is only a representation of his father's healing power. Apollo's kiss may have done it. The interest the gods have taken in you should make your husband very proud."

"Oh, she's not married," responded Myrrhine. "She wishes to remain virgin."

"A little late for that," replied Theognotus. "She's pregnant."

"What!"

"I knew it the instant I first saw her, and thought that was why you worried so about the epilepsy. It complicates pregnancy considerably."

"No! No, I can't be," said Melaina. "It's not possible!"

"How long since you've had the flow?"

She was slow to answer. "Three months…. But that's due to the south wind. The physician said it could make my flow irregular."

The priest smiled. "But not absent entirely. Your abdomen is already distended. The greenness below your eyes, characteristic facial splotches, freckles. You said yourself, that you recently experienced sickness after rising."

"I just can't be."

"How about you eating ashes, and earth?"

"I was starving! The fast!"

"During pregnancy women are close to Gaia, Earth goddess. They've been plowed and seeded same as a field of grain, and so crave earth. "Did you lay with a man?"

Melaina looked at her mother knowing what the answer must be. "No," she said, but her denial hung in the air like a dark cloud.

"At least, I don't believe I did."

"Oh, dear mother Demeter!" said Myrrhine.

"'Twas the last seizure I had at Eleusis. I thought it but a vision."

The Hierophant dropped to one knee before her. "Explain yourself, granddaughter. This is very important."

"The night before you brought the physician to examine me."

"At the winter solstice," added her grandfather.

Melaina's thoughts raced forward, calculating a strategy to omit the episode with Sophocles. "I was tired and went to bed early, didn't sleep well with the lightning and thunder, and woke with someone in the room, in bed with me." She realized how this sounded and raised her arms imploring them. "An apparition! I'm sure of it."

"A man?" asked the Hierophant.

"A vision. No not a vision, just the presence of a man. I was on the threshold of a seizure, and you know the confusion I suffer."

"No, I don't. Tell me," said Theognotus.

"I see the gods, see the world, as they do. It's crowded with people not really there."

Myrrhine spoke up. "I witnessed this seizure. So did the Hierophant. Remember?" she said turning to him.

"This is true," the Hierophant said to Theognotus. "Both of us walked into her room just as the seizure finished with her. She was in bed alone."

"At first, I thought some animal was under the covers with her, killing her," said Myrrhine. "But when I pulled them back, it was just Melaina, alone."

"That tells all," said Theognotius. "The gods evaporate before the eye. Great Zeus! She has a god for a husband! Her seizures are caused by divine possession."

"No!" cried Melaina. "It was a presence without substance. Nothing could come of it."

All the while she was wondering desperately if it had been

Sophocles. Before, she'd wracked her memory out of curiosity, now the answer was crucial. She'd also wondered about Kallias. Could he have raped her? She didn't dare say any of this aloud. Slandering Sophocles would be intolerable, and she realized how her mother esteemed Kallias, though Melaina herself harbored a secret dislike of him.

She cried, "I am a virgin! Artemis is my life." Her face contorted. "I just can't be pregnant!"

"This masculine presence, what was his appearance, demeanor?" demanded Theognotus.

She spoke through tears. "I know nothing of his appearance. Except that he was bearded as are all men. Thick chest. But these I only sensed. I saw nothing. All was shrouded in Erebos, the lightless dark of the depths."

Theognotus turned to her mother. "What the woman sees during intercourse determines in part the appearance of the child," he said. "Women who view monkeys while conceiving have children resembling such both in body and soul. The darkness wiped her sight clean allowing the god to write only his own vision on the child." He questioned her again. "His actions. Was there nothing telling?"

Melaina's cheeks turned bright crimson, and she had to straighten herself to get the answer out, cleared her throat. "When he had his great pleasure, his warm seed flowed into my womb like liquid gold. I felt consumed by fire."

Theognotus remained quiet a moment, measuring the weight of her words. His response came in a whisper. "Those were the words of Perseus' mother when Zeus lay with her." He turned to Myrrhine again. "Your daughter carries a divine child. In the dream last night, Apollo kissed her. She belongs to him, as does the child, the pure seed of the god."

"Check her virginity," said the Hierophant. "If she's physically intact, she can't be pregnant."

"Unless it was a god," replied Theognotus. "But virginity can't be verified physically. Rumors of a thin membrane blocking the entrance to the vagina are not to be believed. I've questioned many midwives. The ones who believe it exists don't agree on the location. Some say it's at the entrance, some midway to the womb and others believe it's even further inside. Most deny its existence. Only the gods can determine virginity, and they've already spoken. She's with child."

The Hierophant's disposition grew grave. Melaina remembered her discussion of virginity with her mother and realized that she could be banished. This has gone too far, she thought. I've got to tell them about Sophocles. But what if it wasn't him? I really don't believe it was, more likely Kallias. He was the one prowling about that night, and Sophocles gave no hint of anything between us in the days following. Oh, it had to be just a phantom produced by the seizure. I must remain silent.

"Just think," said Theognotus, speaking to himself, "a divine conception! The sanctuary will be famous throughout the Mediterranean. We won't be able to keep patients away."

"How could the god do this to me?" asked Melaina.

The Hierophant summed it up. "The gods give us our lot in life, a yoke about our necks."

"Divine Artemis! Do not be angry or destroy me, but forgive. I acted unwillingly!" cried Melaina.

★

Melaina went to the small temple of Artemis beside that of Asklepios, cried long hard tears before the likeness of the goddess, but all her words seemed empty. "Virginity, virginity, where are you? Never again will you come to me, never again."

She went to her mother. Myrrhine was all smiles. "You'd stayed with that virginity business long enough anyway," she said. "I'll have grandchildren after all. Oh, the thrill of it!"

Trying to get her mind off herself, Melaina walked the sanctuary grounds listening to the miracles of other patients. The man with no eye dreamed that the god poured a drug into the empty socket. When he woke, his eye had been renewed. Even his wife couldn't believe it. "I know you have another orb," she said, "but can you see out of it?" The man with the stone in his penis had a dream in which he copulated, and it was ejected.

They spent the rest of the morning sacrificing a cock to Asklepios and awaiting the priest's plans for the Hierophant's unnamed ailment. Melaina sensed a rift coming with her grandfather, and she couldn't stand to be away from him, seeking him out that she might somehow make it right. If he turned against her, he might sell her into prostitution.

"How could this happen?" she asked. "Have I no freewill at all?"

"Those of us called by the gods have no freedom," the Hierophant said. "First wall against it is the body. The soul really is trapped within the flesh."

"The gods have played a trick on me," she said, "giving me this love of liberty but now taking it with a single stroke." She imagined Zeus having a great belly laugh.

★

That afternoon the Hierophant received word that his time had come.

"Are you sure you want to do this?" asked Theognotus.

"By the gods!" answered the Hierophant. "What do I have to do to get treated?"

The Hierophant called the cure, "surgery," but Theognotus called it, "an initiation of sorts," even suggesting that all should undergo the "trial of the irons" once. Melaina took the priest literally and wondered if it was similar to initiation into the Mysteries.

The Hierophant left with the priest for a building outside the sacred glen, and when Myrrhine went down for a nap, Melaina became restless. She walked the grounds alone, and concern over her grandfather's condition caused her to circumnavigate the facility where the priest had taken him. Seeing others enter and exit, she peeked inside, then entered a long empty foyer. She smelled smoke and heard voices from a chamber at the foyer's far end. A female slave left smiling, greeted Melaina as she passed, and entered another room off the corridor. Melaina stepped into the doorway.

Melaina heard voices coming from a room at the end of the hall and peeked inside. It was exactly as she expected, not a surgical facility at all, as the Hierophant had suggested: no hot water or white bandages, no instruments for delicate incision, no prosthetics for limb replacement, no urns of herbs or jars of pungent oils, as she'd seen at Kleito's. She decided that the priest's description had been the more accurate. It wasn't a medical procedure at all, but some ancient rite appropriate to a Hierophant's station, perhaps one divinely inspired hundreds of years before when Kalchas of Megara had divined for Agamemnon's forces at Troy.

A group of men gathered about a circular hearth at the center of the room: Theognotus and her grandfather, who was nervous enough for his limbs to shake, and blind Udaeüs attending the fire as if he had eyes, plus seven burly assistants who seemed to have no function other than to witness the ceremony. Melaina watched Theognotus prepare a set of eight irons, as the blacksmith back at Eleusis might, placing them among coals until the tips glowed, then bending them flat as an obol at the ends. Reluctant to perform before, Theognotus now seemed to relish executing the ritual. Udaeüs boiled a fine broth of lentil and chickpeas on the fire, possibly a divine repast to be ingested during the rite.

Then she heard the name for this healing ceremony and felt bad about it, probably some secret word not to be uttered in the presence of women. "Haemorrhoids," said Theognotus, and Melaina felt sorry but could do nothing to redeem herself, the forbidden ceremonial key forever locked in her memory.

Theognotus laid the Hierophant on his back upon the table and gathered his tunic to the waist. The Hierophant muttered softly to himself, "two trials for every blessing" and "the soul trapped within the flesh," as Theognotus placed a pillow under the naked loins. The attendants then approached, one at the head, one at each arm and two at each leg. Smiling and chuckling they were, as if some pleasant reminder of their own initiation had passed before the mind's eye. They brought the Hierophant's knees to his chest as Theognotus, grabbing a glowing iron from the coals, said, "Shout so they'll pop from the anus like livid grapes."

The Hierophant sang while the attendants held him down, but not until she heard the hiss of hot iron against flesh did he reach full volume, his shriek ringing throughout the sanctuary and scaring Melaina's wits from her. "Louder!" shouted the priest while probing with the iron, the stench of seared tissue drifting about in smoke clouds. Copious sweat flowed from Melaina's brow, her own cry of dismay absorbed in the Hierophant's bellow. Her eyes remained glued on the priest as he brought iron after iron from the glowing coals to renew her grandfather's agony. Finally, the scorching complete, Udaeüs pounded smooth the lentil and chickpea soup and applied it as a plaster.

Melaina fled the scene.

CHAPTER 22: THE WAR MACHINE

The priest at Epidaurus had been correct. After returning to Eleusis, the Hierophant complained of a constant stream of nightmares in which he again underwent the trial of the irons. Melaina had garnered all Theognotus' ministering instructions before they left Epidaurus, and when she heard her grandfather's late-night groaning, took his care upon herself, having, it would seem, unusual sympathy for his condition.

Seven days after he had suffered the irons, she cut a soft sponge six-fingers wide on a side and very thin, covered it with fine linen cut the same size, smeared it with honey and, placing the sweet-covered sponge over her index finger, shoved it up his anus as far as it would go and inserted a woollen plug. To apply a holding pressure, she tied a band round his flanks, ran two strips down the back, drew up the ends between the legs and tied it all at the navel. The contraption stayed in place for twenty days, being removed periodically for an excruciating evacuation followed by washing with hot water and new honey application. Once a day she fed him barley-meal gruel.

His appreciation of the pain she thus inflicted came in a stream of strained warblings, realizing that her soft touch was infinitely kinder than would be a rough slave's. His questioning of the circumstances surrounding her pregnancy weakened as his gratitude strengthened. At times, he muttered words such as "divine conception" and "consumed by fire," having achieved, it would seem, a little sympathy for her condition as well. When he again appeared in public, it was with a new zest for life. He'd given up walking with his staff. Never had anyone seen him hop about so.

Melaina's condition also improved, her abdomen gradually growing, her epilepsy again pronounced cured. She had no seizures, and since few knew she'd ever had the affliction, speculation turned solely to her divine pregnancy, word of which spread like wind waves across Demeter's wheat fields. Occasionally she heard snickers, but accepted the humiliation with the fame, since some came to Eleusis braving the hazards of Persian raiders solely for a glimpse of the maiden blessed beyond common mortals.

Melaina's condition reignited her mother's interest. She wouldn't leave Melaina alone, wishing to do this and that for her and filling Melaina with women's lore of a proper diet of neutral character. "Avoid garlic, onions, and leeks," her mother said, "and be wary of excesses, fright, or sudden joy. The child could become misshapen and of ignoble soul."

Not long after arriving home, Melaina wrote a letter to Keladeine at the Isthmus. She had to tell her about the baby. Would Keladeine understand? She wiped tears from the papyrus, smudging the lampblack.

Melaina developed an unusually powerful taste for pomegranates and frequently made her midday meal entirely of apples and pomegranate seeds, while sitting under the pomegranate tree in the courtyard outback and mulling over one of her grandfather's scrolls. She'd remembered her mother's words while telling the story of Asklepios at Epidaurus, that "all mortals who have a divine father also have a mortal one," and was still trying to reconcile the fact that she didn't believe she'd been visited by a mortal. She confirmed what Perseus' mother had said concerning the god's seed, that it was like the warm flow of liquid gold. But she just simply could not believe she was carrying a divine child.

Melaina remembered her promise to her father and became overly sensitive to the Persian menace. She stood atop the hill for hours, staring north along the road to Eleutherai and the shadowy slopes of Kithaeron, expecting to see the dust cloud and ant trail of troops spelling their doom. She heard her own fear in the frantic cry of birds, croak of frogs, and in the wind's rustling of oak leaves, the gentle tingle of pine needles. She felt more helpless than ever, but watched for a time when she'd be able to avenge her father. She felt the covenant grow stronger.

She seized on her grandfather's convalescence as an opportunity to again request he build a temple for Artemis. She talked to him in the library. "Artemis must have it because of the burning of Brauron. I'll need it to conduct my own graduation ceremonies here at Eleusis. We can't allow our girls to miss the rites of the virgin goddess."

"Wisely spoken," her grandfather said, "but how about the Mysteries? Have you totally abandoned them?"

"Oh, grandfather, no! Demeter and Kore will always be dear to me. They are the soul of my existence. I was brought up on them. As a matter of fact, I've wanted to ask a question. Of late, I've experienced a need to be alone with my thoughts, yet have a powerful love for those around me, all Hellas for that matter. My teachings in the Mysteries spoke of a divine force holding Hellas together, and I've wondered about it and my remoteness. What binds us?"

"That force not only holds Hellas together but makes civilized life on earth possible. You've achieved what some never achieve, and those who do only in life's later years. Most mortals are witless, with their souls in the purse. You're destined for a different path. This fall, you must be initiated into the next level of the Mysteries. I can't divulge its significance now. This can only be revealed in the ceremony, but I will tell you that the soul has come from elsewhere and is always a fugitive, wandering by gods' decrees. You've uncovered your soul's detachment."

"Why can't you tell me more? No one will hear."

"Some things can't be spoken, not because they're forbidden, but because understanding isn't always achieved with words. Sometimes it comes through witnessing. So it is with the deepening mysteries of love, not those of the body, but the beauty of the soul and its longing for reunion with the gods. To experience this eternal oneness is to reach perfect virtue and be a friend of the divine."

Melaina let it go at that. She'd taken to watching the heavens of late, the stars wheeling above. Her stubborn insomnia, unprofitable sleep, and troubled dreams granted her time to relish the rising of the Pleiades, that fuzzy patch of stars embodying the seven daughters of Atlas. She liked to count the six visible and try to find the seventh, Merope, the nymph who married a mere mortal, and blushing from shame, paled from sight. With the rebirth of the Pleiades came the harvesting and threshing of Demeter's grain, slaves rustling about the well-rounded threshing floor. Shortly, following the first real heat, blustery winds brought the picking of peas, beans and lentils, the shearing of sheep.

Melaina, just at the time she first felt the baby move, heard that the king of Thessaly, Alexander, had come to Athens with an appeal to join Persia against Sparta and avoid a second invasion. She realized that this was a result of Mys's efforts. She hadn't discouraged him. Melaina listened quietly in the halls while her grandfather's deep voice wondered over these affairs and which direction the Athenian generals would take. Aeschylus came and went without speaking to her or her mother. Melaina wondered if he felt disappointment over her pregnancy. She heard Hipparete, her uncle's wife, complaining about Melaina's indiscretion and dismissing the rapidly expanding stories of a divine conception.

Kallias, however, spent more time than ever in Eleusis, and not all of it preparing for the Mysteries. He'd been snooping about the family home of late, and a problem had developed between him and the Hierophant. She'd never heard Kallias argue so heatedly, and wondered about her grandfather. Even with his newfound strength, he'd certainly be no match for the younger man if they came to blows. Kallias had won the pancratium in the Olympic Games a few years before. She'd caught her mother trying to overhear their arguments because they had something to do with Melaina's father.

Word finally came that Alexander had returned from Athens

empty handed; this was followed by even more worrisome news. Mardonius had finally put the Persian forces on the move south out of Thessaly. When he reached Boeotia, the Athenians again evacuated to Salamis and Troezen, as they had the previous year. Melaina remembered her own frantic chariot ride with Kallias and worried at the poor souls again fleeing Attica with their belongings. Soon, Persians were again camped out in Athens.

Eleusis, in the stout grip of a rejuvenated Hierophant, stood firmly against evacuation, but Aeschylus was there to help those who were willing. This time he smiled when he confronted the Hierophant. "Evacuate! You're putting people's lives in jeopardy."

Melaina was in the room when Aeschylus arrived. The Hierophant had called her because, as he put it, her closeness to the Mistress of the Underworld bothered him. He'd just told her that he'd noticed several parallels between her life and that of the goddess. She'd listened, then thinking he was through, started to leave when Aeschylus arrived, but her grandfather stopped her with a touch of the arm. She stayed.

"No need for evacuation," the Hierophant replied to Aeschylus. "We'll whip the Persians before they get here. I was right last time. Besides, the Spartans are coming to our aid. Their army is on the march as we speak."

Kallias, who'd come with Aeschylus and had stood quietly by, finally spoke. "Not so, I'm afraid. They're celebrating the Hyakinthia and thinking of nothing but the god. The Sacred Objects must be evacuated. We can't allow them to fall into the hands of Persia."

The Hierophant shook him off. "I'll protect them with my own life, and won't allow them out where their sanctity could be violated. Rumors say Mardonius is repairing the damage done to Athens by Xerxes. Perhaps I was wrong about him. He seemed the evil force behind Xerxes. But when Mys, Mardonius' agent, captured us outside Epidaurus, he could have killed us. He showed great respect for us as sacred officials."

Melaina's thoughts were ever on the tip of her tongue. She'd had strong visions of the world in flames lately. "Would it not be an arrogance, grandfather, to imagine Eleusis immune to worldly dangers?" As soon as the words escaped her mouth, she wished she could retract them. The hurt in his eyes was unbearable. And fear, yes, she saw some of that too. She'd overstepped his trust of her, questioning his judgment in front of these men. Oh, if she'd only left when they'd arrived!

She departed her grandfather's chamber, feeling worse about herself than ever. She remembered her indiscretion at the Isthmus, how she'd embarrassed her uncle. Her habit of introspection had turned on her. She had too much time for it, and now thought she had the answer for everything.

She went immediately to the blacksmith. She'd been avoiding him the last couple of months, not wanting to see his disappointment at her pregnancy. But she knew Palaemon's disposition wasn't toward judgment.

The sun had already set, but a dull yellow glow clung to the sides of stone buildings. Eleusis had again filled with refugees, narrow streets and alleyways clogged with lean-tos and makeshift tents. The desperation in their drawn faces left a sense of hopelessness in Melaina.

She expected to see the smith shutting down for the evening, find him putting away his tongs, cooling fires. Instead the smithy was a volcano, spewing sparks and rumbling, flames of the tortured furnace rising to singe the air white-hot. Hissing clouds of steam billowed from the quenching trough.

Some believed that the fireballs of metal that occasionally fell from the sky were tears of the gods, that all metal was divine. She believed it now herself with what she knew of fire, it being the passage between the worlds of mortals and immortals. The smelter seemed a great birthing chamber of the gods, molten metals pouring there from Heaven's streams.

She heard the grumble of the blacksmith ordering about his two slaves, Akmon and Damnameneus, as they stoked the fire, their shadowed shapes eclipsing the glowing metal. Huge hammers flashed like lightning, rang like thunder. They seemed primordial beings beating a din to drown the birth screams of some great metallic demon taking shape in the flames, the breaths of bellows giving life to a glowing fire-beast. These brothers Melaina feared greatly. Rumor said they'd murdered a third brother years ago, wrapped his head in a purple robe and buried it at the foot of Mt. Olympus.

But the virility of the shop, the masculine, barely-controlled violence, struck flame to Melaina's feminine heart. Around the shop stood the smith's customers: warriors, farmers, and derelicts in rags who'd come to feel the great rhythm of the place, witness the dance of fire. Melaina started to turn back, thinking Palaemon too busy, but he caught sight of her and quickly brought her into his chamber. He made a soft place for her by throwing pillows over the stone couch.

"I've heard the gods have gotten more personal with you," he said.

"They've given me another trial alright. While at Epidaurus, I heard that the gods give two trials for every blessing."

Palaemon chuckled. "If we knew more of the gods' motives, I think we'd find only blessings. But tell me, are you happy?"

Melaina hadn't thought much about happiness. She had to smile, and a tear formed. "I've learned to love being pregnant," she said. "I'd thought all along that virginity and following Artemis was the most glorious path. But I've found great affection for the child growing inside me. How could I ever want anything else?" She fell silent. "Still, I don't have a husband. My baby will have no father."

"A trifle. None are deserving, or the gods would have given you to a man. Zeus himself would be proud. Many the mortal woman hath raised Hera's jealousy."

She felt so womanly in his presence, none of the little girl she'd been. She lowered her head, saw the brooch he'd given her on her breast. "I keep the golden eagle with me always. Arrogance flames forth so frequently, I feel unworthy of it."

"All human beings have arrogance. You've recognized yours very young. 'Tis the power of the words marked on the back."

"Though I view them frequently, I can make none of the sounds."

"The etchings work on the mind even with no comprehension."

"My greatest arrogance is belief that I can see the future."

"And well you might! Remember, Prometheus, Forethought himself, gave mortals the writing craft. The words scrawled on the brooch may have the power to unleash his gift of prophecy."

"But in a woman?"

"All prophets were once women. Even Prometheus received the gift from his mother, Themis."

"Is god-given prophecy an arrogance?"

"Prometheus wraps all his gifts in arrogance. When Zeus discovered Prometheus had such great love for mortals that he stole fire for us, Zeus roared with laughter, realizing the trail of new misery it would bring. Beware Prometheus' gifts!"

A commotion out front cut off their conversation. The squeal of children's voices broke the spell. Palaemon grabbed her hand, squeezed it. She loved his rough-stone hands, his smell of ashes.

They walked from his chamber into the smithy. A new horde had descended on Eleusis and drifted like moths to the strongest source of light, the glow of furnace fire. They were children, wide-eyed little boys and girls of eight, nine years, rushing about screaming like wild animals. Their near-naked bodies were dark with dirt and sun. She heard the rattle of shackles.

"Slave children from the silver miles of Laurium," the smith said.

"I'd not known. We have children in chains?"

"Yes. I saw them while there buying ore for the smelter. Themistocles used the silver of Laurium to finance the building of the fleet that defeated the Persians at Salamis. These kids descend into the depths, crawl through knee-high tunnels to retrieve the ore. They work day and night by light of oil lamps."

"Our salvation at Salamis came from the labor of children?" Melaina couldn't bear gazing upon the desperate cherub faces. "The hands and knees of these dirty, branded children have delivered Hellas from Persia?"

"They call themselves 'worms' because they tunnel the earth."

"They're divine then," she said. "They exist in both worlds, as does Asklepios."

Melaina turned from Palaemon to seek out the owner of the children, but they disappeared as quickly as they'd come, quicksilver before the eyes. They were off west to Megara, the Isthmus. Perhaps Keladeine will help them, she thought. She returned home, but with a stricken conscience. What price will the gods demand for this outrage? she wondered. And a new fear entered her heart. How perilous Greece's safety seemed, perched on the knife-edge of child slavery.

★

In the pink glow before dawn, Melaina saw the rebirth of the glittering Dog Star, Sirius, bringing the new year and the dog days of summer. The Athenians again sent for help from Sparta, but learned that Spartan troops were already on the move to the Isthmus. In spite of this, the Hierophant seemed agitated. He'd heard that the Persians had begun to burn Greek temples, and he reluctantly planned an escape for all of them in case things went sour.

Melaina continued classes for her circle of girls, but her stomach was greatly upset and even rejected fluids. She went to her mother. "Help me," she said. "If I don't keep down something soon, my baby will wither."

"When I was pregnant with you," her mother said, "Kleito was ready with a remedy at the slightest mention of a symptom." Her mother applied astringent embrocations made of freshly ground, unripe olives to Melaina's abdomen and bound it with wool. When that seemed not to help, she applied oil of roses mixed with saffron and pomegranate peel.

"At least this smells better," said Melaina.

As an aid to digestion, she gave Melaina a decoction of purslane, picking the tiny yellow-flowered plant from the garden according to Kleito's instructions, and tried to follow it with sweet Cretan wine, but Melaina protested. "Remember the physician's admonition against wine," she said.

While she suffered one of these bouts of nausea, Melaina asked her mother about arrogance. "Why is it so difficult for me?"

Her mother didn't answer right away, treating Melaina's question more seriously than she would have in times past.

"The blacksmith says arrogance is a deadly defect," Melaina said, "and virtually impossible to guard against. I've found it true. My mouth forever gets me into trouble."

Her mother smiled. "You enjoy these philosophical discussions, the play of ideas men esteem so. The solution to arrogance is within the world of women. Courage that produces arrogance must be woven with moderation that comes with introspection. The two work counter to each other and are the warp and woof of an elaborate fabric that forms the personality. It's the same with marriage. Weaving of feminine warp and masculine woof produces the fabric on which the couple embroiders their lives."

"You make it all seem so simple."

But Myrrhine had fallen silent, heavy thought wrinkling her brow, and Melaina went out to find her circle of friends. They'd been cut to only a few by the evacuation. Today she'd teach them to make themselves more desirable for marriage. She prompted them to concentrate on their looks. "Avoid working wool. It makes the hands hard," she said, and taught them how to apply a little rouge to the cheeks and bleach their tresses in a caustic wash until it was auburn, the preferred hair color. She taught them to construct the ever-fashionable psyche-knots and to plait and crimp the hair. She also warned of the manner with which prostitutes and courtesans wore clothing and fabricated the figure by use of padding. She shuddered to remember what she'd done in her own attempt to snare young Sophocles. "Never present a false front. Never resort to manipulation. Never set in motion what you can't control," she told them.

Melaina loved her days home with her mother. Each brought new movement from the baby, and her mother would feel the swelled abdomen, placing her warm palm against the stretched skin. When something startled Melaina, the baby also jumped. And Melaina would smile and wrap her arms around her abdomen when the baby quaked with tiny hiccups. In the mornings, Eleusis rang with songs of slave women grinding barley meal, and Melaina had taken to eating ripe figs directly from the tree.

One bright summer afternoon, Melaina took her circle of friends into the grass-covered fields across the sacred way that led eastward to Athens and west toward Megara. In the shade of a tall plane tree, they removed their sandals, formed a circle in grass spiced with thyme and bog myrtle, and picked heavy-scented lilies.

Melaina stopped to look at little Agido. How she'd grown in the last year, yet was still such a child. She'd inherited a chiton many sizes too big and frizzled by the wash. She reminded Melaina of the little Bears at Brauron. Agido's unconscious charm was Melaina's delight. Anaktoria was a slender sapling, her chiton a brilliant play of pleats, hair tightly curled. Aristocratic, dignified, that was Anaktoria. Melaina taught them manners, saying, "When anger wells up inside your breast, guard against a biting tongue," and "Wealth without sympathy is a frightful friend."

The noble-peaked landscape to the north towered above the circle of girls, and ever-changing clouds billowed, sailed with the wind, their dark shadows charging across the meadow where the girls plucked flowers in the lush meadow. Melaina had planned to teach them prayer but had put it off until she was sure she had it right, but they forced her hand now. "Teach us to commune with the divine," talkative Dorothea demanded.

Melaina smiled and thought this was probably her most important lesson. "Let you utter no wrong or complaining word, remembering that good speech starts with holy silence. The simplest prayer requires but a small glass of wine spread over sacred fire. First of all, speak the name of the deity, requesting that she hear you. Heap epithets one upon another and speak fulsome descriptions of the goddess' powers. This should be done with raised arms and upturned palms. Call her from her dwelling place that she might hear your plea. You must then tell her why you've inconvenienced her and that only she can help. State the problem quickly, succinctly, and be done with it. Never trouble the divine with trivial thoughts. After learning prayer structure, you can offer up variations and unusual themes."

"Compose one," said normally quiet Euphemia.

"One to gladden our hearts," added Agido.

They were standing in the Rarian meadow beside the river Kephisos, the first field ever sown with wheat, glorious Helios beaming down on the deep-bosomed daughters of Eleusis. Melaina thought perhaps a prayer to the Muses would be appropriate. She composed on the spot, knowing it less than inspired, and formed them into a chorus. "A chorus is the loom of society," she told them. "With dancing and singing we weave the fabric of civilization." She spoke the words once that they might repeat them, and then they all held hands, danced and sang.

"Polymnia, daughter of Mnemosyne and lightning-throwing Zeus, sweet song-addicted, lovely-haired spirit of many hymns, who haunts the misty slopes of Helikon with your eight sisters. Come to us here in the dusty fields of Eleusis. Give us the divine art of prayer that we might better serve the ancient gods on Olympus."

They finished the prayer, twirled and stopped, their laughter ringing. Melaina spotted a yellow narcissus, beautiful, wonderfully radiant, awesome. She bent to pick it, reached out both hands for the sweet-smelling bloom glowing in the orange sunset, when she heard a noise. Startled, she thought a visitor had come among them. But the shout had panicked the girls, and Melaina looked behind her to see a band of men rounding the hilltop, dark men strangely dressed, one's shrill voice rising in a heart-ripping screech.

From the west they came, rounding the crests of hills, sloshing through the waters of the Kephisos, hordes of men on horseback and on foot, a charging mass of humanity with an inhuman thirst for blood. The people of Eleusis scattered before them, some west along the plane, others north to seek the safety of the mountains, and those closest to the city streaked for the safety of stone walls.

Melaina ran after her screaming girls, ran though her swelled abdomen wouldn't allow it. She heard horses' hooves thunder behind as she slowed and stopped, fearing she'd lose the child. Arrows whistled about her, and a spear lodged in the ground at her feet. She smelled smoke from the torches that would soon burn Eleusis, her home. A war machine, a great mechanical monster for crashing gates, rose above the hilltop. As the host of Persians descended upon her, intent on its prey, a great team of horses drew alongside, and all her sight turned dark. Erebos had blacked her mind. "Save me!" she screamed with all her might, screamed again, but knew not for whom she was screaming. She heard a shriek at her ear.

"Father!" she cried, "O dear Lord Kynegeiros, save my unborn child!"

Here ends Volume One, *The Mysteries: Daughter of Darkness*. Volume Two is titled *The Dadouchos*, since Kallias, the Dadouchos (Torchbearer) of the Mysteries of Eleusis, plays such a prominent role in that volume, which concerns the land battles at Plataea and Mykale. A preview that includes the totality of Chapter One is viewable at www.themysteriesofeleusis.com.

THE END

SOURCES

Sources

Cover Illustration

Every cover illustration should be relevant to the subject matter of the book. The statement that "the cover sells the book" is truer than most authors would like to admit. Richard Sheppard created the cover layout, design and illustration for *The Mysteries: Daughter of Darkness*. I provided source material for the cover illustration and designated where each vignette should appear. Richard painted a watercolor that he overlaid with text. We worked closely together. My source material was as follows: The female on the cover represents Melaina, as best we could imagine her. Her hair was taken from Figure XI of *The Thread of Ariadne, A Study of Ancient Greek Dress* by Elsa Gullberg and Paul Astrom, which depicts Kore, Demeter's daughter Persephone. Her attire was taken from a picture I took of an ancient Greek statue of Kore (Persephone) while at the National Archaeological Museum when I was in Athens in October 2009. The statue is from the early 5th Century BC and was found at Eleusis. Melaina, as the priestess of Kore, would have worn similar clothing. The dancing girls in the near background were sketched from an image taken from the ancient Greek vase shown in Figure 38 of *The Dance in Ancient Greece* by Lillian B. Lawler. These dancing girls could represent either Mylaina's girlfriends or the girls chorus during the celebration at the Isthmus of Corinth. In the far background, the depiction of the seabattle between two ships (a Greek trireme on the left and a Persian warship on the right) came from several figures on ancient Greek vases shown in *Greek Oared Ships* by J. S. Morrison and R. T. Williams. The two warships are symbolic of the Battle of Salamis. The coastline was inspired by a trip to Greece the author and illustrator took in October 2009.

Primary Sources

The following sources constitute the primary ancient texts from which I've taken both the idea and much of the plot for *The Mysteries*. Herodotus was my heaviest influence; however, the dialogues of Plato were indispensable, was were the plays of the three great tragic playwrights: Aeschylus, Sophocles, and Euripides. Aeschylus' play *The Persians*, was particularly useful for depicting the Battle of Salamis, after all, he was the only one who was there and wrote about.

Genesis of The Mysteries:

The original idea for *The Mysteries* came from reading Herodotus. Several paragraphs contained, what was for me, a rather startling observation: Three battles (Thermopyle, Plataea, Mykale) were fought in the vicinity of a temple of Demeter. At the time, I'd also become interested in the *Homeric Hymn To Demeter* and the archeological site at Eleusis, just northwest of Athens. The juxtaposition of all the information coalesced, and I decided to write a novel.

The passages from Herodotus are the following:

Herodotus VIII, 65 (the night before the battle of Salamis):

Moreover Dicaios the son of Theokydes, an Athenian, who was an exile and had become of great repute among the Medes at this time, declared that when the Attic land was being ravaged by the land-army of Xerxes, having been deserted by the Athenians, he happened then to be in company with Demaratos the Lacedemonian in the Thriasian plain; and he saw a cloud of dust going up from Eleusis, as if made by a company of about thirty thousand men, and they wondered at the cloud of dust, by what men it was caused. Then forthwith they heard a sound of voices, and Dicaios perceived that the sound was the mystic cry Iacchos; but Demaratos, having no knowledge of the sacred rites which are done at Eleusis, asked him what this was that uttered the sound, and he said: "Demaratos, it cannot be but that some great destruction is about to come to the army of the king: for as to this, it is very manifest, seeing that Attica is deserted, that this which utters the sound is of the gods, and that it is going from Eleusis to help the Athenians and their allies: if then it shall come down in the Peloponnese, there is danger for the king himself and for the army which is upon the mainland, but if it shall direct its course towards the ships which are at Salamis, the king will be in danger of losing his fleet. This feast the Athenians celebrate every year to the Mother and the Daughter; and he that desires it, both of them and of the other Hellenes, is initiated in the mysteries; and the sound of voices which thou hearest is the cry Iacchos which they utter at this feast." To this Demaratos said: "Keep silence and tell not this tale to any other man; for if these words of thine be reported to the king, thou wilt surely lose thy head, and neither I nor any other man upon earth will be able to save thee: but keep thou quiet, and about this expedition the gods will provide." He then thus advised, and after the cloud of dust and the sound of voices there came a mist which was borne aloft and carried towards Salamis to the camp of the Hellenes: and thus they learnt (said he) that the fleet of Xerxes was destined to be destroyed. Such was the report made by Dicaios the son of Theodykes, appealing to Demaratos and others also as witnesses.

Herodotus VIII, 84 (during the battle of Salamis):

It is reported, that a phantom in the form of a woman appeared to the Greeks, and, in a voice that was heard from end to end of the fleet, cheered them on to the fight; first, however, rebuking them, and saying --'Strange men, how long are ye going to back water?'

Herodotus IX, 65 (during the battle of Plataea):

It is a marvel to me how it came to pass, that although the battle was fought quite close to the grove of Demeter, yet not a single Persian appears to have died on the sacred soil, nor even to have set foot upon it, while round about the precinct, in the unconsecrated ground, great numbers perished. I imagine—if it is lawful, in matters which concern the gods, to imagine anything—that the goddess herself kept them out, because they had burnt her dwelling at Eleusis.

Herodotus IX, (just before the battle of Mykale):

The Greeks now, having finished their preparations, began to move towards the barbarians; when, lo! as they advanced, a rumour flew through the host from one end to the other- that the Greeks had fought and conquered the army of Mardonius in Boeotia. At the same time a herald's wand was observed lying upon the beach. Many things prove to me that the gods take part in the affairs of man. How else, when the battles of Mycale and Plataea were about to happen on the self same day, should such a rumour have reached the Greeks in that region, greatly cheering the whole army, and making them more eager than before to risk their lives.

A strange coincidence too it was, that both the battles should have been fought near a precinct of Eleusinian Ceres [Demeter]. The fight at Plataea took place, as I said before, quite close to one of Ceres' [Demeter's] temples; and now the battle at Mycale was to be fought hard by another. Rightly, too, did the rumour run, that the Greeks with Pausanias had gained their victory; for the fight at Plataea fell early in the day, whereas that at Mycale was towards evening. That the two battles were really fought on the same day of the same month became apparent when inquiries were made a short time afterwards. Before the rumour reached them, the Greeks were full of fear, not so much on their own account, as for their countrymen, and for Greece herself, lest she should be worsted in her struggle with Mardonius. But when the voice fell on them, their fear vanished, and they charged more vigorously and at a quicker pace. So the Greeks and the barbarians rushed with like eagerness to the fray; for the Hellespont and the Islands formed the prize for which they were about to fight.

--translated by George Rawlinson

In addition to Herodotus, many other works by both modern classicists and ancient Greek writers have influenced the writing of *The Mysteries*. I have only limited ability in ancient Greek, so I have used many translations of ancient texts, sometimes as many as three or four to find ways the ancients expressed themselves. I've listed a few of my sources by chapter in what follows.

Sources for Chapter 1

To provide the student with some indication of how I plotted *The Mysteries*, I have indicated below the basic milestones as discussed in my book *Novelsmithing*. In keeping with the plotting techniques I suggest there, I've locked the central conflict in this first chapter. The overall struggle in the background of the novel is the conflict between the Greek states and the Persians. This conflict is resolved toward the end of the novel.

1. I was at the Hellespont, or the Dardanelles as it is now called, in the fall of 1993. I spent the night in the coastal town of Canakkale, which is a few kilometers south of where the Persians crossed the strait at Abydos. I was there to visit the ruins of Troy, which are a few kilometers south of Chanakkale, and didn't pay much attention at the time. This was on November 24th, and I remember it being cold, rainy, and above all, windy. When I left Seljuk to go up to Canakkale, the woman in the pension where I was staying told me not to worry about the weather. "It's always bad at Troy," she said.

2. This chapter is primarily a dramatization of material from Herodotus' *The Histories*, Book VII, 33-57.

3. The last line of the chapter comes from Herodotus, VII, 59.

Sources for Chapter 2

1. I visited Eleusis, or Elefsina as it's now called, in the fall of 2009, no more than a couple of weeks later in the year than the time this chapter takes place. A few inches of rain had fallen only a month before, and green grass shoots were standing tall throughout the site. The ruins of the sacred city are marvelous to walk through. The sacred grotto is still there, chiseled into the hillside, although much of the entrance must have crumbled away during the two and one half millennia since the Persian invasion. The semi-sacred quarter, where the Hierophant and priestesses lived, is marked by a sign, as is the home of Kallias. The floors of the Telesterion and Anaktoron are also visible. I climbed the hill to look over the area as all the population of the sacred city must have at one time or another. For images and videos of the ruins of Eleusis, all of which I took while there, go to www.themys-teriesofeleusis.com.

2. For the layout of Eleusis, no reference is as important as *Eleusis and the Eleusinian Mysteries* by George E. Mylonas. Professor Mylonas was among the many who excavated the site. I sorted

through the wealth of information in that book and determined that the basic layout of the temple of Demeter is that illustrated in Figure 25 of Mylonas' book. It is before the statue of Demeter in that figure where Myrrhine prays to Demeter. A larger overview of the town is show in Figure 32. Myrrhine's home would have been in the semi-sacred quarter shown just south of the Asty Gates. This is where Aeschylus would have visited her and the Hierophant. Myrrhine's husband's tomb would have been close by her home, and it is there that she calls upon her deceased husband for help protecting their daughter, who is away from home at Brauron. Eleusis is an amazing site, and my hope is that *The Mysteries* might encourage others to visit it.

3. For much of the setting of this opening chapter, including the layout and functionality of Myrrhine's home as well as the placement of Kynegeiros' tomb, I've used the first forty-two pages of *The Ancient City* by Fustel de Coulanges. Though published in 1864, it is a classic in French literature and retains its value to this day.

4. Myrrhine is a fictional character, but I have her married to a real man, Aeschylus' brother, Kynegeiros who, according to Herodotus (VI, 114), was in fact killed at Marathon. Myrrhine's name was a common one in ancient Greece. Aristophanes used it in his play Lysistrata. The name comes from μυρρινων, meaning a branch or wreath of myrtle. Myrtle was a symbol of love, being emblematic of Aphrodite. At Eleusis myrtle grew in sacred groves, which were used during the Mysteries initiation ceremony. Her daughter, Melaina, is also a fictional character, and her name comes from the ancient Greek Μελαινα, which I've directly transliterated into English. I've taken the name from Farnell, *The Cults of the Greek States*, Volume III, pages 51 and 62/3 (see also Note 40, page 320), where it is shown to be an appellative of Demeter as the goddess Earth in her dark form, or Persephone, goddess of the Underworld. "Melaina" means "black, darkness." Farnell's information comes from Pausanias VIII, 42[1], a cult of Demeter at Phigaleia in the western Peloponnese. (As a curious

side note, see Peter Levi's *The Hill of Kronos*, page 80, for a recent visit to the little village.)

5. For the personality of Aeschylus, I relied primarily on *The Tragedies of Aeschylus* by E. H. Plumptre published in 1897. Page XXXII of his introductory chapter titled "Life of Aeschylos" reads as follows:

> The personal temperament of the man seems to have been in harmony with these characteristics of his genius. Vehement, passionate, irascible; writing his tragedies (as later critics judge) as if half-drunk, doing (as Sophocles said of him) what was right in his art without knowing why; following the impulses that led him to strange themes and dark problems, rather than aiming at the perfection of a complete, all-sided culture; frowning with shaggy brows, like a wild bull, glaring fiercely, and bursting into a storm of wrath when annoyed by critics or rival poets; a Marlow rather than a Shakespeare: this is the portrait sketched by one who must have painted a figure still fresh in the minds of the Athenians. Such a man, both by birth and disposition, was likely to attach himself to the aristocratic party, and to look with scorn on the claims of the demos to a larger share of power. His ancestors had fought against Peisistratos, and he too entered his protest against that form of government which the Greeks called a tyranny, the despotism of a political adventurer, self-raised to sovereign power, without the divine sanction which attached to the old hereditary kings who traced their descent from Zeus himself. Through his whole life, he was faithful to his early creed. There is hardly a play in which some political bias in that direction may not be distinctly traced. The time of his greatest popularity was during the ascendancy first of Aristeides and then of Kimon. When his star waned before the clearer, calmer, less fitful light of Sophocles, the change synchronised with the rise of Pericles to political supremacy. It was natural with such a character that his career as a dramatist and a man should be somewhat more chequered than that of the great successor. Sophocles was from first to last the favorite of the Athenians,--easy, genial, contented. Aeschylos—quick to take offence, quick also to give it; startling men by strange tours de force; coming into direct collision with their feelings, moral, political, and religious; wounding them where they were most susceptible--experienced the mutability of popular favour in a more than ordinary degree. The incidents of his life, so far as they are known to us, seem to point to a series of irritations, misunderstandings, and temporary alienations between him and his countrymen.

Yet having been born and raised at Eleusis, Aeschylus was never initiated into the Mysteries of Demeter, as demonstrated by the fact that he was charged with revealing the epiphany of the Mysteries and brought to trial under threat of execution. He was acquitted by virtue of proving he'd never been initiated. I've used his sons' actual names but taken his wife's from a relative.

6. Myrrhine's prayers here, and all prayers throughout the novel, are in accordance with *Prayer in Greek Religion* by Simon Pulleyn. Not only the prayer itself but also the method of supplication as presented in Chapter 4, along with the language of prayer in Chapter 8 of that book, I've adhered to religiously. See also Burkert's *Greek Religion*, page 74.

Sources for Chapter 3

Relationship of the chapter to the rest of the novel: This chapter locks Melaina's conflict (a subplot) with her mother and grandfather, the Hierophant. She knows they plan to marry her off, and now she realizes she doesn't want the life they have planned for her. Perhaps more importantly, it also sets up her future conflicts with the designs of the gods.

1. I visited the ruins of Brauron on Friday, October 9, 2009. It was a warm, sunny day in the early afternoon. A few tourists, eight or ten, were scattered about. Recently mowed grass covered the site. In ancient times, Brauron was at the edge of the sea, but deposits from the Erasinos have filled in the low-lying areas and changed the coastline considerably. Images and videos I took while there are posted at http://themysteriesofeleusis.com.

2. Euripides provides the story of the founding of the school for girls at Brauron at the end of his *Iphigenia Among the Tauri*. Athena speaks:

> As for thee, Iphigenia, thou must keep her [Artemis'] temple-keys at Brauron's hallowed path of steps; there shalt thou die and there shall they bury thee, honouring thee with offerings of robes, e'en all the finely-woven vestments left in their homes by such as die in childbirth.

This play, along with the *Iphigenia at Aulis*, provides the story of

Iphigeneia as depicted in various places through out *The Mysteries*.

3. Brauron, the archaeological site, is described in *Athens and Attica* edited by Dr. Marianne Mehling, page 239. (It's listed as Vravrona, the modern phonetic transliteration of Brauron.)

4. Many books provide a description of the rites practiced at Brauron, but one of the best is *Iphigeneia, Agamemnon's Daughter* by Maria Homberg Lübeck, published by Almqvist & Wilksell International in Stockholm. Part Three of that book opens with a chapter titled, "The Brauronian Myths, Rites and Cult Customs." It provides a list of references by Classical authors as taken from the Loeb Classical Library's publication of the ancient texts. Included in this chapter is the Arkteia—The Bear Ritual, dramatized in this chapter of *The Mysteries*. Another definitive examination of the rites at Brauron is contained in *Death and the Maiden* by Ken Dowden. See pages 19-32. Additional information is contained in *Pandora*, edited by Ellen Reader, in the chapter titled "Little Bears," pages 321/2.

4. Kallias, the Dadouchos (Torchbearer), was a real person and an actual priest at Eleusis. He was an expert horseman and charioteer as evidenced by his success at the Olympics. See Herodotus, VII, 151; Diodorus, 7.4,7; and Plutarch, *Lives*, "Kimon," 13.

Sources for Chapter 4

Relationship of the chapter to the rest of the novel: This chapter escalates the conflict of the Greeks with the Persians. The Greeks have to evacuate their homeland.

1. Kimon is another character taken from real life. See Plutarch, *Lives*, "Kimon."

2. Traveling in ancient times is described in *Travel in the Ancient World* by Lionel Casson. I've used this work extensively for everything throughout the novel, even down to the ruts in the road. See pages 65-93.

3. The fact that horses can't tolerate the sight or smell of a

camel is document by Herodotus, I, 80.

4. Mnesarchides and Kleito were actually Euripides' parents, and they did have two homes, one on the island of Salamis and the other at Phlya. See *Encyclopaedia Britannica*. See *Euripides and His Age*, by Gilbert Murray for information on his birth, page 9. For a discussion of his mother, see pages 11 and 15. Euripides was laughed at for his mother being a 'greengrocer' but others called her an herbalist. I've taken the herbalist connection because of its usefulness with treating Melaina's epilepsy.

Sources for Chapter 5

1. Xanthippus is another real-life character. He was Pericles' father. Kimon's difficulty with him, and hatred of him, was a fact and not a creation of mine. See Plutarch, *Lives*, "Pericles" and "Kimon."

2. For the Greeks burning Sardis and the temple of Kybele and then the Persians using it as an excuse to burn Greek temples, see Herodotus V, 102 and 105.

3. Myrrhine's prayer is true to the nature of the god Hermes. Many of the prayers throughout *The Mysteries* have been influenced by *The Orphic Hymns, Text, Translation and Notes*, tr. by Apostolos N. Athanassakis.

4. The description of the panic during the evacuation of Attica comes from Plutarch's *Lives*, "Themistocles," page 154.

5. The description of Melaina's epilepsy here in Chapter 5 and elsewhere in the novel comes primarily from two sources. The first is Hippocrates' essay, *On The Sacred Disease*. The second is *The Falling Sickness, A History of Epilepsy from the Greeks to the Beginnings of Modern Neurology*, by Owsei Temkin, my most valued resource on the illness and its treatment by the ancients.

Sources for Chapter 6

1. The Mysteries were indigenous to Eleusis but controlled

by Athens. This was not always the case. See Mylonas, page 229, and *Aristotle, The Complete Works of Aristotle, Constitution of Athens*, edited by Jonathan Barnes, Section 57.

2. The layout of Melaina's home was taken from *A Day in Old Athens, A Picture of Athenian Life*, by William Sterns Davis, Chapter IV, "The Athenian House and Its Furnishings," but has been added to using details from Homer, *The Odyssey*, VII 90–140. Other details and descriptive words were selected from *Life in the Homeric Age*, by Thomas Day Seymour, as well as *The Ancient City, Life in Classical Athens & Rome*, by Peter Connolly and Hazel Dodge, and *Handbook to Life in Ancient Greece*, by Lesley Adkins and Roy A. Adkins.

3. The fact that the Sibylline Oracles were present in "book" form in Melaina's time was taken from *Prophets & Emperors, Human and Divine Authority from Augustus to Theodosius*, by David Potter, which has a lot to say about the prophetic arts during Classical Greece in spite of its subtitle.

4. Much of the description of Melaina's chest came from the one Pausanias saw at the Temple of Hera at Olympia. See Pausanias Book V, 17.5. For the dowries of women, see *Children and Childhood in Classical Athens*, by Mark Golden, pages 132-5, and *Birth, Death, and Motherhood in Classical Greece*, by Nancy Demand, pages 12/13.

5. For the care-taking and visiting of family graves, see *The Greek Way of Death* by Robert Garland, page 104.

6. The blacksmith's name, Palaemon, comes from Apollonius Rhodius, *Argonautica*, I.202-206. Palaemon was a son of Hephaestus and was also lame.

The material contained within the scene at the blacksmith shop came from many sources. First of all, the description of the blacksmith beating the metal, the "woe-on-woe" and "smiting and counter-smiting" were taken directly from Herodotus I, 68 where he describes the discovery of Orestes bones by a blacksmith. Details of the smithy were mostly taken from *Studies in Ancient Technology*, Volumes VIII and IX by R. J. Forbes. The description of the smith himself comes directly from Homer's description of Hephaestus in *The Iliad*, VIII. Palaemon's two workmen, Akmon and Damnameneus (anvil and hammer), have been named for and even their physical details taken from Hephaestus' workers.

7. The name "Agido" was taken from a poem by Alkman in *7 Greeks*, tr. by Guy Davenport, page 118. The name "Anaktoria" comes from a poem by Sappho in the same book, page 76.

8. The speculation that Sappho ran a finishing school for girls is discussed in *Sappho's Immortal Daughters*, by Margaret Williamson, page 80.

9. Sources for the mythical Telchines of Rhodes are contained in *Early Greek Myth* by Timothy Gantz and *The Gods of the Greeks* by C. Kerenyi.

10. The gold work for Melaina's eagle broach was taken from *The Etruscans in the Ancient World* by Otto-Wilhelm von Vacano, Chapter IV, Section 6, "Gold Work, The Art of Granulation." The technique did not come from the Etruscans (Italy) but from the east and was associated by the Etruscans with the workers of Vulcan, the Roman Hephaestus. Undoubtedly this form of gold working had an association with the Telchines, who were also associated with Hephaestus. The script on the broach would be what we now call Linear B, a more ancient form of written Greek (Minoan, Mycenaean) than that used in Melaina's time. See *Linear B and Related Scripts* by John Chadwick.

11. Melaina's poem that young Sophocles overhears has in fact been influenced by Sappho's poem "To Aphrodite," but the heavier influence is "To Artemis" by Callimachus (LCL 129) page 61. See *Sappho's Immortal Daughters* by Margaret Williamson, page 160.

12. Young Sophocles' teachers mentioned here are well documented, if somewhat questionable. See the *Encyclopedia Britannica* and *The Life and Work of Sophocles*, by F. J. H. Letters, pages 33 and 38. Sophocles' home was in Colonus, a suburb north of Athens, and his father was a blacksmith, or at least owned a factory for

making battle armor.

13. The superiority of the "hotness of young men" over that of women was a well-known claim in ancient times. See *Before Sexuality*, ed. by David M. Halperin, et al, pages 139-41. Of course, Melaina's feelings for Sophocles have clouded her perception here.

Sources for Chapter 7

1. While visiting the ruins of Eleusis in the fall of 2009, I walked through those of the Telesterion and Anaktoron. The seats chiseled into the side of the mountains where initiates once sat are still there, but all that remains of the Anaktoron are the stones that formed its floor. I have uploaded images and video clips of these ruins at www.themysteriesofeleusis.com. For descriptions of the Telesterion and the Anaktoron in Melaina's time, see Mylonas, pages 77-105. Although the size of the Telesterion changed from age to age, that of the Anaktoron as well as its location inside the Telesterion remained the same.

2. The idea of a "second fate" for those who had a close brush with death was well known in ancient Greece. See the final pages of Plato's "The Republic." Those given a second fate were called "second-fated ones" (δευτεροποτμοι) or "persons with two fates" (υστεροποτμοι). See *The Greek Way of Death* by Robert Garland, pages 100 and 164. Plutarch also tells us that temples do not suffer the approach of "any person for whom a funeral had been held and a tomb constructed on the assumption they were dead." Plutarch goes on to say they were called, "Men of later fate."

3. The three priestesses of Zeus from Dodona, the "doves," are mentioned in Pausanias 10.12.5 (translated "Rock-Pigeons" by Levi) and Herodotus 2.54/5.

4. For Sappho's finishing school for girls, see *Three Archaic Poets, Archilochus, Alcaeus, Sappho* by Anne Pippin Burnett, pages 209-28, and also *Sappho's Immortal Daughters* by Margaret Wil-

liamson. Another good source on the life of Sappho is *Greek Lyric I, Sappho and Alcaeus*, tr. by David A. Campbell (Loeb Classical Library), pages x-xii.

5. For the aulos being a sordid device, see Plutarch's *Lives*, "Alcibiades."

6. The reference to the Danaïdes and a woman's body as a jar, see *Greek Virginity* by Giulia Sissa, Chapters 10 and 12; also *Pandora*, ed. by Ellen D. Reeder, pages 91-101 and 195-199.

7. The story of the priestess of Athena and the honey-cake is told in Herodotus VIII, 41, which I've embellished a little.

8. The two oracles from Delphi are provided complete in Herodotus VII, 140-3. I've provided the second here as being brought to Eleusis for interpretation.

9. The manner in which Kallias restrains Aeschylus for the discussion, I've taken from Plato, "Protagoras," 335d-e. In Plato's dialogue, this is actually Kallias' grandson, but I attribute the action to Kallias, as if his grandson had inherited his grandfather's mannerisms.

Sources for Chapter 8

1. For Melaina's experience descending into the Underworld, I've consulted Homer, *The Odyssey*, end of Book Ten and all of Book Eleven. In particular I've used Circe's directions for getting to the Underworld and Odysseus' experience descending to the Underworld and the ritual he performed to call the shades. The description of Charon and the Styx comes from Kerenyi, *The Gods of the Greeks*.

2. The description of the Cave of Hades at Eleusis comes from Mylonas, Carl Kerenyi's *Eleusis, Archetypal Image of Mother and Daughter*, and *Myth and Cult, The Iconography of the Eleusinian Mysteries* by Kevin Clinton. Clinton even has a diagram of the interior of the cave showing the smaller portion of the cave where I fictionalize a small, second gate into the chamber where Melaina sacrifices the pregnant lamb. Clinton says of this part of the cave:

"This inner cave, which is little known, obviously had religious significance, and it is hard to imagine what else this significance might be than that of an opening to the Underworld." The remarkable part of this is that I fictionalized that portion of the cave and wrote the scene prior to getting my hands on Clinton's book and learning that it actually existed.

3. The description of Kore (Persephone) came primarily from *The Cults of the Greek States* by Lewis Richard Farnell, Vol. III.

4. The description of the gate of Tartarus comes from Hesiod, *Theogony* 726-835 with additional material taken from Kerenyi, *The Gods of the Greeks*.

5. Melaina's epithets used in her prayer to Hades (Plouton) come from *The Orphic Hymns*, translated by Apostolos N. Athanassakis.

6. All the prayers in this chapter and other chapters are in accordance with Pulleyn, *Prayer in Greek Religion*.

7. The description of Melaina's encounter with her father's shade is patterned after that of Odysseus' encounter with his mother in *The Odyssey*, Book Eleven.

8. The setting for the scene set next to the Anaktoron is based on Mylonas, pages 83-88, Kerenyi, *The Gods of the Greeks*, and other various sources.

Sources for Chapter 9

This chapter is a dramatization of an event from Herodotus VIII, 65. It has been discussed in many places with varying interpretations. See Kerenyi, *Eleusis*, pages 7-12, and Peter Green, *The Greco-Persian Wars*, page 205, who dismisses it as dust raised by a Persian army corps that had set out for the Isthmus. See also Brandford, *Thermopylae*, pages 186/7. What flies in the face of the negative interpretations is the fact that Persians would not have sung the Iachos song.

Of course, the purpose of the previous chapter in this novel along with this one is to provide a fuller dramatization of Herodotus' belief that the dust cloud signified divine intervention in the coming sea battle. Herodotus' belief that the gods intervened on behalf of Greece is well supported if a little more than most scholars can stomach, which is certainly understandable. However, here's what Kerenyi (*Eleusis*, page 10) has to say about it:

> If this mysterious rite which encompassed and concerned the whole world could not be performed by men, the gods had to attend to it. A reason need scarcely be given since the Mysteries concerned the whole world, but an answer is provided by the victory at Salamis. Apparently what happened was that a divine host, a procession of spirits which could not be seen but only heard, replaced the festive throng of the Athenians with the cries of "Iakchos," joined the battling Greeks, and helped them to victory. This miracle has no known parallel, no analogy, in the history of Greek religion.

Sources for Chapter 10

1. The oaring and sailing of boats was taken from *Greek Oared Ships 900-32 B.C.* by J. S. Morrison and R. T. Williams, and *Ships and Seamanship in the Ancient World* by Lionel Casson, and *The Ancient Mariners* also by Lionel Casson.

2. The function of the Aulete (the flutist) in keeping the beat for the oarsmen is best described in *Greek Oared Ships*, pages 196, 256, 266-8, 310, and *The Ancient Mariners*, page 95.

3. The big-headed boy in this scene is actually Pericles and Xanthippus is his father. This scene with Xanthippus' dog actually occurred, (Plutarch, *Lives*, "Themistocles," page 154) and although we have no record of Pericles actually being there, it is reasonable to assume he was with his father. Pericles had such an unusual-shaped head (see Plutarch, *Lives*, "Pericles," the poets of Athens called him squill-head or sea-onion) that he wore his helmet in public, and even sculptures of him show him wearing a helmet.

4. The earthquake that morning actually occurred and is from Herodotus Book VIII, 63. Since Poseidon is the god of earthquakes (the "Earthshaker"), it was natural to have Melaina pray

to him.

5. Sophocles' poem he gave to Melaina is a paraphrase, or perhaps a better word is "corruption" (remember that Sophocles is still very young), of what he would later write for Oedipus as he went to his death in *Oedipus at Colonus*, lines 1549-1555.

6. Melaina's prayer at the end of the chapter is a true reflection of Ajax's life. He was prince of Salamis. The story of his fight with Odysseus, disgrace, and suicide is told by Sophocles (and paraphrased in Melaina's prayer) in his play *Ajax*.

Sources for Chapter 11

Relationship with the rest of the novel. The end of this chapter marks the one-quarter point in the novel, and constitutes what is known in the movie industry as the "1st plot point." See *Screenplay* by Syd Field, pages 7-13. Storytelling in a novel is somewhat different but nevertheless still contains the paradigm talked about by Syd Field. See my *Novelsmithing*, Chapter 2, "Plot." This chapter of *The Mysteries* marks a major turning point in the novel, not only in the war between the Greeks and Persians, but also in Melaina's life, since now she knows she has epilepsy.

1. The argument among the Greeks overheard by Melaina and her mother was told in even more detail by Herodotus, Book VIII, 74-76, although some (Green, 182-4) would have us believe this is all a fabrication. I've kept Herodotus' telling of the night before the battle. Sicinnus was a real person, and according to Herodotus, went to Xerxes under cover of darkness with the message.

2. Aeschylus' attempt to get Melaina and her mother to leave for Italy is a real option considered by many Greeks and is talked about by Herodotus, Book VIII, 62. Aeschylus' argument for the women leaving runs the same here.

3. The vision of Melaina standing at the edge of the cliff appearing as a goddess was taken from Herodotus, Book VIII, 84:

It is also reported, that a phantom in the form of a woman appeared to the Greeks, and, in a voice that was heard from end to end of the fleet, cheered them on to the fight.

4. The description of the sea battle given in the last paragraph comes from Aeschylus' play *The Persians*. He is believed to have actually fought in the battle. He was approximately forty-five years old at the time.

5. The description of Hermes gathering souls comes from Homer's *The Odyssey*, the beginning of Book 24.

6. The details of Melaina's seizure come from Temkin's *The Falling Sickness*. For Melaina's internal experience, I have also used a description provided by Dostoevsky (who was epileptic) in his novel *The Idiot*, Part II, Chapter 5, both toward the beginning and end of the chapter. Nothing like details from those who have suffered through the experience to provide realism.

Sources for Chapter 12

1. The description of hellebore, its medicinal properties, the harvesting and preparation comes from Theophrastus, *Enquiry Into Plants*, Book IX, Paragraphs VIII–XV. I invented none of it.

2. The Herakleia comes from Theophrastus, IX, XII, 5.

3. The prayer to Earth is derived from *The Homeric Hymns*, translated by Apostolos N. Athanassakis, "To Earth, Mother of All," page 67/8 and *The Orphic Hymns*, translated by Apostolog N. Athanassakis, pages 37 and 39.

4. The prayer to Asklepios is derived from *The Orphic Hymns*, Number 67, page 89 and *The Homeric Hymns*, "To Asklepios," pages 60/1.

Sources for Chapter 13

1. Herodotus tells us that Xerxes' brother did die in the sea battle (Book VIII, 89).

2. The words of Darius scolding Xerxes are from Aeschylus' play, *The Persians*.

3. Much of this short chapter is a dramatization of Herodotus, Book VIII, 89-92.

Sources for Chapter 14

1. Kleito's description of the cause of epilepsy comes from Hippocrates' *The Sacred Disease*.

2. The description of the burial/cremation ceremony for the dead is mostly taken from *The Greek Way of Death* by Robert Garland.

3. The philosophy behind cremation and burial provided here by Myrrhine in answer to Melaina's questioning comes from *Studies in the Use of Fire in Ancient Greek Religion* by William D. Furley, but is also heavily influenced by many books on the Mysteries.

4. The scene where Myrrhine and Melaina have difficulty lighting the fire comes from Homer, *The Iliad*, Book 23, around line 220, where Achilles tries to light Patroklos' funeral pyre. The prayer to Boreas and Zephyrus is patterned after Achilles' prayer but also those in *The Orphic Hymns*, Numbers 80 and 81.

Sources for Chapter 15

1. For the details and operation of the trireme, see *Ships and Seamanship in the Ancient World* by Lionel Casson and *Greek Oared Ships* by Morrison and Williams.

2. The destruction of the Scironian Road is told by Herodotus, VIII, 71.

3. The description of the oarsmen rowing from below deck has been taken from *Argonautica*, Book II, Lines 660-8.

4. Kimon's propensity to drink excessively is described in Plutarch's *Lives*, "Kimon."

5. The best reference on the Isthmus and all of Corinthia is *The Land of the Ancient Corinthians* by James Wiseman. I was at the

Isthmus in the fall of 1993 and passed through again in the fall of 2009. A canal slicing across the Isthmus was completed in 1893 after failed attempts that stretch back to 67 AD when Nero failed.

6. Material used in the building of the wall at the Isthmus is also described in Herodotus, VIII, 71. The diolkos is described in many places and some of it survives to this day. For a picture of the diolkos, see *The Peloponnese* by E. Karpodini-Dimitriadi, page 28. See Wiseman also.

7. The description of the temple of Poseidon comes from Pausanias, Book II, 1 [5] through 2 [2].

8. Keladeine's name is an epithet of Artemis as "the noise of the chase." Κελαδος means "noise, den, clamor." See Kerenyi, *The Gods of the Greeks*, pages 100 and 149, and Pindar, *Pythian Odes*, IX, 89 where it describes the Charities (Graces) and where it (keladennan) is uncharacteristically absorbed in the translation.

9. Keladeine's temple of Artemis, along with its ancient wooden statue of Artemis, is that alluded to in Pausanias, Book II, 2 [3]. See Wiseman also for the archeology of the site.

10. Herodotus tells of the celebration at the Isthmus in Book VIII, 123, along with the squabble over the prize for valor. In setting up the scenes of this chapter, I've relied on Burkert, *Greek Religion*, pages 102/3 and 234.

11. Pindar's poem is patterned from his "Isthmian Ode VIII," which was actually written just after the battle of Salamis. Though from Thebes, he stood above politics, as is evident by the thin line he treads in this poem. The description of his style of poetry comes from *Pindar*, tr. by Sir John Sandys, page XXXV.

12. Athenaeus tells of Sophocles dancing nude during the celebration at the Isthmus. See Athenaeus I, 20f.

13. The dancing scene has been carefully constructed from many sources. Probably the best is *The Dance in Ancient Greece* by Lillian B. Lawler. But *Choruses of Young Women in Ancient Greece* by Claude Calame is in a class by itself. It is a brilliant work, and much of the structure of this dance scene comes from it. In particular see Chapter 2.2, but all of Chapter 2 is important.

Sophocles "poses he committed, this way and that," comes from Athenaeus I, 21f with other words taken from I, 22b-c.

14. The affectionate scene between Sophocles and Aeschylus comes from Athenaeus, *Deipnosophistae*, XIII 604, which actually depicts Sophocles seducing a young boy, but the assumption I've made is that Sophocles learned this trick from Aeschylus. Anyway, the scene is pretty much the same as that described by Athenaeus.

Sources for Chapter 16

1. The description of the sacred officials of the Mysteries comes from Mylonas, pages 229-237.

2. The description of women weaving presented here comes from *The Thread of Ariadne* by Elsa Gullberg and Paul Astrom. See also *The Amasis Painter and His World* by Dietrich von Bothmer, pages 185-7.

3. The stigma of having epilepsy is documented in *The Falling Sickness* by Owsei Temkin, page 8:

To the ancients the epileptic was an object of horror and disgust and not a saint or prophet as has sometimes been contended.

4. For the line of descent of the Eumolpids going back to the time Demeter came to Eleusis, see Mylonas, 229/30 and 234; Kevin Clinton, *The Sacred Officials of the Eleusinian Mysteries*, page 10.

5. The ancients told the passage of time through the seasons by the stars. Hesiod in the *Works and Days* Lines 383, 572, 615 and 619 refers to the Pleiades and Orion. The condition of the agricultural crops at that time of the year and the state of the harvest comes from *Classical Landscape with Figures, The Ancient Greek City and its Countryside* by Robin Osborne, particularly pages 14-17. The information is specifically from archaeological evidence found at Eleusis. "First fruits" being offered to Demeter comes from the famine of 760 BC and is discussed by Mylonas, page 7.

6. For references to the significance of Triptolemus, see Kere-nyi, *Eleusis*, 121-130 and Clinton, *Myth and Cult*, Appendix 1, "Triptolemos as Child."

7. The ancient description of Korinna and Myrtis given here by Melaina is provided by Sarah B. Pomeroy in *Goddesses, Whores, Wives, and Slaves, Women in Classical Antiquity*, pages 52/3.

8. The names, "quiet Euphemia and ever-yapping Dorothea" come, interestingly enough, from *Curse Tablets and Binding Spells from the Ancient World* by John G. Gager, page 103. Euphemia in the ancient Greek stood for "religious silence" and Dorothea, "gift of the gods."

9. Aeschylus' description of Dionysus coming to him as a boy and telling him to write tragedies may have actually happened, and has been taken from Pausanias, Book I, 21:3.

10. Aeschylus' comment that "When hastening to your own undoing, the gods take part with you" comes from his play *The Persians*, Lines 741/2.

11. Sophocles wearing "a waxed writing tablet and stylus hanging from his belt" is taken from Athenaeus XIII, 582c, al-though actually it is Euripides whom Athenaeus is talking about.

12. Melaina dressing up as a prostitute comes from Athenaeus, *Deipnosophistae*, XIII 567/8. But her actual wardrobe is taken from *The Thread of Ariadne* by Elsa Gullberg and Paul Astrom, page 32. The way she gathers "the front of her skirt in a vertical column to pull it in and up at the ankles" is shown in Figure IX of that reference. The proper form for this action is from Sappho as told by Athenaeus, I, 21b-c. For the other reference to Sappho, see *Sappho: A Garland*, tr. by Jim Powell, page 5.

13. The scene between the two young people I've patterned after Athenaues, XIII, 608.

14. The slaughter on the island of Psyttaleia is told by Herodo-tus, VIII, 95.

Sources for Chapter 17

1. Oil lamps were commonly used to break the darkness, but they were considerably different than what me might imagine today. They were mostly open, but could have a covering to protect the flame from the wind while walking with one. They used olive oil with a wick made of linen, flax, or papyrus.

2. The ancients frequently compared the actions of the epileptic in a seizure to that of an animal, and I've capitalized on that here with Melaina in the dark and under covers. See *Hippocrates*, LCL, Volume II, *The Sacred Disease*, Paragraph IV, 20.

Sources for Chapter 18

1. For the irritableness (melancholy) caused by epilepsy, see Temkin, *The Falling Sickness*, page 21, 35, 39, and especially 368/9.

2. For the best and only reasonable discussion of the way virginity was perceived in antiquity, see *Greek Virginity* by Giuila Sissa.

3. The name of the physician, Podaleirius, comes from one of the two sons of Asklepios. Both sons were suitors of Helen and fought in the Trojan War as physician soldiers. My sources for the personality and manner of the physician (down to the aroma of sparkenard) are: *Hippocrates, The Physician* (Volume III, LCL), and *Asklepios, Archetypal Image of the Physician's Existence* by C. Kerenyi, pages 20-23. Asklepios was the god of healing and all physicians were considered to be direct descendents of him, as was Hippocrates. For the archeology and history of Kos as a place of Asklepios worship and a treatment center, see Kerenyi, *Asklepios*, pages 47-69.

4. Asklepios' daughter was Hygieia, health herself. I've used her name here for the physician's assistant in the form Hygeiadora, which I take to mean "the gift of health." Hygieia was Asklepios' consort. See Kerenyi, *Asklepios*, and also Emma J. Edelstein, *Asclepius*.

5. The staff with a snake entwined about it is the forerunner of the caduceus, which is the symbol of the physician today. It

has been changed to a winged staff with two intertwined snakes for symmetry but in doing so has actually become the symbol of Hermes, Zeus' herald and guide of souls in the Underworld. The color of the snake and it being friendly to humans comes from Pausanias, Book II, 28[1].

6. The "marking or gnarling of a hand" comes from Hippocrates, *On the Sacred Disease*, XI.

7. References to the winds come from Hippocrates, *On The Sacred Disease*, XV.

8. The "skull-drilling" comes from Temkin, *The Falling Sickness*, page 76 where the "trephining" is describe in gruesome detail.

9. Melaina's description that "It comes like a breeze, an aura. I also see visions in fire," I've taken from *The Falling Sickness*, pages 37/8. Her discussion of the euphoria comes from Dostoevsky, *The Possessed*, Part III: "A Wanderer," V (at the end):

There are seconds—they come five or six at a time—when you suddenly feel the presence of the eternal harmony perfectly attained. It's something not earthly—I don't mean in the sense that it's heavenly—but in that sense that man cannot endure it in his earthly aspect. He must be physically changed or die. This feeling is clear and unmistakable; it's as though you apprehend all nature and suddenly say, 'Yes, that's right.' God, when He created the world, said at the end of each day of creation, 'Yes, it's right, it's good.' It... it's not being deeply moved, but simply joy. You don't forgive anything because there is no more need of forgiveness. It's not that you love—oh, there's something in it higher than love—what's most awful is that it's terribly clear and such joy. If it lasted more than five seconds, the soul could not endure it and must perish. In those five seconds I live through a lifetime, and I'd give my whole life for them, because they are worth it. To endure ten seconds one must be physically changed.

10. The reference to bleeding her comes from Temkin, *The Falling Sickness*, page 71.

11. Epidaurus did claim to have cured epilepsy. See *The Epidaurian Miracle Inscriptions*, by Lynn R. LiDonnici, page 127, Inscription C 19(62).

Sources for Chapter 19

1. For admission of boys in the deme, see *Children and Childhood in Classical Athens* by Mark Golden, page 4.

2. For the tracing of letters as a method of teaching, see Plato, *Protagoras*, 326c-e.

3. For epilepsy "stealing bits of memory" and "causing spider webs before her eyes," see *The Falling Sickness*, page 38.

4. For Myrrhine's statement that "I'm barren. Epidaurus is a great center for curing this problem," see *Epidaurian Miracle Inscriptions* by Lynn R. LiDonnici, page 35/6.

5. For the Hierophant's legend of Saron, the ancient king of Troezen, see Pausanias, Book II, 30[7].

6. Hera's temple, here visited by Melaina, actually existed and is mentioned by Pausanias, Book II, 29[1]. I've taken the description of the priestess and that of the statue of Hera from Farnell, *The Cults of the Greek States*, Volume I, page 214 and page 222.

7. Melaina's aborted prayer to Hera has been adapted from *The Orphic Hymns*, Number 16 and *Zeus and Hera*, by C. Kerenyi, page 121.

8. The Argives' neutrality during the war, and the reason for it, comes from Herodotus, Book VII, 148.

9. The description of the carriage comes from *Travel in the Ancient World* by Lionel Casson, page 179, along with the lubricant, "dregs of animal fat." Page 181 provided the line, "The mules struggled with the increased load, wheezing as the breast bands rode up against their throats." That it was pulled by "quick-stepping" mules is from the same reference and *Engineering in the Ancient World* by J. G. Landels, pages 15 and 173.

10. The description of the ravine between the coast and Epidaurus comes from *The Earth the Temple and the Gods, Greek Sacred Architecture* by Vincent Scully, page 205, and the surrounding countryside by Pausanias, Book II, 26.

11. Mys was a real person, although his appearance in Argos is my own conjecture. Mys did, however, conduct a tour of all Greek oracles that would receive him, and he was trying to learn the will of the gods. See Herodotus, Book VIII, 133-6.

Sources for Chapter 20

1. The boundary stones about the sanctuary at Epidaurus are mentioned by Pausanias, Book II, 27[1].

2. The description of the sanctuary is presented in *Epidauros* by R. A. Tomlinson, *Asklepios, Archetypal Image of the Physician's Existence* by C. Kerenyi, and *The Epidaurian Miracle Inscriptions* by Lynn R. LiDonnici. I visited the ruins of Epidaurus in the fall of 1993. My picturs of the site can be found on the Internet at www.oedipusonapalehorse.com.

3. The Tholos, or Thymele, that peaks the Hierophant's curiosity is a circular building, the function of which remains a mystery although it is of central importance. See Tomlinson *Epidaurus*, pages 65/6.

4. The temple of Apollo on the hill is much older than Asklepios' sanctuary, as shown by Tomlinson in *Epidaurus*, page 22, and in Pausanias (Levi's note 192, page 196).

5. The myth of Asklepios is also told by Tomlinson and LiDonnici, and can also be found in Tripp, *Meridian Handbook of Classical Mythology* along with various references to the ancient texts.

6. The connection between Asklepios and the Mysteries of Eleusis is covered by Kerenyi, *Asklepios*, 39-41, and 91.

7. The dying man being kept out of the sanctuary was realistic. See Pausanias, Book II, 27[1].

8. The character Udaeüs has been patterned after his ancestor, Teiresias (see Tripp), but also from an old blind man I saw in Athens during my few days there in the fall of 1993. See my travelogue *Oedipus on a Pale Horse*, Chapter 23, "Colonus." Here I have Melaina leading Udaeüs about as Teiresias' daughter Manto

led the ancient seer.

9. Pindar is the source for the saying that "the gods apportion two trials for every blessing." See Pindar, *The Odes of Pindar*, "Pythian Odes III," Lines 80-2.

10. The cure of the mute girl is documented in LiDonnici's *The Epidaurian Miracle Inscriptions*, page 117.

11. I have been unable to locate my source for the name for the priest, Theognotus. All I can remember is that it was perfect for him. It would translate something to the effect: he who understands the gods, or is understood of god, or is known of god.

12. The ivory-and-gold statue of Asklepios at the altar is from Pausanias, Book II, 27[2].

13. Theognotus' description of healing at Epidaurus comes from Pindar, *The Odes of Pindar*, "Pithian Odes III," Lines 45-60.

14. Theognotus' reason for not letting childbirth or death occur on sanctuary grounds comes from Pausanias, II, 27[1].

15. The description of other patients' ailments all come from LiDonnici's *The Epidaurian Miracle Inscriptions*.

16. Udaeüs' comment: "Diviners disease. I thought so. It's no boon to see the future. Fools, those who practice the soothsayer's art," comes from Euripides, *The Phoenician Maidens*, Lines 954-9.

17. Udaeüs' teachings on the hilltop come from several sources. Among them, *Encyclopaedia Britannica* (under "Augur"), *The Etruscans in the Ancient World* by Otto-Wilhelm von Vacano, pages 42-5, and *The Bronze Liver of Piacenza* by L. B. Van Der Meer, pages 27-9, which provides a relationship between the Etruscans and Greeks.

18. The statement that "He also revealed which of the crook-taloned and ravening birds the gods marked as auspicious, which sinister, omens of bird-flight" comes from Aeschylus, *Prometheus Bound*, Lines 488-92.

19. The statement that he taught her "to read shape, dappled smoothness, what gall-hue marks the god's pleasure, the speckled symmetry of liver lobe," comes from Aeschylus, *Prometheus Bound*, Lines 490-500.

20. Udaeüs' final warning about being a prophet comes from Euripides, *The Phoenician Maidens*, Lines 954-9. The statement that prophecy comes incomplete is from Apollonius Rhodius, *Argonautica*, Book II, Lines 311-16.

21. The name "Abaton" comes from the ancient Greek, αβα–τον, (see the *Greek-English Lexicon*) means "untrodden", "impass-able", "inaccessible," and for holy places, "not to be trodden upon."

22. Theognotus' final statement that "The Tholos is Asklepios' tomb, represents his dual nature: the aboveground portion, his life here on earth; that below, his life as a god," comes from *Epidauros* by R. A. Tomlinson, page 66/7.

Sources for Chapter 21

1. The building where Melaina and Udaeüs capture the mice is labeled simply "ancillary" by Tomlinson in *Epidaurus*, page 71, and no function provided, so I've adopted it as a rather barn-like structure for collecting mice to feed the snakes, among possible other functions.

2. The Tholos, or Themele, is an important building at the sanctuary for which no function is absolutely known. I've taken the approach of Tomlinson, page 66, that it represented the dual nature of the god, both mortal and divine, since part of it is above and part of it below ground. The feeding of the snake follows the lead of Kerenyi in the Postscript to his *Asklepios*, pages 102-5.

3. The description of the Tholos comes from the reconstruc-tions in Tomlinson, *Epidaurus*, pages 62/3, and Kerenyi, *Asklepios*, page 45.

4. For the chorus singing a hymn by Olen, see Herodotus IV, 35.

5. The line, "I sing the Divine, Glorious Child and great light of mortals, Asklepios" spoken by Udaeüs comes from Aristo-phanes, *Plutus*, Lines 639-43.

6. Kerenyi speaks to the close connection between the Mys-teries and Asklepios. See Kerenyi, *Asklepios*, pages 39-41.

7. For Udaeüs' statement that, "In the end, all deities merge to one. All within mortals' perception is ultimately Zeus," see Burkert, *Greek Religion*, pages 125-31.

8. For the sacrifice before sleeping in the Abyton, see Tomlinson, *Epidaurus*, page 19.

9. For the details of the design and layout of the Abyton, see Tomlinson, *Epidaurus*, pages 67-71.

10. As for Theognotus' comment that, "During incubation, you must withdraw from mankind and surrender to the force within, meet the god halfway for naked, immediate healing," see Kerenyi, *Asklepios*, pages 34/5.

11. Theognotus' statements concerning the signs of pregnancy and that, "During pregnancy women are close to Gaia, Earth goddess. They've been plowed and seeded same as a field of grain and crave earth," comes from *Soranus' Gynecology*, pages 42-4 and 50.

12. For "Women who view monkeys while conceiving have children resembling such both in body and soul," see *Soranus' Gynecology*, pages 37/8.

13. For the words of Perseus' mother, see *Pindar*, Pythian Ode VII, 17, Apollodorus, 2.2.4.1, and Hyginus, *Fabulae*, LXIII.

14. For virginity not thought to be verifiable in antiquity, see *Soranus' Gynecology*, page 15. This is an amazing statement since much of his information came from Hippocrates. Women hadn't been added to the human race so recently, Hesiod's Pandora aside. You'd expect physicians to have a little more knowledge of female anatomy, but such seems not to be the case.

15. The Hierophant statement that, "The gods give us our lot in life, a yoke about our necks," is apt for someone from Eleusis. The statement comes from *The Homeric Hymn to Demeter*, Lines 147/8 and 216/7.

16. The source for the scene where the Hierophant gets the "cure" for his hemorrhoids comes from, *Hippocrates*, LCL Volume VIII, page 381, "Haemorrhoids." Believe it or not, all the details are there down to the lintels and chickpea soup.

Sources for Chapter 22

Relationship with the rest of the novel: The end of this chapter constitutes the midpoint in Melaina's story. That's the reason I've ended the first volume here. In terms of pages, it is within one page of the middle. But more importantly, it constitutes a reversal in the overall plot of her story. The Persians have been chasing the Greeks for the first half, and the Greeks will chase the Persians for the remainder. Eleusis is burned at the end of this chapter, and it stays in ruins throughout the second volume. Other reversals occur here, but to avoid spoilers, I'll not go into further detail.

1. The treatment of the Hierophant continues to be from *Hipprocrates*, LCL, Volume VIII, pages 383 and 385.

2. The Hierophant's comments about "the mysteries of love" come from Plato, *Symposium*, 210a-212a. His comment that, "Most mortals are witless with their souls in the purse," comes from *Hesiod, Works and Days, Shield* Line 685.

3. The reason Merope is not visible as a part of the Pleiades is given by Hyginus, *Poetica Astronomica* II, 21.

4. Melaina's reaction to Palaemon, "the virility of the shop, the masculine, barely-controlled violence, struck flame to Melaina's feminine heart," comes not from ancient Greek literature, but from *Out of Africa* by Isaak Dinisen, Book IV, "From an Immigrant's Notebook," Chapter "Pooran Singh." Just as I relied on Dostoevsky for a firsthand account of the experience of the epileptic, I found it necessary to rely on a description of a woman's feelings about a smithy that comes from a female's heart and not one of my own invention.

5. The blacksmith's discussion of Prometheus and Zeus's laughter comes from *The Religion of the Greeks and Romans*, by C. Kerenyi, page 192-5.

6. The change of seasons as reflected by the stars is illustrated by Hippocrates in the first lines of his *Epidemics*, Book I. See *Hip-*

pocratic Writings, ed. and tr. by G. E. R. Lloyd, page 87.

7. The description of Agido's wardrobe comes from *The Thread of Ariadne* by Elsa Gullberg and Paul Astrom, page 37. The description of Anaktoria is from *Sappho: A Garland*, page 12.

8. Mylaina's lesson on how to pray to the gods comes from *Greek Religion* by Walter Burkert, page 73-5, but is also influenced by the entirety of *Prayer in Greek Religion* by Simon Pulleyn.

9. Melaina's hymn to Polymnia derives from Hesiod's *Theogony*, from the beginning of the poem to line 105, and also from *The Orphic Hymns*, Number 76 and 77. But much of it is my own invention.

10. The scene leading up to and including Melaina's kidnap/rescue is taken from the opening to the *Homeric Hymn to Demeter*. An assortment of translations were consulted, including that by Helene P. Foley in *The Homeric Hymn to Demeter, Translation, Commentary, and Interpretive Essays*.

11. The description of the Kephisos River is documented in Pausanias, 38, 5-7.

www.ingramcontent.com/pod-product-compliance
Lightning Source LLC
Chambersburg PA
CBHW050925120626
46552CB00001B/44